SLAYER OF MONSTERS

SLAYER OF MONSTERS

BOOK TWO OF THE TRIANID

ANNE MOLLOVA

ROSE LEAF PRESS

Slayer of Monsters

Copyright © 2023 by Anne Mollova
Rose Leaf Press, LLC

ebook: 979-8-9857603-3-0
paperback: 979-8-9857603-4-7
hardcover: 979-8-9857603-5-4

Editing: Rebecca Heyman
Proofreading: Lucia Ferrara
Cover Design: Damonza.com

Inquiries: anne@annemollova.com

 Created with Vellum

For My Love,
who lights my fire and calms my storm

ALSO BY ANNE MOLLOVA

Keeper of Scales

NETHERMAIR
NORHELM
ILLYA
DRAGON TERRITORIES
ALYEN'S GORGE
Hammel
EYRIS RIVER
Lake of Leora
SHENEN
DÚRAMAIR
SEARING PLAIN
MOOR OF MOIN
CRANN
Ramsheath
ROYAL WOOD
Castle von Dúr
Doclann
Monstar Abbey
MOUNTAINS OF GEAL
Tiragel
BRANN DALA
SANDAMAR
N
W
E
S

SLAYER OF MONSTERS

I

THE WEDDING

It was the perfect day for a wedding.

The mud of early spring had given way to the lush green of new grass, which covered the courtyard of Castle Dúr in a carpet of soft, spongy freshness. Leaves unfurled on trees and bushes, and spring flowers sent splashes of hopeful color against the castle's stone walls. The fruit trees had bloomed just days before, and one of the first truly warm breezes of the season sent petals of pink and white drifting softly to the ground. In the courtyard, beneath the tall oaks, chairs were gathered around a white archway entwined with flowers and ribbons.

Alyen gazed at it all, thinking it was the most beautiful wedding setting she had ever seen.

Yet all she could feel was unease.

Alyen's brow furrowed as she lifted a hand to her chest, feeling her rapid heartbeat in a body that tingled with alarm.

It had been happening for months, ever since the Battle of the Second Slayer, but had intensified in the past few weeks. Today was the worst yet. It felt like the world was waiting for something just out of sight—something that made the very air quiver with trepidation. And she knew in her bones that when whatever-it-was came, disaster and darkness would come with it.

Strong arms circled her waist from behind. "Pretty, isn't it?" Aaron said, his voice low.

Alyen smiled despite the tightness in her chest. She turned and leaned into the kiss waiting for her, determined to push the discomfort away for a day that was supposed to hold nothing but joy and celebration.

Aaron broke off the kiss and stood back to take in the sight of her. "You look stunning," he said appreciatively. Then his eyes met hers and his mouth thinned in understanding. "You're worried, though."

Alyen sighed. "I can't help it."

"About anything in particular?"

Alyen shrugged one shoulder, squinting at the stone wall that blocked the moat from view. Hundreds of morkshai had poured over that wall just months before, in a wave of terror and death. She shook her head.

"I know everyone says it's normal to feel this way after living through a war, but I just can't shake the feeling that something's not right. That something else is coming. That the fight isn't over …"

Aaron pulled her back against his chest and Alyen closed her eyes, inhaling his familiar scent. He held her for a moment, saying nothing, until Alyen was the one to pull away. She took a deep, bracing breath. "But today isn't a day for any of that. Today is a day to be happy."

Aaron slung an arm around Alyen's shoulders, and for the first time she noticed his appearance.

"You look fantastic, yourself," she said. "I don't think I've ever seen you dressed up before." Indeed, as her eyes took in the fine linen of his shirt, just open at the throat, his laced vest, and his new breeches and boots, her stomach did a flip that sent warmth rushing to her cheeks.

Aaron grinned. "Turns out even a scruffy soldier can clean up nice."

Alyen shouldered him playfully. "Scruffy soldier, indeed. As if you're not the most eligible bachelor in the kingdom now that everyone knows you're the Second Slayer."

Aaron glanced down at her. "But I'm not."

"Not what?"

"Eligible. I'm very much taken." He bent his head to kiss her hair.

Alyen turned to face him and saw how his eyes grew dark as they took her in. How his lips curled as he looked at her mouth. Her own lips parted, and she was just about to tilt her head up for what promised to be a wonderful moment, when across the courtyard she saw a line of people exiting the castle doors and heading their way.

"I'm afraid we'll have to put that on hold. Again," Alyen said with regret.

Aaron let out his breath with a huff and a rueful grin. "You know, with a castle this big, you'd think it'd be a little easier to find some privacy."

"Trust me," said Alyen wryly. "There's *no* privacy in a castle. But cheer up. We have a wedding to celebrate."

They joined the others at the archway and selected two

chairs in the front, clasping each other's hands between them. Mother Brenwyn, Lirianna, and Alyen's parents sat nearby, and castle servants and soldiers filled the rest of the seats. Garret gave Alyen a wave as he sat a few rows back, and Alyen returned his smile before scanning the remaining guests.

"Where's Nah'dar?" Alyen whispered, craning her neck to look over the crowd. "I thought you said he was coming."

Aaron smirked and nodded to the front where the former assassin, clothed for the first time in the ceremonial garb of Castle Dúr's Captain of the Guard, was taking his place under the archway opposite Alyen's former maid, Bridget.

Alyen gaped. "He's Brother Hugh's *witness?*"

Aaron's shoulders were quivering with silent laughter. "I know, I was as shocked as you. But Brother Hugh asked him specifically, and he said yes. Apparently, they're kind of friends now."

Alyen could only shake her head, trying and failing to reconcile her memory of the lethal warrior who had vehe-mently detested Brother Hugh with the captain now standing at attention, waiting to discharge his duty as formal witness to the former monk's marriage vows.

A ripple of music started, and everyone twisted in their seats to see the wedding couple approach the archway, led by the high priestess of Béathan. Cook Nellie, her face pink and smiling, came arm-in-arm with Brother Hugh, who no longer looked like a monk. His robes had been traded in for a shirt, tunic, and breeches, his lightening-struck hair tamed and respectable. His expression, usually joyful in any case, glowed even more as he looked at his bride, clad in a simple gown of elegant cream linen.

"Look how adorable they are," Alyen whispered to Aaron as the ceremony started. "They look so happy."

Aaron nodded and squeezed her hand, and for a moment, Alyen let herself relax into the couple's shared joy among her family, her friends, and the beauty of spring.

But it didn't last.

Something was wrong, and growing more so by the minute.

The unease Alyen had felt—had been feeling for weeks—surged, and she drew in a sharp breath as fear sprang into her throat.

Aaron looked at her, frowning. "What is it?"

"I'm not sure," Alyen whispered, eyes scanning the courtyard and the castle wall as surreptitiously as she could. "But we're not safe."

Brother Hugh and Cook Nellie were kissing, and everyone was clapping and rising from their seats. Aaron scanned their surroundings as they rose as well, clapping absently with the others. "Are you sure?"

"I'm sure. This can't just be battle memories. Something's wrong and it's ... coming."

The guests were starting to mill around, all crowding forward to congratulate the happy couple. No one seemed to notice that the wind was picking up, scattering apple blossoms across the courtyard, and bending the heads of the spring blooms to the ground.

Lirianna came to join them and frowned when she saw Alyen's face. "What's wrong?"

"I don't know. Something's not right. Something's—"

Then she saw it. A massive black cloud was looming from the direction of the Royal Wood, rising over the castle walls like a towering monster. Lightning, tinged a sickly green, flashed from within and a sudden boom of thunder threw a silence over the wedding guests. Everyone turned and gaped at the colossal storm, the clouds now roiling unnaturally as the wind let out an eerie howl.

Alyen stepped away from her friends, moving toward the castle, her eyes never leaving the mass of darkness looming above it. Something about the feel of the storm—dread mixed with malice—struck a familiar chord deep in Alyen's bones. Ice hit her stomach, and she closed her eyes, face turned upward as she sent her mind out toward the towering clouds. Tentatively, she pushed against the magic threading through the tempest, bracing herself for what she feared would come.

Suddenly she felt what she had hoped never to feel again; magic filled with darkness slammed into her own, and she jerked her mind back quickly, eyes fluttering open in alarm.

"Darklings," she breathed.

Another flash and a crash of thunder jolted Alyen from her terror. "Inside!" she cried over the rising howl of the wind. "Everyone get inside! Quickly!"

There was a confused commotion as the wedding guests all started fleeing the storm in different directions. Garret raced for the stables to calm the horses. Brother Hugh clasped Cook Nellie's hand and they bolted toward the kitchens, along with many of the servants. Nah'dar drew his scimitar, his face in a snarl, as if to take on the storm himself.

"Nah'dar, this way! Inside!" Alyen called, and the captain hurried behind Alyen's family and friends as they fled to the front doors.

They filed into the castle, wind whipping at their clothes and hair as it moaned through the castle towers. Alyen entered last, glancing back to ensure that all had made it inside to safety before pulling the door closed.

"Bolt it," she ordered, a tremble in her voice. "The other doors too. And send everyone to shutter the windows. Quickly!"

Pages were sent scurrying through the castle and soon Alyen heard the distant echoes of slamming shutters and the clank of bolts being shoved into place. Seconds later, rain erupted onto the castle with a vengeful fury, sounding like knives hurled at the impenetrable walls.

"Alyen?" Queen Réanna was looking at her daughter with concern. "Are you all right?"

Alyen realized she was clutching her arms around her waist and forced them to relax as she nodded. Her fingers were trembling.

Aaron caught her gaze, his eyes knowing. "It's not a natural storm, is it?"

"No," Alyen shook her head. "No, it's not." She closed her eyes against the fear that rose along with the memories of her last encounter with darklings. Memories of the Royal Wood, of Ylvain and a flashing sword …

She opened her eyes. "It's darklings. They're driving the storm."

The faces around her all fell into expressions of shock and confusion.

"Darklings?"

"But Ylvain's gone …"

"Who's controlling them without her?"

"Alyen?" It was Mother Brenwyn, fixing Alyen with her knowing gaze. "What does this mean?"

Alyen scanned the faces of those closest to her, all

searching for answers she knew she didn't have. The wind roared outside, and she swallowed.

"It means we aren't done. It means … the fight's not over."

2

FAER DINNÁN

The storm raged for most of the day. Castle Dúr had been built to withstand the onslaughts of battle and gale, but even within the thick stone walls, the roar of thunder and scream of wind could be heard, punctuated by the occasional crash or shatter of breaking glass.

Alyen sat with the others, no one bothering to speak much over the noise of the storm. She tried to use the time to calm the beating of her heart that quailed at the malice lacing the very air as the darklings passed overhead. She knew now that this was the threat she'd been sensing since the Battle of the Second Slayer. And while it was somewhat comforting to know there was a true reason for her fear, she tried not to think of what a massive rogue swarm of elementals turned to evil meant for her kingdom—or for her.

When the storm finally stopped, the sudden quiet was deafening. In silent agreement, everyone rose and made their way to the front doors. They emerged to assess the damage, and Alyen's breath caught in her throat.

The courtyard was a wasteland. The gardens were shredded and bare. Branches littered the ground along with a few trees that had been uprooted completely. The limbs of those still standing had been stripped as bare as they had been in winter. Glass from several windows glittered in the grass like strewn ice, and the archway and chairs from the wedding had been smashed against trees and the castle walls.

Alyen licked her dry lips as her eyes settled on the building across the courtyard. "I'm going to see if Garret and the horses are all right," she said, and made quickly for the stables.

Night was falling as she picked her way through the littered grass, the sunset an angry red line on the horizon. Alyen squinted in the gloom, trying to assess the damage done to the stable building. Parts of the roof had been ripped off and one of the doors was hanging half off its hinges. Alyen breathed a sigh of relief when Garret emerged, seemingly unharmed but for a scrape against one of his cheeks.

"Garret!" she called. "Are you all right?"

Garret nodded as Alyen reached him and folded her in a reassuring embrace. "And you, cailínna? Is everyone all right in the castle?"

"I think so. What about Lusa? The other horses?"

"All fine," Garret assured her, turning to the stable. "Though they've all had the fright of their lives. That was a storm to end them all."

"It was darklings. Practically a whole army of them. I don't know how …" Her voice trailed off, and even she couldn't miss the faint note of desperation it held.

Garret turned back to Alyen, understanding in his eyes. "I'm guessing Rowenna never got around to teaching you much about darklings."

Alyen shook her head in despair. "I don't even know if *she* knew much about darklings. I had barely a year of training with her, and now everyone will expect me to be able to fix this."

"No one will expect you to have all the answers, cailínna."

Alyen looked up into the face her oldest friend. "They will. Because there's no one else who can."

Suddenly a heat on the verge of burning flared on Alyen's wrist. She gasped in surprise and looked down to the place where the image of a single green leaf was imprinted on her skin—the mark of Faer Dinnán that all Keepers bore. She'd never felt anything from it before, but now it was glowing with a soft green light.

Alyen looked up and, on instinct or some other inner knowing, looked across the courtyard to where a figure stood beneath one of the great oak trees, illuminated faintly with the same green glow.

"Faer Dinnán," she said. "I'm sorry, Garret, I have to go."

It was fully dark now, the way across the courtyard made treacherous by the fallen debris. Alyen hadn't thought to bring a lantern in her haste, so she paused and whispered into the darkness.

"Salamandars in the night, help me with a guiding light."

At once, a dozen fiery elementals sprang into view around her, each clothed in swirling flames that emitted a flickering orange glow. Together they advanced across the courtyard, the salamandars illuminating a path for Alyen through the wreckage until they came to the oak where the faerie king stood waiting. Alyen whispered her thanks, and the salamandars moved as one to surround their monarch, like moths to a flame.

"Your Majesty." Alyen inclined her head, then lifted her arm to indicate the leaf on her wrist. It was no longer glowing, but when she spoke there was no missing the accusatory edge in her voice. "Is this how it works when you want to see me?"

Faer Dinnán's face was as impassive and ageless as she remembered from the last time she'd seen him after the Battle of the Second Slayer, yet there was a line of worry between his eyes that Alyen didn't remember seeing before.

"Not usually," he admitted, sounding almost apologetic. "But this is a matter of some urgency."

Alyen nodded. "The storm—the darklings. I guess I assumed they would have disappeared with Ylvain …"

Faer Dinnán shook his head as his eyes held hers. "Things, beings, do not just disappear, Alyen. Nor do the problems they create if left unchecked."

"I'm sorry. I didn't know. Rowenna never told me much about darklings."

Faer Dinnán shifted uneasily, his eyes flicking away from Alyen's. "It's not your fault. Darklings haven't been seen in Dúramair for centuries, and I had hoped … I had hoped perhaps I could heal them on my own."

"Heal them?"

"Free them. From Ylvain's darkness. Return them to their original elemental state."

"But you couldn't?"

Faer Dinnán turned his face back to Alyen's, his eyes troubled. "I could not."

A sinking feeling settled into Alyen's stomach. "What does that mean?"

Slowly, Faer Dinnán raised his right arm. Alyen's eyes widened. The lower half of the faerie king's arm was faded, nearly translucent, and his fingers seemed to flicker as though winking in and out of existence.

"What happened?" Alyen breathed.

Faer Dinnán lowered his arm. "When darklings are created, they shift the Balance away from its rightful state. Usually, a dark magician has only enough power to create and control a few darklings, but with the aid of Malscath, Ylvain was able to create dozens throughout the entire kingdom. In the past months, their darkness has spread, and they continue to multiply. The sheer number of them has disrupted the Balance so greatly that not only can I not restore it on my own, but my very existence is threatened. I am fading, Alyen."

"You mean you're … *dying?*"

Faer Dinnán nodded. Alyen closed her eyes, the implications of the faerie king's death racing in her mind.

"So that means that nature—the world—is dying?" Alyen asked, barely able to believe such a statement could be true.

But Faer Dinnán nodded again, and the truth of it hung in the stillness between them.

Alyen's brow furrowed. "There's something we can do though, isn't there? That's why you called for me?"

Faer Dinnán's eyes searched Alyen's as he spoke. "It seems I must call on you to do what no Keeper has done for centuries. I must ask you to break and reverse Ylvain's magic and release my elementals from the evil she has spun. I must ask you to save my life, and with me, the world."

Alyen's head felt light, and she passed a hand across her forehead, breathing in the cold night air. "But if *you* couldn't do it, how can I possibly hope to? I don't have that kind of power."

"You won't do it alone. Your power will combine with mine. The humanness of your magic is better equipped to confront and triumph over Ylvain's than mine alone. If *you* lead the effort, I think we shall prevail."

Alyen shook her head. "I don't know how to do that."

"No, but I do. And I'll guide you as long as I'm able. It is a great deal I ask of you, Alyen, but if I'm right, your powers are equal to it. And even if I am weakened, together we will make a most formidable alliance."

Something in Faer Dinnán's voice made Alyen look up at these words. A glimmer of the faerie king's familiar, curious amusement flickered across his features. It was reassuring, and Alyen took a steadying breath.

"What do I have to do?"

Faer Dinnán absently reached out his hand and touched a place on the oak tree nearest him where a branch had been ripped off by the storm. Alyen felt, rather than saw, his power surge into it, sending healing and strength into the weary wood. A tree elf—presumably, the oak tree's guardian—scampered onto the limb and extended a hand to touch Faer Dinnán's in thanks.

"The first thing we must do is to solidify the new Trianid," Faer Dinnán said. "When the Ceremony of Three takes place, the powers of all the Trianid members are increased, and you will need that power in the ordeal to come. Then you must travel to the Keeper's cottage and claim it as your own, so your new power will ground itself in its home base.

I shall instruct you further once these things have been done."

"And when must they be done? How much time do we have?"

Faer Dinnán looked down at Alyen, serious once more. "We have no time to spare."

Alyen swallowed and nodded. "And what will happen," she asked, her voice low, "if we're too late?"

Faer Dinnán's eyes looked out over the courtyard, as if seeing things Alyen's eyes could not.

"The storm today was only the beginning," he said. "As the darklings' power grows and my own weakens, the storms will become more frequent and severe. If they remain unchecked, I will eventually disappear altogether, nature will tear itself apart, and the world will devolve into a wasteland of chaos and destruction, devoid of life."

Faer Dinnán's eyes cleared, and he looked down once more at Alyen. "It is this that we fight to prevent, you and me. Will you fight with me, Alyen? Are you ready?"

Alyen felt the fear, cold in her stomach, numbing her fingers. The world was hidden in darkness, but she looked out across the courtyard to the castle wall anyway, knowing she gazed in the direction of her kingdom, her home, the people, and the land she'd been born to serve in whatever way she could.

Was she ready?

Did she have a choice?

She turned to look back at Faer Dinnán, unsure of how to answer him, but the faerie king was gone, leaving only the salamandars glowing in the dark. The fire spirits swirled around her, then danced outward into the night, anticipating her need for light to cross the courtyard once more. There they hovered in midair, waiting, it seemed.

With a breath that trembled more than she would have liked, Alyen turned toward the salamandars' glow and walked heavily back toward the doors of Castle Dúr.

3

THE CEREMONY OF THREE

Firelight flickered on the stone walls of the study where Alyen sat, retelling all she'd been told by Faer Dinnán. Aaron and Lirianna sat next to her with Mother Brenwyn close by. Nah'dar, dressed once more in his customary black, listened with narrowed eyes, uneasy as always when matters of magic were discussed. Alyen's parents listened with grave expressions, and beside them sat Merrith, Alyen's cousin and now heir to the throne of Dúramair. He looked young and determined, if not slightly lost.

When Alyen finished speaking, a heavy silence hung in the room. Nah'dar scowled into the hearth, and King Stephan passed a weary hand across his face. It was Mother Brenwyn who spoke first.

"It's my fault it's come this far," she said.

Everyone's expressions registered surprise.

"Why on earth would you think that, Brenwyn?" asked Queen Réanna.

Mother Brenwyn shook her head. "I've neglected my duties. If I'd been weaving as I should have been as Seer, or if I'd instructed Lirianna to do so, we may have seen warning of this earlier. At the very least, I should have arranged for the Ceremony of Three months ago. I must offer my deepest apologies."

"Nonsense," the queen stated firmly. "No one's been working as usual this winter and for good reason. We all needed time after the battle. Time to heal, to regroup, to breathe. The only person to blame for this is Ylvain. And it seems that, too soon, we're once again required to clean up her mess."

King Stephan nodded. "Placing blame won't help in any case. The only thing we can do at this point is to face this new crisis head-on. I know we've barely recovered—the thought of all this makes me weary to the bone. But there seems to be a plan already in place. Alyen ..."

Alyen's father looked at her, his eyes full of feeling. "You've already faced Ylvain once and now you're the one who'll have to face down her evil again. I'd take this burden from you if I could, but as I can't, know that you have our support for whatever you may need. And our love goes with you as well."

The others all murmured words of agreement and Aaron reached over and squeezed Alyen's hand, holding her eyes with his own. Alyen felt a lump of gratitude form in her throat and could only nod her thanks for his reassurance.

Mother Brenwyn shifted in her chair. "Arrangements for the Ceremony of Three will have to be made, and quickly. I won't pretend I haven't let my emotions delay my duties in preparing for this day, but I admit that part of the reason I've been postponing is because there are certain requirements—or at least traditions—that I'm not sure how to get around."

"What do you mean?" asked Alyen.

Mother Brenwyn smiled sadly. "The Ceremony of Three is a transfer of power from the old Trianid to the new. Each member of the Trianid has a role to play, but we're short a Keeper and a Slayer."

A moment of silence followed; the air felt suddenly heavier from grief. Mother Brenwyn cleared her throat.

"Of course, the magic of the Trianid exists apart from its members. We merely borrow it for the time we serve. Naturally, I will still play my part in bestowing the title and powers of Seer to Lirianna. And if we can find two suitable people to stand in for Morten and Rowenna, perhaps the magic will see fit to overlook the technicality."

"Suitable people?" asked Queen Réanna.

Mother Brenwyn nodded. "I think we'll have the best chance of success if the substitutes possess at least some of the traits or talents as the true Keeper and Slayer would have. So, for instance, Aaron would need someone who is a warrior—a good one. A warrior who shows not only skill, but discernment and discipline …"

The abbess's voice trailed off.

Nah'dar broke the silence. "I will do it."

Everyone's eyes lifted to the Captain of the Guard, most showing some degree of surprise.

"You don't have to do it," Aaron said. "We're talking about a magical ceremony, and I know how much you dislike magic."

The muscles in Nah'dar's jaw twitched, but his words were collected as ever. "It was people that led to my discomfort with magic, not magic itself. It would be foolish for my personal history to hinder our progress in a time of crisis. Apart from that, it would be an honor to assist Aaron in this rite of passage." He turned to Mother Brenwyn. "If you will instruct me, Abbess, I will execute my part to the best of my ability."

"Thank you, Nah'dar," said Aaron, his voice slightly hoarse. "It will be an honor to have you standing beside me."

"Well then," said Mother Brenwyn, "all we need is someone to stand in for Keeper, and honestly, I have no idea who that could be. A village healer might be more familiar with nature and healing than most, but I know of no one with any knowledge of the elemental world. Alyen was the only candidate for Keeper. Rowenna never found anyone else with the Sight."

There was a troubled silence as everyone cast about in vain for an answer, but the void only served to remind Alyen how very alone she was in this endeavor, in her work, in the world. Her heart began to sink, but a voice suddenly cut through the quiet from the corner of the room. A voice that was soft, yet unfathomably strong.

"I will stand for the Keeper. I will ensure that the power passes to Alyen."

Faer Dinnán stepped out of the shadows, his dark eyes dancing as they held Alyen's, despite the visible flickering of his right hand.

The king and queen glanced at each other, and Mother Brenwyn looked almost flustered. "Your Majesty. We would be most honored by your presence. This is surely unprecedented."

"Not at all," the faerie king replied, looking as though he was enjoying the reaction to his unexpected appearance.

"Who else would have instated the very first Keeper of Scales in the initial Ceremony of Three? I can think of none more worthy than Alyen, nor any circumstance more dire, to call upon my participation once more."

His face turned more serious as he turned to face Alyen. "You have my word, Keeper of Scales, that as long as there is life in me, you will undergo no part of this journey alone."

It wasn't the first time Alyen had the impression that the faerie king knew more of her thoughts than she had shared, but gratitude stung the corners of her eyes as she bowed her head in thanks. "It will be my honor," she said.

The faerie king held Alyen's eyes a moment longer, his gaze unreadable. Outside of Alyen's vision, Aaron's eyebrows drew closer together as he studied the expression on the faerie's face, but the moment was soon over, Faer Dinnán turning away to address Mother Brenwyn once more.

"Tomorrow evening, then. In the courtyard at sunset."

And just as suddenly as he had appeared, he was gone, leaving only the scent of spring leaves lingering in his wake.

The full moon hung over the oak trees, a bright coin against the dusky sky, as eight people filed out the doors of Castle Dúr into the courtyard. Mother Brenwyn led, a lantern held in one hand, a basket slung over the other. Behind her came Alyen, Aaron, and Lirianna, each with their own lanterns, closely followed by Nah'dar, who carried a sheathed sword that glinted in the half-light. The king and queen came last with Merrith, a lantern shared among the three of them. They shut the castle doors behind them and followed the others toward the oak tree where Alyen had met Faer Dinnán the night before.

The faerie king was waiting. He stood, regal and otherworldly, beneath the budding branches, the fading of his hand invisible from the distance. Alyen glanced toward the stables and saw Garret's silhouette, dark against the light from within, watching their progress across the grass. Mother Brenwyn saw him, too, and raised her lantern in invitation. He crossed over to join them, and stood just apart with the royal trio, scarred hands clasped silently behind him.

I wonder if he saw Rowenna's Ceremony of Three, Alyen pondered, feeling a twinge through her heart for her friend who was surely feeling the grief for his sister more keenly today.

The lanterns were set in a circle, then Nah'dar and Mother Brenwyn took their places, one on either side of Faer Dinnán under the oak. Alyen, Aaron, and Lirianna joined them, forming a circle within the ring of lantern light. For a moment no one spoke, everyone looking to Faer Dinnán. He suddenly seemed to realize that everyone was waiting for him to say something, and his mouth twitched upward. He turned to Mother Brenwyn.

"As a true member of the Trianid, Seer of Strands, perhaps it would be best for you to lead the ceremony."

"Thank you, Your Majesty," Mother Brenwyn murmured, then turned to the three apprentices. She took a breath that shuddered as she exhaled, and Alyen saw a host of emotions flicker over her face: pride and grief, joy and regret, each in turn until they stilled, and only the abbess's eyes shone with the fullness of what she carried and what she now must do.

"For thousands of years," Mother Brenwyn began, "the

members of the Trianid have dedicated their lives to upholding the Balance for Dúramair and all its people. Through the Keeper of Scales, we are kept in harmony with nature and the spirits that tend it, remembering always that we are part of the same rhythm as the trees, the wind, the mountains, and the seas. The Slayer of Monsters has guarded our people against threats from any beastly foe, while ensuring we live in peace with the magical creatures who share our land. And the Seer of Strands has forever kept an eye to the future, weaving visions of things to come so we may be forewarned of any danger to our land and its people.

"To be part of the Trianid has always been a path of discipline, bravery, and humble service, and each Trianid has made its own contribution to the legacy of power and wisdom carried by its members throughout the ages. Yet, I think that never before has so much been asked of any Trianid—and certainly not of its apprentices—than what has been asked of the three of you who stand here tonight.

"And so, we celebrate," she continued. "We celebrate the rise of a new Trianid. A Trianid that has already proved its worth and loyalty many times over. We celebrate the passage of power and the security of knowing that that power carries on to the next generation. We celebrate the lives of dear friends whose service demanded the ultimate sacrifice, and we feel their presence from the world beyond, knowing the joy and pride they would have felt on this night."

The sun had fully set now, and the courtyard was dark but for the light that shone from the lanterns. Mother Brenwyn paused and reached into her basket. She drew out two items, both of which gleamed in the firelight. She stepped into the center of the circle, nodding to Lirianna. As her apprentice joined her, Mother Brenwyn held out the larger of the two items she carried.

"Lirianna of Tiragel. From this night forward, you shall take your place as the Trianid's Seer of Strands. I give you this shuttle, passed down through generations of Seers, engraved with our highest law, Purity of Sight. May it bring you clarity as you gaze forward, and forbearance as you feel behind you the love of all those who've walked this path before.

"And this," Mother Brenwyn held out the second object with her other hand, "is the key to the Seer's workroom in Monstar. It's rightfully yours now. I hope you find as much joy in its sheltering beauty as I did."

Lirianna reached out her hands and laid them atop the gifts in Mother Brenwyn's outstretched palms. For a moment, both their hands and the objects between them seemed to glow. The two women caught their breath, and when the light dimmed, both their eyes were shining. Mother Brenwyn embraced the new Seer, then both stepped back to rejoin the circle.

Nah'dar stepped forward then, his movements betraying only a hint of unease. Aaron joined him in the circle of light, and Nah'dar extended his arms, holding out the sword he carried between them. Its hilt gleamed red and orange as it caught the lantern light, and Alyen saw recognition spark in Aaron's eyes.

"Aaron of Doclann, Second Slayer of Dúramair," began Nah'dar in his soft, accented voice. "I hold before you the sword of the Slayer of Monsters, carried by generations of warriors before you, and wielded last by Morten of Hammel. On its hilt is engraved the creed of Dúramair's Slayers, Integrity of Might, that you are bound from this day forward to uphold as your highest law. May you wield this sword with the valor and honor you have already shown, and may each blow it strikes ring for justice and the continued peace of this land."

Aaron stepped closer and took the sword from Nah'dar's grasp. Emotion flashed across his features as he paused, looking down at it. Of all the apprentices, Aaron had been closest with his mentor, and the pain of Morten's absence showed keenly on his features. He drew a breath, then reached behind him, fastening the sheath to his waist.

As soon as it was securely in place, Nah'dar suddenly drew his own scimitar in a gleaming arc. "Ready yourself, Slayer! Defend yourself and your kingdom."

The ringing of steel cut the air as Aaron drew his blade. Nah'dar swept his scimitar down as Aaron raised his sword in response. The two blades met in the air between them with a clash, steel upon steel, and as the two warriors strained against each other's strength, the swords began to glow. Aaron's eyes widened as the light reached his arms, and Nah'dar's face curled in a snarl as the magic he feared channeled through him into the new Slayer.

Then the glow faded, and the blades slowly lowered. Breathing somewhat heavier than usual, Nah'dar extended his hand and clasped the arm Aaron offered in return. The two warriors bowed their heads in mutual respect, then stepped back to join the others in the circle.

For a moment, Alyen caught Nah'dar's gaze. As the captain's black eyes held hers, she could have sworn she saw something flicker in their depths. Was it fear or pain? But just as quickly as it had come, it was gone, and Alyen couldn't even be certain that it wasn't just a trick of the lantern light in the darkness. Nah'dar averted his gaze, and Alyen turned her attention back to the ceremony.

Now it was Faer Dinnán's turn to step forward. He did so, eyes locked on Alyen's, and she suppressed a shiver as she joined him in the center of the circle.

"Alyen of Dúr," the faerie king began. "I have known a great many Keepers of Dúramair, all worthy, all talented, all wise in their own ways. Tonight, you join their ranks with less than two years of training—the least of any upon initiation—yet having already demonstrated more power, more courage, more resilience against more perilous odds than I believe any Keeper has before you. And as we all know, your work is not yet done.

"You have shown yourself to be both worthy and talented. Your own wisdom will come with age, and in the meantime, the collective wisdom of all the Keepers of Dúramair is waiting for you in the Keeper's cottage. I regret I cannot present it to you tonight, as it is not my place to remove things from a space not my own. But I do have this to offer you …"

The faerie king extended his arms before him, and Alyen caught her breath as the lanterns illuminated the object in his hands. It was a pestle and mortar, beautifully crafted of milky white stone and intricately carved with leaves and vines entwined around the words "Sanctity of Life."

Faer Dinnán studied Alyen's face as her eyes took in his gift. "A small token from the elemental realm, crafted of the purest marble by the gnomes, imbued with the magic of all four elements, and blessed by the faerie nobility. Please accept it as a gesture of good will and camaraderie from nature, and may it aid you in your healing work as Dúramair's Keeper of Scales."

Alyen's eyes shone as she raised them to meet the faerie king's. "Thank you," she whispered, and reached out to place her hands around the gift still resting in Faer Dinnán's palms.

The moment her hands touched the smooth marble, a jolt raced up her arms. A sudden flurry of elementals rushed into the ring of light. Circling sylphs set a vortex of wind around their king and the Keeper, while flashing undines sent a patter of rain splashing over their hands and into the marble mortar. Salamandars swirled in the air above, sending drops of fire raining down around them, and from deep below, Alyen felt the earth tremble as gnomes sent their magic up through the layers of rock and soil.

Faer Dinnán began to glow, a golden-green light that radiated from within, spreading throughout his body and down his limbs. The light reached his hands, then continued to advance, first engulfing Alyen's hands, then her arms, until her entire body pulsed with the glow of magic that surrounded and infused her. She felt her own magic rise to meet it, and suddenly the pestle and mortar burst into light, a white-gold ball of magic resting in its receptacle. A singing note hummed in the air around them; Alyen felt a final thrill of power before the magic began to fade. The elementals receded, the light dimmed, and all was dark and quiet once more in the lantern light.

Alyen cupped her gift in her hands, holding it close as she stepped back to rejoin the circle, limbs trembling slightly, but feeling the new strength of her power within. Faer Dinnán likewise retreated, and Mother Brenwyn, face shining, lifted her arms toward the three initiates.

"Alyen, Aaron, Lirianna: may your paths be guided by Béathan, the One, as your light shines throughout our kingdom, preserving the Balance as you carry the ancient powers bestowed on you this night. From this moment, all shall hail you as the Keeper, the Slayer, and the Seer: The Trianid of Dúramair!"

It was over. Alyen suddenly found herself buried in a cascade of embraces, first from her fellow initiates, then her parents, Garret, Mother Brenwyn—even Nah'dar placed a congratulatory hand on her shoulder, followed by a quietly sincere handclasp from Merrith.

It was several minutes before the commotion subsided. When she finally found a moment to breathe, Alyen suddenly thought of Faer Dinnán and turned to look for him in the circle of lanterns.

She found him, standing near the tree just outside the fire's glow. He was watching her, his expression evaluating, amused. And there was something else in his gaze—something she couldn't name—that made Alyen's stomach squirm. Their eyes met, and the faerie king's mouth lifted a fraction. Then, without speaking, he melted into the shadows and was gone.

4

MAIDEN'S CHOICE

awn broke in a sheen of golden spring sunlight, beautiful enough to make even the remaining signs of storm and destruction seem inconsequential, but the stillness of early morning didn't last. The courtyard was busy with preparations. A small wagon was being loaded with Mother Brenwyn's and Lirianna's looms and other belongings, while guards saddled horses, making ready to ride as their escort.

Alyen and Aaron had saddled their own two horses, packing clothing and food into saddlebags and lashing blankets to the backs of their mounts. Finding herself done with time to spare, Alyen stood apart, surveying the activity in the courtyard before her.

"You look thoughtful." Aaron appeared next to her, his new sword hanging at his waist.

Alyen gave the Slayer a quick smile before returning her

gaze to the preparations underway. "I suppose so. I was just thinking back. The last time I left Castle Dúr, I was on my way to Monstar to decide whether or not to give up the throne. My Sight hadn't even fully emerged yet. And now here I am again, not even two years later, leaving as the Keeper of Scales. It just feels … strange."

Aaron nodded. "It is strange. I never imagined things turning out this way either." He squinted up at the sun, just visible over the castle wall. "But it's a beautiful morning. And a beautiful ride ahead. And I get to spend it with you."

Alyen looked up to meet his smile with her own. "Sounds pretty good when you put it that way."

"I'll see how close we are to getting started," Aaron said. He gave Alyen's hand a squeeze, then headed over to see if he could help load the wagon.

King Stephan and Queen Réanna emerged from the castle accompanied by Merrith, who headed for the stables to visit his stallion. Alyen joined her parents on the castle steps, watching the young heir to her former throne as he chatted with Garret and played with one of the hunting hounds.

"How's he doing?" she asked.

The queen nodded thoughtfully. "Well, I think. He has a quick mind and a kind heart, which will serve him well. He does lack your natural confidence. But hopefully that will come with time."

"I think *my* confidence has waned with time." Alyen smiled ruefully at her mother.

The queen reached out her hand and smoothed the hair from her daughter's face. "That's not waning confidence, Alyen. That's *wisdom*. Life teaches us caution, but I have no doubt your fire's burning as strong as ever beneath it."

The king placed a hand on Alyen's shoulder. "As I said, focus on feeling the support of those who love you. You are not facing this alone."

Alyen smiled. "It's been good being back. I'll miss you both," she said, and embraced each of her parents in turn.

The preparations were complete, and many of the castle staff had gathered to see the caravan off. Alyen found herself occupied with what seemed like endless farewells to her parents, Nah'dar, Brother Hugh, Cook Nellie, Garret, and Merrith, all smiling with wishes for good luck and fair weather. Alyen wondered if the rest were trying not to think about when the next time they might meet would be, or what would happen if their quest failed.

At last, Garret gave her a leg up onto Lusa's back, the drawbridge lowered, and the air was filled with the sounds of hooves crossing over the moat, the creaking of the wagon wheels, and final shouts of farewell.

Alyen passed through the outer wall onto the road crossing the Moor of Moin. She turned Lusa, seeking out her parents' faces, echoing their smiles and waving as the bridge slowly rose and finally shut with a clang. Then, for the second time in her life, she turned toward the moor and rode into the unknown.

For a time, Alyen and Aaron traveled with the caravan, but it wasn't long before they had reached the fork where they would continue north, while Mother Brenwyn and Lirianna turned east for Monstar.

Aaron dismounted to say his farewells to Lirianna, and

Alyen slid down from Lusa to make her own goodbyes. Mother Brenwyn wrapped her in a firm embrace, wishing her luck, safety, and a swift return. Then she turned to Aaron, and only Lirianna was left.

"I wish you were coming with us," Alyen said.

"No, you don't," Lirianna teased. "You and Aaron, together at last, without a whole castle of people crowding you? Please, you'll never want to come back."

"Not true. I'll always need my dearest friend. And I'll always come back."

Lirianna's face grew serious. "You'd better. Once this is over—*really* over—I'll be expecting a visit at Monstar, and we can sit up on the wall with cider and talk about silly things like we used to. Promise me that'll happen?"

Alyen nodded, blinking back the sting in her eyes. "I promise."

The two friends embraced, then broke off as Mother Brenwyn climbed back into the wagon. Lirianna joined her, and the caravan creaked into motion, heading east. Lirianna's hand went to the pendant around her neck, and suddenly Alyen's hearing stone grew hot around her chest. She clasped it in her hand as Aaron reached for his own hearing stone.

"*And don't forget to fill me in along the way,*" Lirianna's voice sounded in their heads. "*I want to know everything!*"

"*Of course,*" Aaron's voice replied.

"*Travel safe!*" Alyen added with a wave that Lirianna returned as the caravan receded and finally disappeared behind a swell in the moor.

Alyen and Aaron remounted and turned to face the north fork.

"Just us now," Alyen said with a grin.

"It's never been just us," Aaron said, his eyes dancing. And just as he shifted to move toward her, Alyen kicked Lusa into a run, her laugh ringing across the countryside as Aaron shouted indignantly and gave chase.

It was a glorious ride. The sun was warm, but the rushing of the wind kept them cool as they flew over the swells and creeks, keeping off the road to avoid colliding with any other travelers. But they needn't have worried. The world around them was empty of all but themselves and their horses, the land, and the sky. After the initial burst of speed, they eventually settled into a rolling canter, allowing them to enjoy the sight of the moor sliding past as the distant smudge of trees marking the beginning of Sheanen Crann grew slowly more distinct.

By late morning they had reached the edge of the forest. They slowed their mounts and entered the trees at a walk. Alyen breathed in the leafy coolness with a sigh of pleasure, feeling the relief the forest always brought spread through her limbs and belly.

They stopped at a creek to let the horses rest and drink. Aaron spread a blanket on the bank while Alyen retrieved bread, cheese, and dried fruit from the saddlebags. She joined Aaron by the creek and had barely deposited their food on the blanket when Aaron's arm suddenly hooked around her waist, sweeping her backward into his lap. Alyen could utter only a small squeak of surprise, then his mouth was on hers, his free hand in her hair, his lips warm and earnest, tasting faintly of mint and raspberries.

Alyen felt as though she were falling, drowning, as all the

desire they'd had to keep bottled up at Castle Dúr came rushing out of them. Aaron's hands moved over her hair, her waist, her legs, sending first shivers then heat racing through her. She twisted in Aaron's arms until she was facing him, pulling him closer, hearing his breath intake sharply as her tongue found his. Her lips curved upward, and she pressed closer, but this time she felt Aaron pull back, his arms gently increasing the space between their two bodies.

Alyen opened her eyes and looked into Aaron's face. He was breathing hard, his cheeks flushed and his eyes dark. He swallowed, and when he spoke, it sounded as though it took considerable effort for him to do so.

"We should eat," he said, and swallowed again.

"Eat?" Alyen repeated blankly, her head in a daze.

Aaron nodded, his eyes still fixed on her face. "We want to get to the cottage by nightfall. So we should eat and keep going."

"Right," Alyen said, and slid off his lap.

Aaron reached for the packages of food, and after a moment, Alyen followed suit.

She was confused. Why had he stopped so suddenly? Had she done something wrong? Mortified, she glanced up at Aaron as he handed her a chunk of bread. But no, his expression was warm as ever, and there was no mistaking the hunger that lingered in his eyes. *He wanted me*, she thought. *Just as much as I wanted him. Which was a lot*, she realized as her heart slowed and her thoughts cleared.

The strength of her desire for him had caught her off-guard. She'd been completely swept up by it, washed away—it had felt almost beyond her control. Had it been the same for Aaron? Had he felt the world tilting, the same need drowning out all sense of restraint or rationality? What might have happened if they hadn't stopped?

"Alyen?"

Aaron's voice jarred her thoughts back to the present.

"Mmm?"

"Are you all right? You've been staring at your cheese for a while now."

Alyen blinked at the cheese in her hand and looked up. "I'm fine. Just daydreaming."

Aaron nodded, a faint line between his eyebrows. "I'm sorry if I came on too strong," he said, his eyes searching hers.

"You didn't. And you're right. We should keep moving."

Aaron nodded and Alyen watched as he continued to eat, his body positioned carefully so they never felt too close together. And Alyen finally understood.

He's being considerate. He doesn't know what I want, or what I'm comfortable with, and he's trying not to push too fast.

Alyen finished the last of her bread and stood up, brushing crumbs from her dress. "I'll be right back. I saw some herbs I want to collect before we go."

"Do you want me to come with you?"

"No need. I'll only be a minute."

Alyen retrieved an empty jar from her healing bag and retraced their steps toward the edge of the forest. As the trees began to thin, leaving sunny patches between the shadows, she squinted around, her eyes trained for one plant in particular. One she hadn't actually seen, but that she hoped to find.

There!

Alyen sank to her knees next to a patch of greenery dotted with red flowers. She reached out and fingered the soft leaves, memories flooding her mind.

Rowenna teaching her lessons at night as she slept.

Walking together through the dreamland forest.

Rowenna pointing at just such a patch of green and red growing where sunlight filtered through the branches. Her surprise when Alyen confessed to never having heard of it before. The Keeper's impatient huff at Alyen's sheltered royal upbringing.

Maiden's Choice. The plant that allows a woman to choose if and when to become a mother.

She hadn't given the plant another thought since that lesson. Had never considered that *she* might be the one to benefit from its gifts. But if their pre-lunch activities were any indication of how things were likely to go now that she and Aaron were together and alone … Perhaps it would be wise to be prepared.

Just in case.

Because next time, she wasn't sure she wanted it to stop.

Alyen returned to find the food and blanket packed away and Aaron waiting with the horses ready.

"Did you find what you needed?" he asked as she tucked the jar full of green and red sprigs into her pack.

"I did."

Aaron came to help her mount, but before he could, Alyen wrapped her arms around his neck, kissing his bottom lip softly. Aaron's mouth smiled against hers, his hands at her waist, and she drew back, looking into his hazel eyes.

"What was that for?" he asked.

"Nothing," she said, returning his smile. "And now we really should go."

Aaron helped her into her saddle, his hand lingering briefly on her leg before he turned to mount Soran. Then, side by side, they turned their horses back down the path toward the Keeper's cottage.

5

THE KEEPER'S COTTAGE

Twilight was making the forest shadows darker and the sunbeams more golden when the trees opened onto a quiet clearing bathed in the soft colors of early sunset. Immediately, Alyen gasped, hand flying to her mouth, eyes wide as they took in the sight before her.

Aaron's head whipped back and forth between her and the clearing. "What? What's wrong?"

"Nothing's wrong," Alyen almost whispered, her hand lowering from her mouth to her heart. "It's just … It's real. I never realized this place was real."

She nudged Lusa forward at a slow walk, entering the clearing and drinking in every detail with her heart in her throat. There was the well, the woodpile, the herbs Rowenna had grown in the sunny patch by the fallen log. And there was the cottage full of so many memories, so many lessons. Alyen brushed a tear off her cheek as Aaron pulled Soran up beside her.

"You know this place? I thought you said you'd never been here."

"I didn't think I had." Alyen shook her head. "But this is where Rowenna taught me every night in the dreamworld. I guess I always assumed it was just an imaginary place she'd somehow created there. I didn't know it was her home."

Aaron nodded his understanding, then studied Alyen's face. "It's your home now."

Her home. Her own home. The realization settled into her with a sighing breath she hadn't known she was holding. Suddenly she was smiling, laughing through tears. "It doesn't feel like mine."

Aaron leaned over and pulled Alyen into an awkward one-armed hug, planting a kiss on top of her head. "It will. Want to go in?"

Alyen nodded, and they dismounted to remove Lusa's and Soran's tack.

When the horses were cared for and grazing in the clearing, Alyen and Aaron collected their things and turned toward the cottage.

"After you," Aaron said, grinning as he held an arm out toward the entrance.

The door had no lock, so Alyen turned the handle and pushed it open, stepping into the cottage she hadn't seen in months.

It was exactly as she remembered it. The hearth, the table, the stove with the kettle sitting on top. The shelves lined with jars of dried leaves and roots. All was just as it had been—and yet it felt so different.

"It feels empty. Lonely," she said.

Aaron's arm circled her waist, and she leaned her head

into his shoulder. "You'll fill it up again. Just as every Keeper has before you."

They stood a moment in silence, then Aaron drew back and looked down. "Shall we eat? I'm starving."

"You're always starving," Alyen smirked.

"True," Aaron agreed, and they set about unpacking the food from their bundles.

There wasn't much left. Aaron pulled their remaining bread and cheese from his pack, and Alyen dug in her bag for the last of the dried fruits. Her hand touched the jar of maiden's choice, and she glanced up to find Aaron spreading his blanket by the hearth. She frowned. "What are you doing?"

"Getting my bed ready." Aaron motioned to the hard floor. It looked terribly uncomfortable.

Alyen looked through a door to an adjoining room and saw a beautiful, quilt-covered bed, easily large enough for the two of them. "That's silly," she said, trying to sound matter-of-fact. "We can both share the bed."

Aaron straightened slowly and looked at Alyen in cautious surprise. "Share the bed?"

"Of course," Alyen said, needlessly rearranging the bread and cheese so as to avoid looking directly at him. "We've slept right next to each other in the forest dozens of times. The bed won't be much different. And it's much better than the floor."

"All right," Aaron said after a moment's hesitation. "If you're sure."

"I am." Alyen threw him a quick smile and turned to the stove, taking a silent, deep breath to calm the fluttering in her stomach. She whispered a few words to the salamandars to ignite the flames inside the oven and filled the kettle from the pump at the sink. She began to pinch leaves off the maiden's choice, adding them to a mug as she glanced up at the jars of herbs and teas on the shelf above her. "Do you want some tea?" she asked over her shoulder.

"Sure. I'll have whatever you're making."

Alyen froze momentarily. "I don't think you want this. But Rowenna had lots of other options."

"Why don't I want yours? What is it?"

Alyen swallowed, her breath quickening once more. "It's maiden's choice."

Aaron was silent for a moment. "Maiden's choice? The tea that women drink when they don't want to get pregnant?"

"Yes," Alyen said, willing her face not to flush.

Aaron was silent for so long she finally turned around to look at him. He was staring at her with an expression somewhere between shock and hope and trepidation.

Alyen's eyes lowered to the floor in front of her. "I'm not expecting anything," she said softly. "And I'm not asking for anything either. I don't know how you feel about—things— but I just thought that, given the way it's been going … And now we're here with a comfortable place to ourselves … I just thought the tea might be … wise."

Aaron crossed the room to stand in front of her and his finger lifted her chin. Their eyes met, and Aaron's were dark as they held hers.

"Nothing has to happen if you don't want it to," he said, his voice deeper than usual.

"Do you want it to?"

Aaron's forehead touched her own and his eyes closed. "I've wanted it to for years."

A soft whistle started behind Alyen, growing quickly to a whine, and Alyen broke the moment to turn and tend the kettle. Aaron withdrew to refold his blanket, then studied the jars of herbs while Alyen found a second mug.

"Here," he said, taking down a small jar and holding it out to Alyen. "I'll have some of this."

Alyen took the jar and read the label, then looked up with a grin. "Emberleaf." It was the equivalent of maiden's choice for men.

"I thought it might be wise," Aaron said with a quirk of his mouth.

Alyen measured out a pinch of the dried leaves, then poured the steaming water into both mugs. "To your health," she said, raising her mug in salute as she handed Aaron his tea.

"And yours," Aaron returned, his eyes sparkling as they held hers over the rim of his mug.

There was little to tidy when dinner was done. They washed out their mugs and tossed the crumbs out the window, then made their way silently into the bedroom. Alyen coaxed the salamandars to start a flame in the hearth, but there wasn't enough wood to last the night.

"I'll be right back," Aaron said. "You make yourself comfortable."

He left to collect the wood, and Alyen heard the door open and shut behind him.

Alyen looked around, not sure what to do. Anticipation left her feeling too jittery to sit down, so she fumbled in her bag for her comb and ran it through her hair to stop herself from fidgeting.

In a moment, Aaron was back with an armful of wood, and he bent to lay some across the fire. Alyen turned to put away her comb, the soft crackles and snaps of the fire somewhat calming the butterflies in her stomach.

Suddenly, Aaron was behind her, closer than usual. "Do you want me to help you unbutton?" he asked, a catch in his voice making it sound almost tentative.

Alyen paused, her eyes closed. She knew what he was asking—what he was *really* asking. She'd never had help undressing in all their travels together. Not unless you counted the weeks she'd been unconscious after Norhelm, but Brother Hugh had cared for her then. This was a different question altogether.

"Please," she whispered, lifting her hair to reveal the back of her dress and the nape of her neck.

She heard Aaron inhale, then felt his hands slowly unfasten the buttons one by one. His fingers traced lightly down the skin of her back, sending shivers through her limbs. His lips brushed her neck, then he brought his hands down and slid her dress off her shoulders. The fabric fell around her feet in a rippling heap, and she waited for the stab of embarrassment she was sure would accompany her nakedness, but it didn't come. Instead, she felt her neck arch in response to Aaron's lips once more on her skin as his hands glided down her sides to her waist, barely grazing her skin, sending shocks and ripples of want through her body.

"You don't have to be so careful," she said, relishing the sensation and aching for more.

"I want to be respectful," Aaron murmured in her ear. "And I don't want to hurt you. I'm new to this."

Alyen froze momentarily, and her eyes opened. Until now

she'd assumed—

She turned to face him. "You mean you've never …?"

Aaron shook his head, his eyes reflecting the firelight as they held hers.

Alyen smiled slowly, and she reached up to bury her fingers in his hair. "Then we'll learn together," she whispered and pulled his mouth to her own.

Suddenly she was drowning in his kisses, her skin fire under his fingers. She pressed her chest against Aaron's, feeling the taut lines of his warrior-trained muscles against her. A ragged noise came from Aaron's throat, and he lifted her easily and carried her to the bed.

Alyen barely had time to register the sensation of cool sheets on her bare skin before Aaron was there beside her, clothing discarded, smelling of the forest and tempered steel. His hand cupped her face, their lips met once more, and for a space of time Alyen was lost to the world and everything in it.

Later, when the fire had dimmed to a cozy glow, and their breathing had slowed, Alyen lay, curled against Aaron's warm skin, her finger slowly tracing designs down the arm that held her close.

"Saints, Alyen," Aaron breathed. "I had no idea."

Alyen smiled and turned to look at him. "Neither did I."

Aaron's gaze traveled over her face as if she were something rare and precious, resting finally on her own eyes. "I love you," he whispered.

"And I love you."

Aaron bent down to kiss her gently, lingering in the feel of their lips pressed together. Then he leaned back on his pillow, pulled Alyen close, and they drifted to sleep as the logs in the fire slowly burned down to embers.

6

THE KEEPER'S BOOK

Alyen woke in the morning to sunlight streaming gently onto her face through the open window. She kept her eyes closed, her body loose and languid beneath the soft warmth of the sheets and quilt. Slowly she rolled over, reaching an arm out to the side of the bed Aaron had occupied. It was empty.

Thnock. Thnock.

The noise was coming from the clearing outside the window. Alyen's eyes fluttered open, and she stretched lazily, arching her back like a cat before sitting up and pulling the sheet up around her still-naked torso. She looked out the window and smiled. Aaron was in the clearing, also bare from the waist up, an axe held easily in his hand. Beside him, a pile of split logs was growing, and she watched as he continued to chop their firewood, his movements rhythmic and graceful, his lean muscles rippling in the early morning light. He was smiling.

Alyen considered going out to join him but decided against it. Somehow, she didn't want to intrude on his solitude and the flow of his work, and she was enjoying the moment she had to herself as well.

She rose from the bed and stepped into her clothes, still strewn on the floor. In the main room, the salamandars helped her coax a fire into the stove. She set a kettle of water on top and nodded in satisfaction; they could have tea with their breakfast when Aaron came in. She almost chuckled aloud, enjoying the simple coziness of this new life she found herself in—a life in a woodland cottage with kettles and rumpled bedsheets, breakfast for two and a lover outside fetching firewood. She savored the moment of true and genuine happiness before turning her attention to the rest of the cottage.

Her cottage. She'd been there countless times before in the dreamworld, but this was different. Then, she'd been a guest and an apprentice, and she'd only ever been in the main room with the large worktable, the hearth, and stove. But now it was hers. And she was the Keeper of Scales. It was time to get to know her home.

In truth, it *was* small. The main room had a doorway on one side leading to the bedroom with a small lavatory attached. These she'd already become familiar with, Alyen thought with a smirk. There was only one other door on the other side of the main room, which she pushed open.

It was a study, simple and lovely. A writing desk against one wall, a shelf holding jars, boxes, and a few books. A lute leaned in one corner—had Rowenna played? Alyen hadn't known. A smaller worktable stood against another wall with a window looking out to the forest. Two chairs stood empty, looking as though they were expecting occupants that had failed to arrive. Alyen stared at the chairs, waiting still and silent in the inviting room, and brushed a tear off her cheek.

She took a breath and shook her head to bring herself back to the present. Grief was patient and could wait for a morning less happy than this one. Thinking of searching for something to go with their tea for breakfast, Alyen turned to leave when her eye caught on a thick, ancient-looking book on the writing desk. With a start of curiosity, she realized there was a note resting on it in Rowenna's handwriting. Alyen pulled out one of the chairs to the desk, her heart fluttering when she saw the note was addressed to her. She sat down, and with eager fingers she lifted the letter and read.

My Dear Alyen,

If you're reading this letter, it likely means the worst has happened, and I am dead. I regret more than I can say leaving you with so little training at so difficult a time. But know that I have complete faith in you and your abilities. You will be a gifted Keeper, and I'm proud to have been your mentor.

I hope your reading this also means you and the others have found a way to defeat Ylvain and whatever dark plans she's put in motion. It is my great hope that this letter isn't needed, but either way, there are two things I must relay to you.

The first is regarding this book on my—your—desk. It is the collected notes of all the Keepers for generations back. You will find it to be an invaluable resource in your work. Study it well, glean all the wisdom you can, and when the time comes, add your own contributions to be passed to your successors. It is possibly the Keepers' greatest treasure.

Secondly, and along the same lines, this book contains information that may be of immediate and crucial value to you. I don't yet know Ylvain's full plans, how you will succeed in defeating her, or what will happen when you do. But we do know she's been creating darklings. One of the kingdom's earlier Keepers wrote an entry on how to break and reverse darkling magic; I've marked the page for you toward the front. Again, I hope you won't need it, but if you do, it may provide the answers you seek.

My blessings go with you, Alyen. Good luck on your journey, and know I will see you again, if not in this world, then the next.
—Rowenna

With equal parts excitement and trepidation, Alyen set down the letter and turned her attention to the massive, leather-bound tome before her. Gingerly, she opened the cover that crackled as it bent outward. She began leafing through the pages; those near the front were the oldest, dating back hundreds of years, but the writing was still well preserved. She passed by headings such as "New Remedy for Winter Fever," "Working with Undines to End Drought," and "The Importance of Leaving Faerie Food for Maximum Harvest Yield." Alyen knew that she would later spend many nights curled up by her hearth with this book—perhaps Aaron would be there as well—but for now she skimmed the pages until she came to one marked by a ribbon that bore the heading, "Darkling Magic Reversal."

Alyen pulled out the ribbon and smoothed the page, wetting her lips in anticipation. In the top corner was penned a date some 1,500 years prior by a Keeper named Noth of the Southlands. With eager eyes, Alyen read:

It is with a heavy heart that I, Noth, Keeper of Scales, do write this entry with the sincerest hope that it never be needed for practical use.

However, should dark times befall our kingdom once again, may these words serve as historic record, useful instruction, and dire warning to any Keeper seeking salvation in these pages.

In recent years, Dúramair has been plagued by sorcerers wielding the darkest of magics, culminating in the corruption and enslavement of the nature spirits with whom we share this world. These darkling elementals with their defiled magic posed such a grave threat to our kingdom that it was necessary in my role as Keeper to take immediate and drastic measures to ensure the safety and, indeed, continuation of our world. I thereby took it upon myself to seek out the source of the darklings' creation, and to reverse the evil powers that held our kingdom in peril.

The process of reversing this magic was simple in concept, yet vile and taxing in the extreme. I was able to locate the enchanted cauldron from which the darklings were created. I was then able to bind myself to the dark magic by spilling a few drops of my own blood into the cauldron, accompanied by a command in the singing speech. Once bound to the magic, communication with the darklings was possible. It was then a matter of pulling the darklings back to light, freedom, and their true nature by coercion and by the force of my own will. Once the darklings had reverted to their original elemental state, I destroyed the cauldron past any repair.

I did not engage in this endeavor lightly. I am aware my actions bordered on conducting dark magic myself, which is the ultimate abomination of the Keeper's vocation and powers. Yet it was the only way I knew to avoid the much greater calamity that would certainly have ensued if left undone.

But this event did not pass without tragedy.

Anticipating the difficulty of the task ahead, and unwilling to underestimate the lure of the dark magic's pull, I felt it would be wise to be joined by a companion who would serve as an anchor while I struggled with the darkling force. This person, I reasoned, should be familiar with the singing speech so that, should the evil prove too great a force for me to overcome, the anchor could entreat the elementals to aid in pulling me away from the dark magic before it consumed me.

To this end, I implored my wife, Runa, to accompany me. Before engaging with the dark magic, we asked the elementals to form a bond betwixt ourselves, and Runa was thus connected to me as I confronted this evil. At one point, witnessing my struggle and greatly fearing for my safety, she threw herself into the vortex of dark magic alongside me, intent on my rescue as planned. However, her fear for me left her unbalanced and vulnerable, and the darkness overcame her.

Since that day, despite the abolishment of the evil we faced, Runa is with me no more. Her eyes stare into a void, recognizing nothing around her, and she refuses both food and water. I have tried every remedy I can think of and some that I invented out of desperation, but she will take no potion, and nothing has restored her. It is as if her soul has already left, and I fear the shell that remains will not be long for this world.

If only I had found an apprentice who could have joined me in her stead. If only there had been someone who lacked the love for me that was her doom. The guilt of her fate will follow me to my grave.

I have saved our world, Future Keeper, but in doing so, I have lost my heart.

Alyen's fingers trembled on the pages of the book as her eyes stopped at the end of the entry. She was suddenly cold and felt slightly ill. She flipped hastily through the pages of the book, eyes scanning for any mention of darklings or a different method of addressing them. But the heaviness in her chest told her she already knew the truth: Rowenna had marked only one page, and there was nothing left to find.

Alyen felt the air shift, the scent of forest green wafting in the room. She looked up to find Faer Dinnán seated in the other chair, arms crossed, his eyes watching her.

"Is this true?" Alyen asked softly. "Is this the only way to rid the kingdom of darklings?"

"It is," came the faerie king's reply.

"So, I need someone to act as my anchor? Someone who knows the singing speech?"

"You do."

Alyen could see from Faer Dinnán's expression that he already knew where her train of questioning was going, but she continued, unable to stop herself or her rising fear. "What about you? Can you serve as my anchor?"

Faer Dinnán shifted in his seat. "It would be unwise for us to depend upon that strategy. I can't guarantee that I'll have enough strength remaining to serve as your anchor by the time you reach Illya."

"So, it can only be Aaron. Aaron is the only other person in the kingdom familiar with the singing speech."

The faerie king nodded slowly, studying Alyen's face.

Alyen felt the fear twist in her stomach—fear for Aaron, yes, but also a deeper, intuitive dread that there was something more to this seemingly hopeless situation that she didn't yet know. Something that, once discovered, would shatter her world. She fought to keep her voice steady. "But Aaron loves me. If he serves as anchor, he'll be in the same danger as this Keeper's wife." Her fingers tapped the pages of the book. "Not to mention the whole endeavor could fail entirely if his feelings for me get in the way of doing his job. So, if this strategy isn't any better, what is it you aren't telling me?"

Faer Dinnán's face was unreadable. "I believe you've identified the solution, Alyen. You've correctly stated that Aaron's feelings for you endanger our efforts."

Alyen shook her head, impatient. "But that's not a solution! I can't *make* him not love me anymore—" She stopped abruptly upon seeing the look on Faer Dinnán's face, comprehension hitting her with a force like a blow. "But you can," she breathed. "You can make Aaron not love me anymore?"

"Love is beyond even my powers," Faer Dinnán replied, and for a second, a wild hope flamed in Alyen's chest before his next words extinguished it. "I cannot make anyone love or stop loving. But I can make someone … forget."

Alyen's brow drew together. "You want to make Aaron forget me?"

"Not you. Just his love for you."

Anger erupted in Alyen's chest. She rose abruptly from her chair and strode across the room to the window, her breath quick and her face hot.

"If forgetting is undesirable, I can instead make Aaron believe you no longer love him," the faerie king suggested behind her.

Alyen spun around to face him, her voice dripping acid. "It's a little late for that, don't you think?"

Something like a warning flashed across Faer Dinnán's face. "What is it you truly wish to say to me, Alyen?"

"You knew," she said flatly, too angry to care about the glint burning in the faerie king's eyes.

"I did."

"You didn't tell me. Didn't stop us …" She bit down on the ire rising in her throat. The anger was easier to feel than the pain that threatened beneath it.

"Should I have?" he asked.

"Of course you should have," Alyen snapped. "How could you do this to me? To Aaron? How could you let us be together so long—fall in love so much, knowing that ..." She couldn't bring herself to finish the thought, to say the words aloud.

Faer Dinnán leaned forward, his face intent. "But I thought only of your own words, Alyen. Your claim that human love is that which makes human living worthwhile. Was it not kind of me to let you and the Slayer have that love, brief though it must be, rather than never know it at all?"

"And if I refuse to sacrifice that love?" Alyen asked, knowing already that the question was futile.

The faerie king's eyes narrowed, and he rose slowly from the chair. "Would you refuse, Keeper? You have your Slayer now because I saved him for you. You've had your time together because I allowed it. Now, when I have need, will you refuse to give him up to save me? Will you put your *love* before the fate of the world?"

Alyen's gaze burned as she took in Faer Dinnán's form. She didn't want to acknowledge it, but the flickering had crept farther up his arm in the last two days. He was fading, and fast. She looked away.

"I'll speak with Aaron," she said, her voice flat and bitter.

Faer Dinnán made no reply, but vanished, the scent of forest green with him.

7

BETRAYAL

When Aaron entered the cottage, Alyen was sitting at the table, tea brewed, cups waiting. Aaron smiled at her and hefted an armful of wood into a rack by the hearth. He turned, brushing the dust from his clothes—Alyen was relieved to see he'd put his shirt back on—and leaned down to kiss Alyen's hair.

"Good morning, love," he spoke in her ear, then sat across from her, his eyes still warm, his face open and trusting. Alyen tried a thin smile, but it faltered. She looked away, no more able to look at him than she could look directly into the sun.

Aaron's brows drew together, his hand with his teacup pausing on the way to his mouth. "Alyen? Are you all right?"

Alyen drew a breath. "I found something this morning." She pushed the Keeper's book toward Aaron, open to the entry Rowenna had marked. "Read this."

Aaron set down his teacup, glanced once more at Alyen,

then studied the page. Alyen waited as he read, sipping her tea and trying to remain calm as she braced for his reaction.

But to her surprise, once he'd reached the end of the entry, Aaron looked up at her with an expression of tentative excitement.

"This is good, isn't it?"

Alyen stared at him. "Aaron, how is this good?"

"Well, now we know what we need to do, right? You know how to connect to the darklings, and I know the singing speech, so I can be your anchor."

Irritation scratched at Alyen's belly. "Did you read to the end? Did you read what happened to Noth's wife?"

"Of course," Aaron said, reaching for Alyen's hand. "What happened to her is tragic, but Alyen, that doesn't mean it'll happen to me. We can do anything together. It's *us*."

"Aaron, the same thing could happen to you *because* it's us," Alyen said, snatching her hand away impatiently. "The whole reason Runa was vulnerable was because she was in love with the person she was trying to anchor."

"But we're stronger than that!" Aaron said, and Alyen felt him recoiling under her glare. "Remember, we're not just any Keeper and her anchor. We've already saved the world together once before, and, not to put too fine a point on it, I *am* the Second Slayer."

"Aaron," Alyen sighed, closing her eyes. He wasn't going to like what she was about to say, but it had to be said. She leveled her gaze at him. "Yes, you are the Second Slayer, and you absolutely saved the world. But the only reason you survived that day is because Faer Dinnán saved you. Without him, you would be gone, and this time, we can't count on his help. We have to be practical and take precautions."

Aaron had bristled during this speech—Alyen could see it in the hardened line of his shoulders and the set of his jaw. He shrugged, challenging her. "What precautions? If we can't count on Faer Dinnán, then I'm the only person left to anchor you. We feel what we feel. What's left to decide?"

Alyen took a breath, praying Aaron would heed the logic of her next words and knowing already that he wouldn't. "Faer Dinnán can … enchant you. Make you forget that you love me."

Aaron's chair scraped against the floor as he rose out of it, his face incredulous. "You want me to agree to have my memory magically altered? By Faer Dinnán?"

"It's to *protect* you—"

"This was his idea, wasn't it?

"Aaron, slow down—"

"Absolutely not!" Aaron's hand pounded down on the table, making the teacups rattle. "I will *never* agree to that!"

"Aaron, it's not just about you!" Alyen shouted, rising out of her own chair, hot tears pooling in her eyes.

Aaron stopped and stared at her, and Alyen sniffed, blinking away the sting. "Do you think I want to do this? That it doesn't break my heart just as much as yours? Or did you stop and think about what it would mean for me if we chanced for everything to work out, and I had to worry about losing you at the same time I was trying to save the kingdom? The whole thing is terrible for both of us, but in the end, this isn't about you, or me, or us together. This is about Dúramair. It's about the people who live here, the ones we've sworn to protect. It's about whether the *world* continues to live or not. And as awful as it is …" Alyen's voice broke, and she crossed over to take Aaron's hands in hers. "We have to make the choice that's best for them. The safe choice. The one that ensures we have the best chance of success. It's what we have to do."

Aaron's eyes searched Alyen's, a storm of hurt, anger, and desperation in their depths. "I won't lose us, Alyen," he whispered. "Not when I believe there's another way out of this. Together."

Alyen shook her head, tears now tracing her cheeks. "The only other way is for Faer Dinnán to make you believe I don't love you anymore."

Aaron held Alyen's eyes a second longer, then dropped her hands with a huff of disbelief and strode toward the door.

"It's the choice we have to make, Aaron," Alyen said to his back, frustration rising.

Aaron turned, his face hard. "Then it's a choice you'll have to make on your own."

"Is that so?" Anger hit her stomach like ice. "And if I choose the way that seems safest?"

Aaron studied her. "I don't think you will."

He turned and stalked out, banging the door shut behind him.

Alyen had returned to her chair, tea forgotten, along with the magic that had infused the early morning. She rubbed her forehead with one hand, hoping Aaron would come back once he had cooled down and seen reason. But the minutes slid by, and he didn't return.

Suddenly, Aaron's chair was occupied once more, this time

by Faer Dinnán. "The Slayer has not taken your news well," he observed.

Alyen lowered her hand with a sigh. "He just needs some time. We both do."

"Unfortunately, time is not a luxury any of us have," Faer Dinnán said. Something in his voice made Alyen look up and her heart sank. The flickering had spread to the faerie king's other hand, both now appearing to wink in and out of existence. Alyen met his gaze, his expression sending dread through her once more.

"You must decide, Alyen," he said, his voice quiet but firm.

"I can't," Alyen protested. "I can't decide something like this on my own ..."

"If Aaron will not hear reason, you must be the one to ensure the survival of our world. By whatever means necessary."

"If I could just have a couple more days. Even just one ..."

"You cannot!" Faer Dinnán's voice cracked like breaking ice, and outside the trees rustled in agitation. "You see how quickly I'm fading, Alyen. I don't have months or weeks—I may not even have days. You must choose now."

Alyen stood from her chair and walked to the window. Outside, she could see Aaron tending to the horses. Unhappiness showed in every line of his face, but his hands were gentle as they stroked the horses' noses and untangled their manes. Alyen's heart swelled, even as she felt it begin to break.

She couldn't believe she was even considering what she was about to say. But she couldn't lose him. Not again. And it would give them a better chance of success. In the end, that's what mattered the most.

"Fine," she whispered, feeling her heart shatter with the word. "Do what you must."

Faer Dinnán studied her, his voice softer when he spoke. "And how do you wish me to enchant him? Shall he forget his love for you, or shall he believe your love for him has ended?"

Aaron was brushing Lusa's coat, his movements gentle and graceful. Even in his anger, he still treated her horse with the same love and care as his own.

He hadn't wanted to lose the memories they shared. She could at least give him that.

"Make him—make him believe I don't love him," she said, her voice shaking.

She turned away from the window to find Faer Dinnán's eyes upon her and was surprised to find sorrow pooled in their depths.

"I shall do what must be done, then," he said, and disappeared.

Unable to watch, Alyen sank back into her chair, buried her head in her arms, and sobbed softly into her sleeve.

It wasn't long until Faer Dinnán was back in the room. Alyen had attempted to collect herself but had been largely unsuccessful, her cheeks still wet with tears she couldn't seem to stop for more than a few minutes.

The faerie king hovered in the doorway a moment, his expression almost tentative as his eyes traced over Alyen's slumped figure. Finally, he crossed the small distance to the table and sat once more. "It is done," he said.

Alyen couldn't bring herself to meet his gaze. She nodded. "And—what does he remember of this morning?"

"He remembers reading the Keeper's book and the role he is to play at Illya. But nothing of your conversation afterward." Faer Dinnán paused, still studying Alyen's face. When she said nothing, he continued. "Aaron now firmly believes that this morning you left him for me."

Alyen's head snapped up, her eyes wide with shock as they latched onto Faer Dinnán's. "He thinks *what*?"

"He believes you have split with him in order to be with me instead," the faerie king repeated in a voice that was infuriatingly calm.

Alyen rose from her chair, anger and panic making it impossible to remain still. "You never told me you were going to do that! Why would you make him believe that?"

Curiosity flickered over Faer Dinnán's features as he took in Alyen's reaction. "To be honest, I don't believe I had much choice. Aaron is young, strong, handsome … He's not only the Slayer of Monsters, but the Second Slayer of legend, and you, yourself, have vouched for the quality of his character. There had to be some explanation for the waning of your love, and given his significant desirability, there are few scenarios that would have proved believable. Your love wouldn't disappear on its own and, if it's not too bold," Faer Dinnán's eyebrow quirked upward, "I thought perhaps I might be one of the more plausible alternative candidates for your affection."

If Alyen had been angry before, it was nothing compared to the rage that surged through her now. Had Faer Dinnán been anyone else, she would have made no effort to stem the wave of fury that pushed against her clenched teeth, demanding to be released. Yet somewhere in her mind, a quiet voice warned that perhaps unleashing uncontrolled ire on the faerie king was not a good idea. So, in a monumental feat of self-control, Alyen forced her voice to be deadly quiet as she spoke.

"You had no right to do that without consulting me first."

"As I said, Alyen—"

"No," Alyen cut him off. "I understand the need to betray Aaron to save you and to ensure that the world doesn't end. But you've doubled my betrayal with a lie that I didn't know about and never agreed to."

Faer Dinnán regarded Alyen from his chair as her eyes burned into his. After a few moments, he inclined his head. "My apologies, Keeper. Perhaps I have erred in my haste. I meant no offense to you, or the Slayer. Are you suggesting I alter the enchantment to something you find less vexing?" He looked up again, his face impassive and unreadable.

Alyen warred with herself, struggling to master the storm of emotions so she could reach a logical decision. She wanted to say yes, to erase the lie Faer Dinnán had planted without her consent. But she also knew he was right. She had chosen the enchantment, and she had no other believable explanation for it. As much as she wanted to blame Faer Dinnán for deceiving her, she was the one who had failed to consider the full ramifications of her choice.

Alyen swallowed, a bitter taste in her mouth. "No. What's done is done. Is the enchantment … Is it permanent?"

Faer Dinnán shook his head. "It will break if Aaron is told the truth."

"So I need to continue the lie. Until all this is over."

"Until it's over, yes. Will that prove difficult?"

Alyen tamped down the retort that rose in her throat and looked away. "I'll do what I must."

"Then it would seem I shall be in your debt," said Faer Dinnán, and Alyen couldn't tell if it was irritation or regret she heard in his voice. She looked back but caught only the lingering scent of leaves and a glimpse of green eyes before she was alone in the cottage once more.

Alyen sank into her chair, her whole body trembling from the events of the morning. She wanted nothing more than to crawl back into the bed, pull the quilt over her head, and fall to pieces. Instead, she concentrated on collecting herself for another conversation she knew she needed to have, and quickly. Lirianna wouldn't like this any more than she did, but Alyen needed her friend to know the truth and to hear it from her first, rather than Aaron.

After a few more steadying breaths, she fished her hearing stone out from beneath her dress and sent her thought out. *"Lirianna?"*

"Alyen! Did you get to Rowenna's? Have you found anything?"

"Yes, we're here. Lirianna, I have a lot to tell you."

"Are you all right? You don't sound good."

"I'm … It's a lot to explain and I might not have much time."

Alyen related everything that had happened that morning, from the discovery of the book and Rowenna's note, to Faer Dinnán's visit, to the argument with Aaron, to the choice she'd made and the lie that came with it.

"Alyen." Lirianna's voice sounded shocked when Alyen finally reached the end. *"This is … I mean, this is bad."*

"I know. But there was no other choice."

"You made him believe you had feelings for Faer Dinnán?"

"It wasn't my idea, but that's what he thinks, yes."

"Well …" Alyen could tell from her friend's voice that Lirianna was casting about, trying to find something to say that would make it better. *"At least it happened early on. I mean, it's not like you've been together for years. It's only been a few months, right? So it's not as bad as if things had gotten really serious."*

Alyen was silent.

"Alyen, why aren't you saying anything? What happened?"

Alyen took a breath. *"Things* had *gotten serious, Lirianna. Things just got serious … last night."*

There was a pause.

"Oh Saints, Alyen." Lirianna's voice was appalled.

Alyen bristled. *"What? I didn't plan it that way."*

"So, you're telling me that, according to Aaron, you split with him the day after you slept with him?"

Alyen's eyes closed again as the awful realization hit her.

"Oh, curses. I didn't even think of it that way."

"He must feel terrible!"

"Well, he's not the only one, Lirianna," Alyen snapped, her eyes stinging once more. *"Or are you too busy scolding me to care?"*

There was silence for a moment.

"I'm so sorry, Alyen," Lirianna whispered at last. *"I shouldn't have scolded. How* do *you feel?"*

Alyen struggled for control against the tears she couldn't hold back. *"I'm heartbroken,"* she whispered. *"Last night was perfect. And now … I don't know how I'm going to face him."*

Her voice broke, and for a few moments nothing could be heard but her quiet sobbing.

When Lirianna spoke again, her voice was resolute. *"Alyen, you can't just leave things like this. There has to be another way."*

Alyen shook her head. *"There's not. Faer Dinnán confirmed it.*

I'm the only Keeper, there were no other candidates, and Aaron's the only other person alive who's ever used the singing speech. There's no time to find or teach anyone else—not with the darklings spreading as fast as they are. This is just how it has to be, or Dúramair is ruined."

There was silence again and Alyen knew Lirianna was fighting inwardly against the logic she didn't want to accept. She took a breath, hopeful she could steer the conversation away before Lirianna started trying too hard to fix things. *"I'm glad you at least know the truth. One way or another this will all end soon, but it helps not being the only person who knows what's really going on. And now that you know, I need your help."*

Lirianna's voice was wary. *"Why do I have the feeling I'm not going to like this?"*

Alyen swallowed. *"We need the enchantment to last until every-thing's finished at Illya, and the only way it can break is if Aaron finds out the truth. So, I need you to help me make sure that doesn't happen."*

"You want me to lie to him?"

"I'm already lying to him, Lirianna, but you might not need to lie outright. I'm sure he'll tell you what he thinks happened at some point, and I just need you to go along with it. Don't act too shocked, don't tell him he must be mistaken, don't try to come up with a different explana-tion or tell him you're sure there's a way to mend things. Just let the story be."

"You mean 'just participate in the torture of my closest friends,'" Lirianna grumbled.

"Please, Lirianna," Alyen pleaded softly, not having the energy to keep up the conversation much longer. *"Please, just help me make this work. I need you on my side."*

And finally, Lirianna's voice held the solidarity Alyen needed to hear. *"Of course I'm on your side, Alyen. I'll do whatever you need me to do."*

Alyen nodded, knowing the tears were close again. *"Thanks, Lirianna."*

"Will you be all right?" Her friend's voice held concern.

"I'll be fine. Promise."

She tried to believe the words were true, but one question kept echoing in her mind, making her wonder if it was yet another lie she was telling herself. *"Lirianna,"* she asked, unsure if she really wanted to hear the answer. *"Do you think Aaron will ever forgive me?"*

To her credit, Lirianna barely paused. *"Of course he will. Aaron loves you, Alyen. He'll always love you."*

But as Alyen ended the conversation and dropped her hearing stone back under her dress, she couldn't help but feel that love and forgiveness were two different things entirely.

Half an hour later, Alyen was sitting at the table, quietly sipping tea. She'd done her best to hide any evidence of her weeping, splashing cold water on her face until the puffy redness had all but left her eyes. Then she'd tidied the cottage and prepared to leave.

The Keeper's book had given her pause. She'd debated taking it with her, but much of it was so old, she worried about the damage a journey might do to it. Besides, what little instruction Noth had given was easy enough to remember. So, she had read the accursed passage through twice more to ensure the words were imprinted forever in her mind, then stashed the book alongside the others in the study and closed the door behind her as she left.

The cottage door swung open abruptly and Aaron stood

in the doorway. Anger radiated from every line of his body, and the look on his face made Alyen's limbs quail.

"The horses are ready. Let's go," he said, voice flat.

He turned and left.

Alyen felt her body shrink into itself. She rose and watched him stalk across the courtyard to the horses, her heart a stone. She rinsed out her cup, gathered their few belongings, and made to follow Aaron outside. At the door she paused and turned to glance one final time at her cottage, empty once again. *Perhaps next time I'll make it feel more like home,* she thought, hoping that with time it would be more to her than just the scene of her greatest betrayal and heartbreak. Then she turned, closing the door firmly behind her.

Aaron was already waiting on Soran, and Alyen didn't miss the fact that he hadn't offered to help her mount as he usually did. She stowed her things in her saddlebags and hoisted herself into the saddle.

She looked at Aaron and for a moment he met her gaze. His eyes were hard, his face expressionless.

Without a word, he turned Soran and rode out of the clearing.

Alyen drew in a shuddering breath, steeling herself for the journey ahead as she nudged Lusa into motion.

Illya seemed very far away.

8

DISTRACTION

Lirianna sat uneasily on the seat of her wagon, barely noticing the towers of Monstar Abbey just starting to peek through the trees from the cliffs above. She tilted her head to one side as if listening to something in the wind, her brow drawn into a frown. She could feel it. Something in the Balance was shifting, and not in a good way.

"Lirianna? Are you well?" It was Mother Brenwyn, studying Lirianna's face with the gaze that always saw more than most would. For some reason, Lirianna hesitated.

"Yes, I'm well. Just tired from the road, I expect."

If Mother Brenwyn noticed the pause, she didn't comment, but her eyes were evaluating as she nodded. "It's a long time to sit in a wagon. It'll be good to be home."

Lirianna smiled her agreement, then turned away as if to watch the abbey come into view.

But she wasn't looking at the turrets on the cliff. Instead, she closed her eyes, sending her mind down the invisible strings of past and future stories that formed the vast web of the Balance.

It was as she'd feared. Without a loom to guide her vision, the images and sensations were fuzzy. But there was definite unease in the web. Almost like a sickness.

Surely, that could be caused by the darklings, she thought, trying to reassure herself. *All of nature is off-balance right now. We know that.*

But something told her it was more than just the darklings. Ylvain had created them months ago. This was something new. Something that had just happened this morning.

Like the fact that the kingdom's Keeper and Slayer were suddenly no longer on speaking terms.

Lirianna felt a sigh rise in her chest and tried not to let it out. She wasn't sure why she didn't want Mother Brenwyn to know everything that had happened between Alyen and Aaron. Surely, the abbess would understand. Alyen had her reasons for what she'd done, and they were good ones.

But something about it didn't sit right, and she suspected the Balance agreed.

I'll know more when I can weave again, she thought, suddenly anxious to be back at her loom, where perhaps some clarity could be found. If she could glimpse where their current course was headed—if she could prove that Alyen's choice had been a mistake—perhaps a new plan could be made and her friends reunited.

The thought bolstered Lirianna's spirits, and she sat a little straighter in her seat. The important thing now was to prevent any further hard feelings between Alyen and Aaron until she'd had time to weave.

That wouldn't be easy. Her mouth pulled down as Lirianna imagined her two friends traveling alone together, hour after hour, with nothing to distract from their anger and heartbreak.

Suddenly her eyes widened as an idea came to her.

Distraction! Now that *I may be able to do something about.*

As the wagon started up the winding path that scaled the cliffs of Monstar, Lirianna surreptitiously reached for the chain around her neck and clasped her hearing stone.

9

THE BERTH AND BREAD

Aaron didn't speak to Alyen the entire day. He rode ahead without looking back once, leading the way through Sheanen Crann until the trees thinned and opened once more to the Moor of Moin and the main road. They stopped briefly to water and rest the horses, but as they'd eaten all their food, they didn't linger and were soon riding once more, heading north toward the Searing Plain.

By late afternoon, Alyen was feeling weak and shaky from hunger and frayed nerves, her stomach an empty pit beneath her ribs. She let out a silent sigh of relief when they came to a crossroads, and Aaron brought Soran to a halt before a stone building with a sign that read "The Berth and Bread Inn" in red lettering.

Alyen slid down from Lusa and unbuckled her saddlebags. Aaron had done the same and was handing Soran's reins to a stable boy, along with a coin from his purse. A small jolt of panic stabbed her stomach as she realized she didn't know the customs around payment for such services. She'd traveled little in her life, and when she had, logistical affairs had always been handled by stewards or the Master of Coin.

Alyen hastily fished out her own leather purse, her fingers fumbling around the coins until she settled on a small silver one. She placed it in the stable boy's outstretched palm, hoping it was both enough and not too much. The boy's expression didn't change as he took Lusa's reins, which Alyen took to be a good sign.

Aaron had already entered the inn, and when Alyen stepped inside, she found the innkeeper greeting him with a handshake and a familiar clap on the shoulder. *Of course, they know each other,* Alyen realized. *Aaron probably knows all the innkeepers in Dúramair. He's been traveling with Morten since he was a child.* She glanced around the comfortable room with its stone hearths and long wooden tables, still empty, early in the day as it was. *This is already Aaron's world,* she thought. *And now I'll have to make it my world as well.*

"I was sorry to hear about Morten," the innkeeper was saying, his voice a low rumble as he held Aaron's gaze with sympathy. "A finer man I've never known."

"Thank you, Gellik," Aaron said. "We'll drink to him tonight, shall we?"

"Indeed, we shall. And a game of Quivers on me, as we used to. I'll have your room readied; food as well. And your companion …?"

Gellik turned to Alyen, his eyes flickering over her fine clothing, realization dawning on his face. His shoulders stiffened, and his voice lost its easy familiarity when he spoke.

"Your Highness." He gave an awkward nod of his head. "It's an honor to have you at the Berth and Bread."

Alyen glanced at Aaron, hoping he would smooth things over with an introduction, but he had turned his attention to counting out coins from his purse, presumably to pay for his room. Alyen wet her lips and gave the innkeeper what she hoped was a warm smile. "Please, call me Keeper. Or … or Alyen, if you prefer."

Gellik nodded, but his face remained wary. "Will you be needing a room as well, then … Keeper?"

"I will, thank you. And dinner and breakfast, too. How—how much do I owe you for the night?"

Gellik's brow pulled together, and he held his hands up in front of him. "No, I couldn't be asking money from you. Your stay will be on me."

"That's very kind—" Alyen began but cut off as her eye caught Aaron's face just behind the innkeeper. His eyes had narrowed, and his head shook nearly imperceptibly from side to side.

Alyen cleared her throat. "No, really, I insist. Your inn is the closest to the Keeper's cottage, after all. I'm sure this is just the first of many times we'll meet. Please," she added as she saw the man hesitate.

Gellik relented with a reluctant nod. "In that case, it's two silvers for the room and four coppers for food. Two coppers extra if you want a bath brought up."

Alyen fished in her purse, relieved. "I'll take it all," she said, giving the innkeeper another smile. Though he returned it with a nod as he took her coin, the uneasiness never left his shoulders or his eyes.

Moments later, Alyen followed Aaron up a wooden stairway to a corridor with rooms on either side. Aaron stopped before one with a number seven carved into the wood, and Alyen quickly found the door bearing an etched five, as Gellik had instructed.

"Aaron," Alyen said, before he could enter his room. Aaron paused and gave her a blank look.

"Thank you. For the hint, downstairs. I guess …I'm a little out of my element."

Aaron considered her for a moment, then looked down to fit a key into the lock of his door.

"I've known these people most of my life, Alyen," he said as the key rattled and the lock clicked. "I've spent a lot of time building relationships with them, and I can't have you messing it all up by being …" He gestured toward her in a motion that seemed to indicate her entire being.

He pulled out the key and the door swung open. Without finishing his sentence, he shook his head, entered his room, and shut the door behind him, leaving Alyen alone in the corridor.

If Alyen hadn't already been starving, she would have seriously considered skipping dinner and staying in her room. The bath that was brought up was warm and soothing, and the room, while somewhat sparse, was comfortable and clean. Loud voices and the scrape of chairs and benches against the stone floor floated up from downstairs as she soaked in the copper tub, the noise advertising the fact that customers were arriving for dinner. Soon a steady drone of talk and laughter streamed through the building. Alyen groaned at the thought of redressing and joining the crowd—and facing Aaron again. But her stomach was rumbling at the smell of stew and fresh bread seeping under her door, so she got out of the tub and prepared herself for dinner.

When she came down the stairs, the noise in the room didn't die out altogether, but it quieted enough to be noticeable. All heads turned her way, and whispers wove through the buzz of more general conversation. Aaron, who was already seated at the tavern counter, talking with Gellik over a tankard, looked up and caught her eye, but turned back to his host almost immediately. Alyen gritted her teeth under the stares of the other patrons. *Fine. He's punishing me, and I suppose I can't expect much different. I'll leave him to his drink and his game.*

Instead of joining him, she found a place at one of the long tables where no one else was sitting, and soon a bowl of stew, a plate of bread and butter, and a tankard of ale was brought. She ate in silence, not looking up, aware that eyes were always on her and the chatter in the room had remained subdued. Occasionally she glanced up at Aaron, hoping against all hope that he would come sit with her, even just for a little while. But he was engrossed in what was apparently the promised game of Quivers, and never once looked her way.

This was supposed to be different, Alyen thought, staring hard into her stew to stop the sting in her eyes. *If I'd never seen that book, if the darklings had gone with Ylvain ... If we were still together, this would have been so much different.*

They would have been sitting together, legs touching lightly under the table. They would have been talking. Laughing. Maybe even enjoying the reactions from the room around them. Basking in their first journey together, both as members of the Trianid and as a couple.

One of their rooms would have been empty.

It didn't take long to finish her meal, and with Aaron

ignoring her and the rest of the room uneasy in her presence, Alyen saw no reason to stay. She nodded her thanks to the woman who came to collect her dishes and retreated to her room, Aaron's eyes flitting her way only for a second as he registered her exit. Once in her room with the door closed, she heard the noise downstairs rise, the sounds of boisterous talk and laughter once again echoing against the walls. Alyen stripped to her undergarments and flopped onto her bed.

She'd been right. The journey to Illya was going to be long, indeed. And she'd never felt more alone in her life.

IO

CONFESSIONS

lyen slept fitfully, unused to the constant drone of noise from the hall below. When she finally did fully wake, the sun through her window told her she'd slept later than intended, and she hastened through her preparations for the day.

Once dressed and packed, Alyen braced herself, fully expecting a repeat experience from the night before. But when she descended the stairs and entered the dining hall, a most welcome sight met her eyes.

"Alyen, my dear! Come and sit and have a bite. The porridge here is really quite good!"

Brother Hugh sat at one of the long tables, raising a mug in her direction, his face beaming beneath his once again disheveled hair. And next to him, greeting her with a silent nod, was Nah'dar. His always-ominous presence attracted a few nervous glances from the other patrons.

Relief flooded Alyen's body, so strong she could have

cried. "Brother Hugh! Nah'dar! What—"

"What are you two doing here?" Aaron's voice cut over hers. Alyen spun to see him standing behind her, a confused frown on his face.

"Couldn't let you two have the adventure all to yourselves now, could we?" Brother Hugh said around a mouthful of porridge.

Nah'dar gestured at the seats opposite them at the table, which Alyen and Aaron took. Aaron scooted down the bench to leave extra room between them—a fact that Nah'dar took in with a flick of his gaze before he spoke.

"It seems that the Seer has had a vision. She insisted we leave immediately and accompany you to Illya. Our presence will apparently be necessary to the success of your journey."

Lirianna. Gratitude swelled in Alyen's chest. *She knew we'd need some company.*

And now that she looked closer, she could see from the flushes on the faces of her companions, and Brother Hugh's generally unkempt state, that their journey had likely been rushed. *They must have ridden through the night to catch up with us so quickly, even if they did stay on the main road.*

On impulse, Alyen reached out and grasped Brother Hugh's hand, catching Nah'dar's gaze with her own. "It's wonderful to have you both."

Nah'dar nodded in acknowledgement, and Brother Hugh patted Alyen's hand before pulling away to redress his breakfast. "Well now, wouldn't be a proper adventure without the four of us together again. And I daresay I've missed it. Been bitten by the questing bug, I have!"

Aaron said nothing, but with a quick glance in his direction Alyen noticed the faint traces of relief lining his face as well.

"We also come with news," Nah'dar said as he sipped his tea. "Messengers from the Brann Dala region arrived not long after you departed. It seems they, too, have fallen victim to the darklings' storms. Several villages have suffered great damage. Many were injured."

Fear sliced through Alyen's heart. "What's being done for them? If there were injuries, I should be there to help ..."

Nah'dar shook his head. "I have sent a contingent of warriors to aid in repairs, and there are no injuries that the local healers cannot handle themselves. The greatest help you can offer, Keeper, is to make haste to Illya."

"Best eat up, then!" Brother Hugh encouraged as porridge and tea arrived for Alyen and Aaron. "It seems we're in a bit of a hurry!"

Breakfast didn't take long, even with Brother Hugh's insistence on second helpings, and soon they were saddled and heading north once more. Alyen had guided Lusa to follow just behind Soran when Nah'dar pulled his stallion level with her, reining the horse in at a slower pace than the others.

"May I have a word, Alyen?" he asked in an undertone.

Alyen glanced at the warrior in surprise, realizing it was perhaps the first time she'd heard her former bodyguard use her actual name. She slowed Lusa to match the stallion's pace, and soon Aaron and Brother Hugh were a fair distance ahead of them. Brother Hugh seemed to be extolling the beauty of the springtime surroundings so loudly to a sulky Aaron that

Alyen doubted either would be able to hear whatever it was Nah'dar wanted to say to her.

"I know it is not your wish to be separated from Aaron," Nah'dar said without preamble. "You carry a secret."

Alyen looked up sharply. "How do you know that? Did Lirianna—"

"The Seer told me nothing. I can see it on your face. The way you move. The way you speak. The patterns of your gaze. You are unhappy."

"Am I that obvious?" Concern prickled at her neck. If Nah'dar could see through her so easily, she'd have to do a better job of upholding the pretense.

"Not exactly. I was First Assassin of the Bahari—I was trained in more than just combat. I know the signs to look for, how to read a person as one might read tracks in the mud, or the weather before a storm. And in you, I see the storm."

He glanced at Alyen before adding, "You needn't worry. I shall tell no one, least of all Aaron. And he is too angry to notice."

Alyen nodded, not trusting herself to speak. When she wasn't forthcoming, Nah'dar spoke instead.

"I assume this split is necessary to your mission?"

Alyen nodded once more, tears standing in her eyes.

Nah'dar nodded as if this confirmed more than he had asked. "Then I shall do what I can to smooth your way. I may at least provide the Slayer with some distraction while you do what it is you must do. Perhaps this will bring you both some peace."

Alyen looked at Nah'dar in surprised gratitude. "Why?" she finally asked.

Nah'dar looked confused. "What do you mean, 'why'?"

"Well, it's just … I didn't take you for one to concern himself with other people's love problems."

"Ordinarily, no," Nah'dar confirmed. "But your wellbeing is now my foremost priority, and if heartbreak is what stands in the way of your happiness, then I must do what I can to remedy it. You are my sanahara."

"Your what?"

Nah'dar shifted in his saddle, his eyes focused forward. "There is a tradition in Sandamar —a code of honor, if you will—that when a person's life is saved, a bond is created between that person and his savior. He lives now on gifted time that he would not have had if his savior—his sanahara— had not given him this second chance, and with this blessing comes obligation. He must now use the time he has to ensure the happiness and wellbeing of his sanahara in whatever way he can. To return the debt of life by filling his sanahara's life with as much joy and comfort as possible. Therefore, if my sanahara's happiness is threatened, I must do whatever I can to alleviate her suffering. Even if it means entangling myself in the snare of a lovers' quarrel."

Alyen shook her head. "Nah'dar, I didn't save your life. It was Faer Dinnán."

"It was you who petitioned him on my behalf."

"Yes, but only because I tried and failed to save you myself. Really, you don't owe me anything."

Nah'dar looked at Alyen frankly. "My life was saved, Alyen, so I must repay the debt to someone. To be honest, I would much rather be indebted to you than to the faerie king."

"Ah," Alyen nodded her understanding. "In that case, I accept your help with gratitude."

Nah'dar nodded. He hesitated a moment, then added, "Even if you were not my sanahara, Alyen, I would still desire your happiness. And Aaron's. I am sorry to see you both this way."

Alyen swallowed the lump in her throat and tried to make her tone light. "Any advice?"

Nah'dar shook his head. "Love is not an area I can advise on."

"What, no girl ever caught your eye in Sandamar?" Alyen teased half-heartedly, hoping to divert the conversation away from the rawness around her heart.

"No."

"Why not?"

Nah'dar was quiet for so long that Alyen assumed he was ignoring the question, as she'd suspected he would. But suddenly he said very quietly, "Because I do not think of women in that way."

"Oh ... *Oh.*" Realization dawned. Then shock that he'd confided in her. As far as she understood, such things were not widely accepted in Sandamar, and as such, Nah'dar wouldn't have taken the decision to tell her lightly.

Alyen hesitated a moment, then reached out a tentative hand to touch the captain's arm. "Thank you for telling me. You didn't have to—even if I am your sanahara."

Nah'dar nodded once, then cleared his throat, looking uncomfortable. "It feels proper that you should know, but I would appreciate your discretion," he said, eyeing her.

"Of course. You can always trust me. Besides, you're keeping my secret, too." Alyen offered him a weak grin, and Nah'dar's lips twitched in the closest thing she'd ever seen to a smile upon them.

"Nah'dar?"

"Yes?"

"Thank you. For being my friend." Nah'dar met her eyes, and Alyen hoped he could see the sincerity in them.

Nah'dar held her gaze a moment, then looked away. "You are my sanahara. We are more than friends." With that, he nudged his stallion to pick up the pace to catch up with Aaron and Brother Hugh.

The day passed much more pleasantly than the last. Nah'dar and Brother Hugh alternated riding next to Alyen and Aaron, and Alyen was grateful for the respite from constantly hovering alone under Aaron's cloud of ire. Still, she watched him as they moved through the day, often wishing she knew what was taking place in his mind behind the hardness he'd thrown up like a wall around himself. Was he simply angry, or was he perhaps tormented by memories implanted by Faer Dinnán—memories that had never actually taken place? He didn't talk much to anyone, which didn't come as a surprise since she didn't feel up to conversation either, but it didn't seem to bother either of their companions. Nah'dar was usually silent to begin with, and Brother Hugh either talked enough for everyone, or was content to hum, often inventing new verses to his standard adventuring song.

> *"Ooooooooooooh, I quest to save the faerie king,*
> *A derry derry dally,*
> *His darklings still to evil cling,*
> *'Tis storming in the valley!"*

As the day progressed to evening and the shadows lengthened, the group began to search for a place to camp for the night. The next inn was too far off to push the horses, and they'd passed the last one two hours before. After Nah'dar's report of Brann Dala, no one had felt they could afford to stop early, so Alyen prepared herself to spend the night in the open.

They found a place to camp behind a swell just off the road where a few trees grew around a meandering brook. Once the horses were unsaddled and tethered to graze, Nah'dar drew his scimitar and nodded to an expanse of open terrain adjacent to the camp.

"Come, Slayer. Training awaits."

Aaron didn't question the statement, and soon the campsite was filled with the familiar sounds of clashing metal punctuated by the occasional shout.

"Well, this certainly brings back memories, doesn't it?" Brother Hugh had appeared by Alyen's side as she watched the two warriors dance, dark silhouettes against the rays of the setting sun. The corner of her mouth twitched up.

"I never thought I'd miss preparing to battle morkshai. But I suppose I do." She lowered her eyes and turned away to busy herself gathering twigs for a fire. "I guess a lot has changed."

Brother Hugh joined her, fishing in his saddlebags for a pot and a cooking spoon. "Indeed, life does seem to surprise us with its twists and turns. Look at me! A year ago, I'd never have thought that I'd be where I am now, married, yet separated from my lady love on a quest to save the very world."

Alyen felt a pang of guilt. "That's right, you're a newlywed. I'm sorry—you should be with Nellie."

"Not to worry, my dear. Our separation will only make our reunion all the more joyous. True love such as ours lasts forever, after all." Brother Hugh glanced in the direction of the sparring warriors and continued, his voice suddenly tentative. "Speaking of which, my dear, how are you finding your first days as the Keeper of Dúramair?"

Alyen decided to avoid the question she knew he was really asking. "Actually, it—it hasn't been very fun," she admitted, and she explained to Brother Hugh about the innkeeper's discomfort around her at the Berth and Bread Inn, and the way the other patrons felt ill-at-ease whenever she was present. "I suppose it's because of what I did at Norhelm," she concluded heavily. "I think everyone's afraid of me."

Brother Hugh shook his head, his lips pursed. "Oh, no, I don't think it's that at all, my dear. At least not entirely. No, I think it likely has more to do with the fact that you're a royal."

Alyen blinked. "What? But I'm not anymore. And the Keeper gets almost as much respect as a royal anyway."

"Ah, but there's a difference!" Brother Hugh brandished his spoon in her direction. "The Trianid has always been comprised of common folk—a powerful trio rising from the masses to serve the needs of the people they came from. It made a nice counterbalance to the power wielded by the throne—kindly wielded, mind you, but still, wielded by those born to privilege. Now, you've mixed the two up. It's never happened before. And I daresay, no one really knows what to do with you."

"Do with me?"

"You know." Brother Hugh gestured vaguely in the air with his spoon. "How to act around you. What to say and how to say it. Are they supposed to treat you like a princess, or like one of their own? Neither one seems right, does it?"

Alyen was at a loss. "But how do I fix that? Obviously, they should treat me like they've always treated the Keeper, but I can't very well go around issuing a proclamation to that effect."

"Oh, no, no," Brother Hugh chuckled. "No, that would rather defeat the purpose, wouldn't it? I think what you must do, my dear, is set the tone yourself. Let the people see you acting as one of them. You'll have to be patient, of course, but over time they'll come to see you that way themselves."

"But that could take *years*!"

Brother Hugh looked thoughtful. "Well, a few maybe, but there's really no rushing these things. Humans aren't very good with change, you know. But the less known a person is, the easier it is to accept change in them. So you've got that going for you."

A particularly loud clash of steel accompanied by a ferocious shout drew their attention to the two warriors, now straining against each other with weapons locked. Alyen took in the sweat pouring down Aaron's face, his muscles quivering until finally he released with a shout of frustration, throwing his sword to the side to stalk away and shake out his arms.

Nah'dar simply stood and met Alyen's eyes in silence.

"Like I was saying, my dear," came Brother Hugh's soft voice. "The real difficulty comes when those closest to us change."

Alyen let her eyes drop. When she spoke, her voice sounded sullen. "Change happens, though. No one stays the same forever, so they shouldn't be expected to. People in *my* life have changed. And I've always accepted it."

At this, Brother Hugh chortled.

"What?" Alyen said, indignantly. "When did I try to stop someone from changing?"

Brother Hugh looked at Alyen with fondness. "Perhaps you didn't *try*, my dear, but look at me. I'm a married man and haven't worn my monk's habit in months, yet still you call me *Brother* Hugh."

Alyen frowned. "Oh. I suppose I do. I guess I didn't think …"

Brother Hugh merely smiled and shrugged.

"Well, what *should* I call you? Master Hugh? Cook Hugh? Just … Hugh?"

Brother Hugh squinted up at the sky, then shook his head. "No, I don't think 'Hugh' would do. That's what Nellie calls me, and I rather like it that way. Let's just stick with Brother Hugh for now, shall we? Perhaps I, myself, haven't quite grown out of it yet. Change, you know!"

Alyen watched Brother Hugh go about his work for a moment, reflecting. In a perfect world, Rowenna would have been the one to introduce her to the world of their work as they traveled together, apprentice and mentor. Since her death, Alyen had always pictured Aaron as the one to fill that role, but fate had not favored that plan either. Lirianna might know what to do, but she was at Monstar, and Nah'dar—well, he hardly qualified as someone who knew how to avoid being intimidating. But Brother Hugh …

"Brother Hugh," Alyen said suddenly. "I think I need your help."

Brother Hugh looked up from preparing the fire. "Do you? With what, my dear?"

"I need to gain people's trust, and I'm not sure how to put

them at ease until they're more used to the idea of me as Keeper. Do you think you could … guide me?"

Brother Hugh's chest swelled with pride, and he gave such an enthusiastic bow that it almost sent him toppling into their pile of cooking gear. "I would be most honored to be of service, my dear! We shall start immediately. Now, let me think …" He tapped his cheek thoughtfully with the end of his spoon. "In my expert opinion, the first thing that will help you in establishing trust will be for you to show a willingness and a capability for what the common folk refer to as 'real work.'"

"*Real* work?"

"Yes. Real work is the work of everyday living that people spend most of their lives doing. Cooking, cleaning, caring for animals and livestock, growing and storing food … The things most assume royalty know nothing about, consider below them, and have servants to do for them."

"So, what, I just let people see me making tea?"

Brother Hugh nodded vigorously. "Yes! You must show the people that you are self-reliant without expecting special treatment. Whenever the opportunity arises, you should make a point to be seen saddling your horse, washing clothes, cooking meals …"

"But I don't know how to cook!"

Brother Hugh paused and blinked at Alyen. "You don't know how to cook?"

"Well, —no. We *do* have servants to cook at the castle. And at Monstar, the sisters did the cooking."

Brother Hugh's eyes moved from side to side before resting on Alyen's face. "My dear, as Keeper of Scales, do you not intend to live in the Keeper's cottage?"

"Yes."

"Alone?"

Alyen swallowed, willing herself not to glance in Aaron's direction. "Yes."

"And how were you planning to feed yourself?"

"I … hadn't thought about it."

Brother Hugh's back straightened, his nostrils flaring. "My dear, as a matter of survival, it is time you learned to cook. And as your most recently appointed tutor, I will teach you!"

Thus began Alyen's education in the culinary arts.

For the remainder of the evening, Brother Hugh instructed Alyen as she boiled water, chopped vegetables, sprinkled spices, and stirred. At one point, seeing the flames dipping low, she started to ask the salamandars to assist, whereupon Brother Hugh whirled around, brandishing a finger in her direction.

"No!" he exclaimed. "There will be no cheating on my watch!"

"I'm not *cheating*!" Alyen protested. "I'm just fixing the fire."

"*You* are not, the fire spirits are. Do you think this will help you cultivate an image of self-reliance?"

"No, but everyone knows I'm the Keeper, don't they? Aren't I expected to do stuff like this?"

Brother Hugh's eyes narrowed. "Do you know *how* to do it yourself?"

Alyen held his gaze silently for a moment, then looked away. "No."

"Very well, then. No more elemental help! You must arrange the wood just so."

By the time Aaron and Nah'dar abandoned their sparring for the night, Alyen, under Brother Hugh's enthusiastic supervision, had managed to produce a very passable stew. It was a small accomplishment, perhaps, but she still felt a glow of pride as she watched the others eating it contentedly, enjoying the savory warmth spreading through her own belly as well.

It would have been pleasant, cozy even, had things been different. But despite Brother Hugh's cheerful chatter, the air remained thick with Aaron's silence, and in the distant darkness of night falling, green-tinged lightning flashed ominously over the moor.

II

TRAINING

Night had fallen, the fire faded to embers, and a spray of stars cascaded across the sky, still clear above their camp. Alyen straightened from preparing her blankets to look out at the moor, the place where a deeper blackness blotted out the stars, punctuated by angry flashes of lightning and the distant rumble of thunder. An uneasy breeze wafted past her ear, sylphs scattering before it, devoid of their usual playful cavorting. Then a glow caught her eye from the field where Aaron and Nah'dar had trained just hours before.

Faer Dinnán.

The faerie king stood alone on the moor, gazing in Alyen's direction in silent summons. She sighed inwardly. After the considerable tension between them at the Keeper's cottage, she wasn't sure what to expect from their next encounter. Alyen glanced at the others, preparing their sleeping spots for the night, and cleared her throat.

90

"I'm going to be up awhile—just out on the moor. You don't need to wait up for me."

Nah'dar straightened and Aaron glanced up, pausing in his own work, his expression suspicious.

"It is not wise to venture out alone at night, Keeper. If your business cannot wait for morning, I will accompany you."

Alyen swallowed, her eyes flitting to Aaron. "It's all right Nah'dar. I'll be with Faer Dinnán."

With a soft noise of disgust, Aaron abruptly turned back to his bed, his back to Alyen.

"Very well," Nah'dar said. "If you have need of me, I'll be taking the first watch."

Alyen gave him a grateful smile, and, glancing briefly at Aaron's back, turned to the darkness of the moor.

She could see nothing, her eyes still attuned to the glow of the fire. A few whispered words brought the salamandars to light her way once more, and she picked her way slowly over the ground to the faerie king. Her chest tightened as she saw that now both arms were fully translucent, flickering like a dying flame.

"It's getting worse," she observed by way of greeting.

Faer Dinnán nodded. "It is. And for this reason, I fear we cannot delay your training."

"Training?"

Faer Dinnán looked perplexed. "Of course. You need to practice connecting with so many elementals at once—and darklings at that. How else are you to succeed in turning so many across such vast distances back to their natural state? You will recall what happened the last time you attempted a similar feat."

A shiver ran up Alyen's spine, guilt settling like rocks in her stomach. "I do."

Faer Dinnán's gaze held a hint of compassion, and Alyen was relieved that the anger and impatience he'd shown at the Keeper's cottage seemed to have dissipated. "It will be different this time, Alyen. This time you will be prepared. But only if we train, and we have little time. You will reach Illya before the new moon. And we will have to practice with Aaron as well so he is prepared to be your anchor."

Alyen glanced back at the glow from the campfire. "I don't think he's going to be very happy about that," she said.

"He has not taken things well." It was a statement, rather than a question.

Alyen looked back at the faerie king. His eyes, fathomless as always, seemed troubled, but it wasn't enough to stop the sting of anger rising in Alyen's chest. "No. But that was to be expected," she said briskly. "So, how shall I practice?"

Faer Dinnán turned to face the moor, his eyes reflecting the stormy blackness that shrouded the sky. "The first thing you must do is ensure that your understanding of the darklings—and our work—is correct. Otherwise, you've lost before you've begun."

Alyen frowned. "Darklings are elementals turned to evil, and I have to try to turn them back. Isn't that what we're doing?"

Faer Dinnán turned to face her, his eyes earnest. "Exactly so. But we must be sure the accuracy of your words is not an accident. You say the darklings are elementals *turned* to evil. They are not evil themselves. It's crucial that you understand this distinction and what it implies."

"It makes a difference?"

"It is the entire point."

"Why?"

"Because your understanding will dictate your strategy. And only one approach will work."

"I don't think I understand."

Faer Dinnán looked once more to the distant storm, a gust of air blowing the hair back from his timeless features. "When you were faced with Malscath and his horde of morkshai, did you see them as evil?"

"Of course."

"And how did you seek to rid yourself of them?"

"We fought them. Killed them."

Faer Dinnán's head turned quickly to Alyen, his eyes flashing. "Precisely."

Alyen's mind ignited with understanding. "You don't want me to fight the darklings."

"They are my children. They suffer from what Ylvain did to them. I would have them healed. Saved."

Alyen took in the faerie king's face, a sadness deep as the oceans tracing his features. She drew in her breath, gazing at the darkness stretching over the land as she felt the malice lacing the wind. "I won't plan to fight them, but that might not be easy. The darklings will certainly fight *me*."

"They are victims as much as any of us are, Alyen. Perhaps even more so, as they are powerless to help themselves."

Faer Dinnán lifted a translucent hand, and in an instant it was surrounded by a cluster of sylphs. Alyen watched them weave playfully through his fingers, their affection for their monarch apparent in the dance of their flight. After a moment, Faer Dinnán spoke, his voice laced with tenderness.

"What do you feel when you see these little ones, Keeper of Scales?"

Alyen kept her eyes on the sylphs. "I feel … joy. Affection. I suppose … love." She almost whispered the word.

Faer Dinnán met her gaze, his eyes fierce beneath their warmth. "Then you must practice feeling this love for the darklings you seek to save."

Alyen looked at the faerie king, incredulous. "You want me to *love* the darklings?"

"It's the only way."

Memories of the few times she'd encountered darklings flooded Alyen's mind, sending the terror she'd felt on those occasions searing through her body once more. "I—I don't think I can."

"If you cannot, we shall fail."

Panic rose in Alyen's body like a storm. What the faerie king asked was completely unrealistic. No one could expect her to be able to love creatures that tainted the very air around them with terror and malice. Creatures that sought her own life and the lives of those she loved.

And yet, if she could not …

She had failed already, and she knew it.

Faer Dinnán watched Alyen's face in silence as she fought against the fear in her throat, her mind racing in a vain attempt to find a loophole that would save her world—or at least release her from the responsibility for its destruction. Finally, he spoke, gesturing to a large boulder nearby.

"Perhaps you would like to sit down?"

Alyen sank onto the cold stone, and Faer Dinnán settled himself next to her. He studied her face once more.

"You forget, Alyen. We face this task together."

Alyen hoped her eyes didn't look too accusing. "But you can't make me love the darklings."

"That's true, I cannot. But I think perhaps you misunderstand my meaning. I tend to forget that humans are very dramatic about their definition of love."

Alyen snorted. "And faeries aren't?"

Faer Dinnán shook his head. "Love means many things to nature. The turn of the seasons, waves caressing the shore, rain falling on growing things, the passing smile of a stranger … all these things can be love. As can accepting the existence of one—or many—with whom you find yourself in conflict."

Tentative relief sparked in Alyen's chest. "So, I don't have to *love* the darklings? Not like I would my friends or my horse or even the other elementals? Or …" Alyen's eyes drifted to the glow of the campfire in the distance.

Faer Dinnán's gaze followed Alyen's, and when his eyes returned to her, his voice was soft.

"The love I ask you to find for the darklings most closely relates to the law you already follow: Sanctity of Life. Recognizing that the sacred spark of light within each being, no matter how deeply buried, grants them a right to life that none may touch save Béathan and the Balance itself. To allow them this right despite their darkness—what greater gift can you give?"

One of Alyen's eyebrows quirked upward. "In that case, I believe what you want me to feel is *compassion*."

Faer Dinnán's eyes were quizzical. "Exactly. A form of love, is it not?"

Alyen exhaled. "One I can work with."

Faer Dinnán's mouth twitched and he stood from the rock,

pulling Alyen with him. "Come, Keeper of Scales. The hour is late and we have work to do."

The faerie king led her away from the rock, salamandars flitting before them to light their way, then forming a circle, their fiery glow in sharp contrast to the darkness of the moor. He stopped when they reached the center of the circle and turned to Alyen, his face intent.

"To heal the darklings, you will have to form a bond between them and yourself. We will speak later how this is to be done, but first we must build your stamina and control. The guardians of the four elements are the strongest of the elementals and the hardest for humans to connect to without losing control, so we will practice with each group one by one, beginning with the sylphs. When you are ready, extend your mind to them, and connect with as many as you are able, from as great a distance as possible. I will be here to aid and anchor you should it become necessary."

He nodded and stepped back expectantly.

Alyen took a breath and closed her eyes, trying to clear her mind and calm the fluttering of her stomach. *It won't be like Norhelm,* she told herself. *This time I have Faer Dinnán to guide me.* Despite her remaining resentment, the thought bolstered her courage and, pushing away all thoughts of Norhelm, of Aaron, of her people who might never trust her, of failing to save her world, she brought her mind only to this moment, this place on the moor with the darkness around her.

Then, her eyes still closed, she turned her thoughts to the air around her. She felt the way it caressed her skin, listened to the hush of it dancing through the grasses at her feet. She imagined it whispering miles away as it rushed through the trees of Sheanen Crann, or whipped over the sea toward Illya.

She remembered its biting cold as they approached the mountains of Norhelm, and the way it had woven around her hands as they clasped Rowenna's the night of their binding so long ago. She seeped herself in each thought, each memory, until they belonged not only to her mind, but to her entire being, her body feeling each gust and breeze as though it were the only thing in the world.

Then, once she was filled with the essence of air and wind, she sent her mind out across the vast distances of her kingdom, and opened her mouth in the singing speech.

"Sylphs who ride the waves of air, wind and storm and breezes fair, join with me to take delight in magic shared upon this night."

The rush of magic nearly took Alyen's breath away, and she felt one leg nearly buckle. A jolt of fear speared her heart as the memories of Norhelm slammed back into her mind. Her eyes flew open as she gasped, all concentration lost, her connection to the sylphs broken.

Faer Dinnán was watching her, a faint line between his eyes.

"I'm sorry," Alyen panted. "It was too much, all at once."

"It wasn't nearly what it will actually be with the darklings."

"I'm doing my best!" Alyen snapped, then immediately regretted her tone. She took a breath, then spoke more calmly. "This is hard for me. Particularly after Norhelm. I'm trying."

Faer Dinnán was silent for a time, observing Alyen as she collected herself. She expected him to say something to instruct, encourage—perhaps even scold. But he simply waited until her breath had slowed before asking, "Are you ready to try again?"

Alyen nodded reluctantly, and, as the faerie king said nothing more, closed her eyes again.

Once more she gathered her memories, filling her body and thoughts with the wind. Once more she sent her mind out and beckoned to the sylphs in the singing speech. This time when the magic hit she was prepared for it, but still the force of it was staggering as it crashed upon her. She felt the panic begin to rise, and she nearly abandoned her cause again.

Then Faer Dinnán's voice sounded in her mind. *"Hold fast, Alyen. You are equal to this task, and on the other side of struggle is great beauty."*

Alyen gritted her teeth and fought to steady her breath. Sweat beaded on her brow as she struggled to grasp on to the enormity of the magic pressing around her. The air seemed to pick up on her agitation and rushed restlessly around her, whipping her hair across her grimacing face.

"Magic is an ocean, Alyen, and you cannot fight the sea. Ride it instead, and you will learn how to harness its power as your own. Control is found in release."

Faer Dinnán's words echoed through her body as the magic crushed against her, threatening to consume. She couldn't release. If she did she would lose herself to the power and be drowned by it. Or worse, create a repeat of Norhelm. The wind grew stronger, moaning as it raked against her skin.

"Think, Alyen. What is it you must give up in order to let go?"

Alyen forced her mind to work despite the growing pain in her head. If she really was equal to this task, why couldn't she do it? What was stopping her? What did she need to give up to release and find control?

Fear.

It was her own voice she heard this time, and the thought

settled into her bones with the weight of its truth. Fear was the only thing holding her back, the only thing that stood between her and her true power. It was no revelation. She had always known it was so and had spent her lifetime pushing fear away so she could do what must be done.

Because she had always done what needed to be done.

She had given up her throne, torn apart her kingdom, killed Ylvain, and broken Aaron's heart—all in the name of duty and survival. All while hoping her will would be enough to overcome the fear that rose and fell like a storm within her.

But if shoving fear aside didn't work, what would? If she didn't change something, all her efforts—including what she'd done to Aaron—would have been for naught. The thought sent a pang through her heart, and she felt resolve rise within her like fire. Too many had suffered for it all to amount to nothing, so, fear or not, full power or not, she would do what she could to make it count. Still bracing against the weight of magic and the howling wind, Alyen focused inward and found her fear.

"I don't know what to do with you," she told it. *"I won't push you away, but until I figure you out, there are things I have to do. Let me do them."*

Then she turned her mind back to the magic, the wind, the sylphs … and released.

It felt as if her body flew to pieces, expanding ever outward into a vast and boundless void. She floated for a moment, utterly free from any sensation, thought, or care. Then slowly, she felt the pieces of herself begin to latch, one by one, onto the tiny pinpoints of magic that surrounded her. The pieces of herself drifted inward, at first unhurried, then with greater speed as they began to coalesce back into the being that was Alyen. Yet this version of her was infused with the magic of air and wind, each spark of power a sylph firmly tethered to the core of magic that was her own. Her body, her mind, her entire being felt weightless and airy, and she felt laughter bubble up within her as she realized she'd never in her life felt so *free*.

"*Alyen.*"

It was Faer Dinnán's voice, but something in his tone had changed. She didn't much care. She wanted to stay as she was, floating and free forever.

"*Alyen, do not lose concentration, but open your eyes.*"

Alyen nearly laughed at the words. *Concentration.* This was the opposite of concentrating. Perhaps she'd never concentrate again. But she opened her eyes as he'd asked …

And saw the moor stretching beneath her at least twenty feet below.

Her consciousness slammed back to reality and her eyes flew wide as she suddenly dropped several feet before stopping herself. Stopping herself how? She had no idea. She simply wished for the air to hold her, and it did. Sylphs, flighty and playful, darted all around her, weaving the currents of air that drifted and spun as she willed them. They were a part of her, yet separate—or was it she who was a part of them? They were so closely enmeshed, there was no way to tell.

Tentatively, she held out her arms, willing herself to turn in a circle, and slowly, her body complied. Wonder and joy filled her, and a cool breeze caressed her fingers and cheeks as she drifted and spun far above the world beneath.

"*I'm flying!*" She sent her jubilant thought to Faer Dinnán.

"*You are,*" came his voice, still with the altered tone she didn't know how to interpret. "*Can you make yourself come down?*"

"I suppose."

She didn't want to. She wanted to stay aloft, to dance with the sylphs in the eddies and waves of air. But suddenly an icy breeze sent a shiver of dread up her spine, and her eye caught the darkness of the storm across the moor. The fear within her nudged, and, remembering that this was no game, she turned her gaze downward and gently sank to the earth.

As her feet touched down in the circle of the salamandars' glow, she felt her connection with the sylphs waver. She released it and stood, simply herself once more, next to Faer Dinnán. The faerie king was looking at her with an expression she couldn't decipher. He seemed almost unsure of what to say.

"Did I do it right?" she asked in jest, knowing she had. But Faer Dinnán didn't share her levity.

"You ... *melded.*"

"I what?"

"I'm not sure I can accurately describe it. You became one with the element. You became part of the air."

Alyen frowned and looked down at her body. "I became a sylph?"

"No," Faer Dinnán said, shaking his head. "You were at once yourself *and* the air. I have never seen another human work such magic."

Alyen swallowed, unsure of what to make of his statement. "Surely it was the aid of your magic that gave me the boost."

Faer Dinnán shook his head once more. "I gave no magic to you, Alyen. What you did was entirely your own."

Alyen didn't know what to say, and a silence stretched

between them. Finally, Faer Dinnán asked, "Do you think you have the stamina to try it once more?"

Alyen paused to take stock of herself. She felt fresh, light, rejuvenated. As if she could run for miles without stopping. "Yes."

An eagerness flitted across Faer Dinnán's features—excitement perhaps, Alyen thought. He looked around at the circle of salamandars and nodded.

"Whatever you did, do it once more, but this time connect to the salamandars. Those around us, and those far away, just as with the sylphs. Again, I shall be here to aid you if necessary."

Alyen nodded, and closed her eyes.

This time, she addressed her fear first. *I'm doing it again. Stay and watch if you will, but leave me to my work.*

Then she turned her thoughts to fire. Blazing fires in the hearths at Castle Dúr. The crackling fires they'd slept around on their quest through Sheanen Crann. Lighting strikes flashing across a storming sky. The soft glow of candles in her room at Monstar.

The fire she'd watched from the embrace of Aaron's arms in the Keeper's cottage.

She filled her body and mind with warmth, heat, and flame, feeling the glow of the circle she stood within intensify. Once she was filled to bursting with fire, she spoke again in the singing speech.

"Guardians of the flame and light, heat and lightning burning bright, join me with your fiery power, dance with me this midnight hour."

Then, feeling the near burn of flaming magic pressing

about her, she spread her arms, and let herself fall apart into its heat.

As before, the void came first—an emptiness devoid of thought or care. Then suddenly, the space was filled with the infinite sparks of flame and light that were the salamandars. They hovered a moment, then began to attach themselves to the pieces of her consciousness, at first just a few, then more and more by the second until Alyen was overcome with a wave of heat and power that filled her being, blending with her magic until she couldn't tell where she began and the fire ended. She stretched her arms upward, glorying in the vibrancy of the energy that pulsed through her.

"Alyen," breathed Faer Dinnán's voice in her mind. *"You are magnificent."*

Alyen opened her eyes and looked at her arms. Her skin was glowing as if a thousand stars dwelt within her. Flames, gentle to the touch as the sun's morning caress, licked up and down her limbs and through her hair. If she looked closely, tiny spiderwebs of lightning flickered just beneath her skin.

Faer Dinnán was looking at her with something close to awe. "I have never seen the likes of this. Keeper of Scales, you have *become* the fire."

The intensity of the faerie king's gaze and the way he was looking at her with near adoration unnerved Alyen. "But you must have known this was possible. You must have known I could do it. You chose me for the Sight, after all."

Faer Dinnán's brow furrowed in confusion. "Chose you? It was not I who gave you the Sight, Alyen. The choice has never been mine."

"But if not you … who?" It was Alyen's turn to look confused.

"It was born with you, Alyen. It's a gift bestowed by Béathan and none other. It's a part of who you are. As is this wondrous magic."

Alyen looked once more at her shining, flaming body and again, she had to resist the urge to laugh aloud. She flexed her fingers and felt the power coursing through her surge in response, the flames on her arms flaring higher.

Caution flickered through Faer Dinnán's expression. "It would be best to break the connection now, Alyen. This is a new magic and we don't know how exhausting it may be for you."

Alyen hated the thought of severing herself from the fire rushing through her, but she knew the faerie king was right. Reluctantly, she turned her mind back to the salamandars, loosening them gently from the core of her magic as she bade them a grateful farewell. Slowly, the glow beneath her skin dimmed and the flames died down. Soon even the lightning had left her, and she stood as herself once more in the glow of the salamandars' ring.

"How do you feel?" Faer Dinnán asked her, his eyes searching.

Alyen considered. "Alone. And small. But well."

Faer Dinnán nodded, looking as if there was much he wanted to say. But when he finally spoke, his words revealed nothing of his thoughts.

"We will continue tomorrow. Rest and recover. You wrought great magic this night."

Alyen nodded, suddenly glad at the thought of sleep as exhaustion settled upon her. She turned to go, but Faer Dinnán's voice stopped her.

"And Alyen—the fear you felt tonight? Keep it. You will need that, too."

His words sent a chill down her spine and into her stomach, but when she turned to respond, she found she was alone on the dark moor.

12
MIDNIGHT

It was late, and the corridors of Monstar Abbey were silent. Lirianna stifled a yawn as she entered her room, careful to latch the door quietly behind her. The doors she'd passed on the way were all dark, devoid of any candlelight spilling out from the cracks into the shadowy corridor. Her lamp had been the only light; everyone else was asleep.

She pulled off her clothes and shrugged on her nightgown, sinking gratefully onto her soft bed. She wrapped a shawl over her shoulders—the one her mother had sent her, patterned in the style of Tiragel—and inhaled its comforting scent of home. She was exhausted, but she didn't want to sleep just yet. She needed to let her mind settle.

She'd been weaving most the day, and all night, until her fingers cramped and her back protested too loudly to ignore anymore. She'd stretched her mind out across the web of the Balance, searching for a vision or even just a clue of what was to come. She'd seen the darkling clouds raging over the land,

and she'd seen Castle Illya. But none of that was new information, and her visions hadn't divulged anything more. The only constant was the same strange unease she'd felt on their journey back to the abbey, running across all the threads of the Balance, like a wrong note struck in a chord.

Lirianna leaned back to rest her head on the wall, gazing out her window at the darkness that hid the forest stretching below the cliffs. Darkness as black as the yarn she'd woven with all day—and for so much of the previous year—as she'd strained to catch glimpses of Ylvain and her monsters. *Once this is all over, I hope I never have to weave with black again,* she thought. *I've had enough darkness for a lifetime.*

Suddenly, her hearing stone grew hot against her skin. Her eyebrows lifted in surprise, then drew together in concern. It was late; had something happened? She groped at the chain around her neck and clasped the stone in her palm.

"Lirianna?"

It was Aaron's voice sounding in her mind.

"Aaron! Is everything all right?" she asked.

"Everyone's fine, sorry. Did I wake you? I know it's late."

"No, I'm still up. H-How are things?" Lirianna winced, hearing how awkward she sounded.

Aaron paused. *"Not great, honestly. Nah'dar's on watch, but I couldn't sleep, and ..."* His voice trailed off. *"I was just wondering, did Alyen tell you anything? About us? About why she ...?"*

Lirianna's pulse quickened. She'd been expecting Aaron to ask something like this eventually. She mustn't weaken the enchantment, but she didn't want to lie either. She chose her words carefully.

"You think she hasn't been honest with you?"

"I don't know." Aaron's voice was laced with frustration. *"If*

you'd asked me last week, I'd have said the whole idea of her wanting to be with Faer Dinnán was ridiculous, but she just came back to camp after meeting with him out on the moor and she was practically floating. She looked so … happy."

Lirianna's heart ached at the misery in her friend's voice. She frowned. Alyen certainly hadn't been happy the last time they'd talked. What had happened?

"Maybe I shouldn't be surprised, though." Aaron's voice was bitter now. *"I always knew he had a thing for her."*

Lirianna's eyebrows shot up. *"Faer Dinnán?"*

"Of course, couldn't you tell? It's written all over his face when he looks at her. And he's the faerie king. I suppose any girl would be tempted, it's just that—" He paused, and when he spoke again, his voice was softer. *"It just seemed to change really fast. So, I wondered if she said something to you. Maybe something I missed."*

"You're right, Aaron," Lirianna said, shaking her head sadly. *"It was really fast. I'd be confused too."* She grimaced, hoping he would interpret her empathy as ignorance.

"All right. Thanks anyway. I guess it's some comfort knowing I'm not the only one who found it strange. Get some rest."

She heard his mental sigh, and let her breath out in relief.

"You, too, Aaron. Goodnight."

Lirianna dropped her stone back beneath her nightgown and rested her hand over the lump where it lay against her skin. Her heart ached for Aaron, and though she hadn't really lied, she still felt that she'd deceived him. How would he react when he found out the truth? Somehow she didn't think his relationship with Alyen would be the only one at stake.

Lirianna rose from her bed and stalked to the window, one hand raking through her tangle of curls, all thoughts of sleep abandoned. She hated this. She hated seeing her friends in pain, hated the secrets and the lies, hated the dance she had to do between them, hated watching everything fall apart without being able to do anything about it. And if she was honest, it wasn't only her friends' feelings she was worried about. What would happen to the Trianid if things got too far out of hand to be repaired? What would happen to the friendship between the three of them?

What would happen to *her*?

That was the curse of being the Seer of Strands: fated to watch people and events come and go for good or ill, without ever being able to do more than issue warnings. An essential role, yes, but always on the sidelines and never part of the action.

Lirianna scratched at her hands. Suddenly they felt hot and itchy. Likely she'd dried them out weaving all day. She reached for a cream to rub into them before attempting sleep once more and did a double take.

She could have sworn she'd seen something on the skin of her fingers. Something that had … *glowed*.

She stared at her hands, turning them this way and that in the pale light filtering through her windows. She saw nothing.

Probably just a trick of the moonlight, she thought, and rubbed the cream into her fingers and palms. They already felt cooler, the itch subsiding.

Lirianna turned back to her bed and slipped beneath her warm quilt. She'd have to talk to Alyen tomorrow and see what was going on. She couldn't imagine there was any truth to Aaron's suspicions about her friend and Faer Dinnán. Still, he *was* a faerie, and, if stories were to be believed, Alyen would be wise to exercise caution around him. If he was truly pursuing her, and she was feeling vulnerable …

She'd talk to Alyen in the morning.

Lirianna watched the moon rise higher over the forest, grateful that no black clouds obscured it this night. She sighed and rolled over, turning her back to the window and everything beyond. She shut her eyes, determined to sleep. Her loom would be waiting tomorrow, and visions always came more easily if she was rested.

After all, it was the only thing she could do to help.

13

DARKNESS

Alyen woke early feeling refreshed and rested. It surprised her, honestly, how well she felt. With all the strain she'd already been feeling, she'd expected the prior night's activities to drain her, as newer, bigger magic always had in the past. Instead, she felt better than she had since they'd left the Keeper's cottage, and she was grateful for it.

She peered around their campsite, noting that Nah'dar and Aaron were both still sleeping, and that Brother Hugh had taken the last watch—a further surprise. She rose and stepped quietly to the edge of their camp to join him.

"Good Morning, Brother Hugh."

The former monk gave a little start, his tuneless humming cut short. "Alyen, my dear! How lovely to see you on this glorious morning! What brings you out of bed so early—or have you come to enjoy the birdsong at dawn?"

"I don't know," Alyen said, lowering herself onto a rock

beside him. "Just done sleeping, I suppose. But since when do you take a shift? I thought Nah'dar insisted only trained warriors should be on watch."

"Ah," Brother Hugh said, waggling his eyebrows conspiratorially. "But I *am* trained now, my dear. Nah'dar has been teaching me the art of self-defense over the winter. Apparently, I've made sufficient progress to be promoted to campsite protection!"

He looked so pleased with himself that Alyen had to smile. "Well, congratulations, Brother Hugh. But I have to say, it doesn't seem fair for me to be the only one sleeping all night."

"Not at all, my dear! You are to sleep as much as possible and preserve your strength. Nah'dar told us all about your new magic when we switched shifts last night. He insisted we let you rest. He sounded quite serious, actually. You know how our friend in black can be."

"He saw me?" Alyen asked, feeling a sudden twinge of concern.

"He did," Brother Hugh confirmed. "And it must have been quite a thing to see. He looked like he'd seen a ghost."

Alyen sighed and glanced over at the former assassin's form, still asleep on the ground. She hadn't spoken to Nah'dar when she returned to the campsite last night. She'd been so distracted that she'd only nodded her goodnight and hadn't really paid attention to his response or his mood.

Since his participation in the Ceremony of Three, she'd hoped the captain's intense dislike of magic had softened, but it seemed it hadn't. Perhaps accepting this new form of magic was simply too far a stretch. She'd have to talk to him later and see if she could put his fears to rest. Not for the first time,

Alyen wondered what had made the steely warrior so afraid of magic.

Suddenly she felt her hearing stone hot against her chest. She excused herself from Brother Hugh and wandered toward their horses as she clasped the stone in her hand.

"Alyen? Are you awake?" It was Lirianna, her voice urgent.

"Yes, good morning. What's wrong? You sound worried."

"I wanted to talk to you before everyone was up. Nothing's wrong, but I have to ask you something. It's a little ... awkward."

Alyen frowned. *"What is it?"*

"Are you ... um ... Is there actually anything going on between you and Faer Dinnán?"

Alyen's eyes flew wide. *"What? No! Why would you ask that?"*

"Would you tell me if there was?" Lirianna pressed.

The words stung. *"Of course I would,"* Alyen replied. *"But I can't believe you think I would do that. What's this about?"*

Lirianna's voice sighed in Alyen's head. *"It's Aaron. He talked to me last night, asking questions, and he said you looked really happy when you came to bed after meeting with Faer Dinnán."*

"I ... he saw me? I thought he was asleep." It was Alyen's turn to sigh, the levity she'd felt that morning slipping away. *"It's not like that at all, Lirianna. I was happy, but it was something completely different."* And she proceeded to tell her friend about the melding, as she greeted Lusa with a pat and a handful of fresh grass.

Lirianna didn't sound reassured when Alyen finished. *"Alyen, that's ... that sounds big."*

"I guess it is," Alyen replied. *"But it felt amazing, and that's probably why I looked happy. If he was awake, why didn't he just say something?"*

"Alyen, you need to be careful." Lirianna's voice sounded more

serious than Alyen had ever heard it. *"You want to be able to get back together with Aaron at some point, don't you?"*

"Of course. You know I do."

"Then you need to be sure you don't do anything that will push him away permanently."

"I didn't! I told you, it had nothing to do with Faer Dinnán—"

"Listen, you need to be smart about this. Think about the state Aaron's in right now. He's confused and he's hurting. A lot. I know it's important to preserve the enchantment, but someday that enchantment will be broken, and when Aaron thinks back on these days, you want him to realize how much you hated seeing him hurt like this and how hard it was for you to be apart from him. You going off with the faerie king and returning like you've just come in from a ball isn't a memory that's going to work in your favor."

"All right," Alyen said, bristling at her friend's tone. *"There's no need to lecture me."*

"I'm sorry." Now Lirianna's voice sounded tired. *"I'm just worried about you two. And the Trianid, to be honest. There's been a strange energy in the Balance ever since you two split up, and I don't like it."*

"Neither do I," Alyen replied quietly. She stroked Lusa's nose absently, taking comfort in her horse's soft huffing.

"I know you don't," Lirianna said. *"Just don't drive Aaron away any more than you need to."*

"I'll do my best. Thanks for letting me know."

Alyen dropped her hearing stone back beneath her clothing. Over Lusa's back, she could see Nah'dar stirring, and Brother Hugh at the fire with his pot and spoon, putting breakfast together. But where was—?

"Alyen?"

Alyen started and whirled around, making Lusa snort and

paw the ground. Alyen put out a hand to calm her. "Aaron! I didn't hear you."

"Sorry." Aaron stood at a bit of a distance with his arms folded, but there was a new look in his eyes. The anger was still there, but it had been joined by something tentative and wary. The Slayer cleared his throat. "I just wanted to ask if … if you were all right."

Alyen nodded cautiously. "I'm all right."

Aaron looked off at the moor. "Nah'dar said you were doing something new last night." His eyes turned back to Alyen's. "He said you glowed. And flew."

"It's true," Alyen confirmed. "It surprised everyone. Even Faer Dinnán."

Aaron seemed to stiffen at the mention of the faerie king, but he said nothing about it. "And you're sure you're all right? Magic has exhausted you before."

"I'm sure. Really, I feel fine."

"All right, then." Aaron nodded and turned back to the campsite.

"Aaron?" Alyen's voice stopped him and he looked back. "Thank you for checking on me."

Alyen's breath stuck in her throat as Aaron paused, his face unreadable. Finally, he simply nodded and returned to the fire and Brother Hugh's breakfast.

Lirianna is right, Alyen thought. She'd have to try to find a way to mend things with Aaron, if only so they could exist comfortably around each other again.

At least he'd spoken to her. That was a good sign. He couldn't hate her too much if he wanted to see if she was all right. Perhaps she could find a way to build on that.

Alyen turned to Lusa. "Think you can ask Soran to put in

a good word for me?" she asked her horse wryly. Lusa merely nickered, so Alyen gave her a final pat, then went to join the others for breakfast.

It was another long day of riding. Alyen had hoped there would be more opportunities to improve things with Aaron, but their stops were brief, and despite their conversation that morning, Aaron seemed content to revert to one-word answers any time Alyen made an attempt to connect.

Instead, she sought out Nah'dar, pulling Lusa alongside his stallion shortly before noon. The captain had avoided her gaze all morning and even now acknowledged her presence with only the smallest of nods.

Alyen decided to be blunt. "Nah'dar, we need to talk about last night. You can't keep avoiding me like this."

"I avoid nothing, Keeper. Least of all my sanahara." His words were clipped.

Alyen ignored him. "It was new magic. *Strange* magic. Anyone would be uncomfortable the first time they saw it. And I know your relationship to magic is complicated to begin with."

Nah'dar said nothing, so eventually Alyen added more calmly, "Look, I don't know what happened that made you feel this way about magic, and you don't have to tell me. But I don't really have a choice about doing it, and I don't like feeling as if I'm putting you through ... whatever it is you feel, just because I'm your sanahara and you feel obligated to be around me. We need to find a way to make it more comfortable for you. Otherwise, I don't want to be your sanahara anymore."

Nah'dar finally glanced sharply at her. "I would not have you think me a coward, Alyen."

Alyen was surprised by his words. "I don't! Whatever it is you feel about magic, I'm sure there's a good reason. I just don't want to cause anyone pain by being who I am. Especially not my friends," she added, gently.

Nah'dar's expression softened a bit, and for a time there was silence between them. Finally, he spoke again, his voice quiet. "Sandamarians have many beliefs about magic. I assume you are familiar with them?"

"To an extent," Alyen said. "I know they think everyone possesses magic within them to varying degrees and that it plays a big part in determining a person's opportunities."

Nah'dar nodded without looking at her. "I do not wish to go into details. Suffice it to say that those who are not blessed with an abundance of magic are likewise not valued by Sandamarian society. I was deemed to possess very little magic. As a result, I came to the conclusion quite early in life that magic makes people cruel."

Alyen was silent as she turned this revelation around in her head. Finally, she said softly, "I would never be cruel to you, Nah'dar."

The warrior finally looked at her fully, his eyes deep pools of black. "I know," he said.

"Then, from now on, let Brother Hugh take the first watch," Alyen said, lightening her tone. "He's still getting used to a warrior's life, after all, and he'll be more alert in the evening than in the middle of the night. I think I shall feel most safe with the Captain of the Guard on watch while I sleep."

Nah'dar looked over at Alyen, and she lifted one of her eyebrows. Nah'dar didn't look exactly pleased, but he nodded his agreement. "But only because I do not wish to cause you additional stress, Keeper. Your new magic is impressive. I imagine it must demand a great deal of strength to achieve."

Before Alyen could reply, he urged his stallion forward to ride at the front, leaving Alyen to wonder if he truly thought her strong, or if he simply saw himself as weak.

Villages were scarce on this part of the moor. Again, there was no inn convenient as evening fell, so they prepared once more to set up camp and sleep under the stars.

As before, Aaron and Nah'dar began their sparring as soon as the horses had been cared for. Alyen had half-hoped she would see a change in Aaron's fighting, that his control and natural grace would have returned. But he continued to rain blows against Nah'dar's scimitar in an angry frenzy, and soon Alyen turned away, not wanting to watch any more.

Brother Hugh was eyeing her, but said nothing about the battle their companions were waging. Instead, he held out a mixing bowl. "Bread time, my dear! Not real bread, of course, as we've no oven. But I shall teach you to make travel biscuits that can be baked on a heated stone next to the fire. A highly useful recipe for a traveler such as yourself!"

In the end, it was nice to have the distraction of cooking, and Alyen discovered that she rather enjoyed making the biscuits to accompany Brother Hugh's stew. Dinner was mostly silent again, aside from Brother Hugh's humming, and it was night by the time they'd cleared away the meal.

Alyen had been glancing out at the surrounding terrain more and more frequently as the evening wore on, and now, as darkness fell, she could see the light where Faer Dinnán was waiting for her. Remembering Lirianna's words, she tried not to look too eager as she turned to the others.

"I'll be out again, training. No need to wait up for me."

She tried to catch Aaron's eye, but he met her gaze only briefly before turning to his bed. She sighed and headed out onto the moor.

Faer Dinnán waited, surrounded, as usual, by glowing salamandars. There was an eagerness in his eyes as he watched her approach that Alyen hadn't noticed before—or perhaps it was hope?

"How do you feel?" he asked as soon as she had reached the salamandars' light.

Alyen shrugged. "I feel fine."

"You are not strained or fatigued in any way?"

"No."

Faer Dinnán nodded. "Good. That is good for both of us."

The faerie king studied Alyen's face for a moment as if calculating his next words, then motioned for her to sit. "I wish to speak with you, Alyen. I believe there may be cause to change our strategy regarding the darklings."

Alyen sat in the cool grass, Faer Dinnán sitting across from her. The salamandars surrounded them, casting flickers of orange and gold across their faces.

Faer Dinnán hesitated, then began. "When you read the Keeper's book, it described the process of connecting to dark magic by means of blood, did it not?"

Alyen nodded. "It said that blood and a command in the singing speech would connect me to the magic that had ensnared the darklings."

"Exactly," Faer Dinnán said, sounding excited. "It's the only way I have ever known a human to be able to connect with darklings, but it's forceful and crude. And it has its limits. I must admit to you, Alyen, that despite your considerable talents, I have had grave doubts as to whether one human—*any* human—would be able to succeed in turning so large a darkling force as Ylvain's magic has created. That is, until last night."

"And now?" Anticipation or apprehension—she wasn't sure which—fluttered in Alyen's stomach.

Faer Dinnán held her gaze. "Now, I see a new path forward. One that, I believe, has a much greater chance of success. There will be no need for blood, or connecting to the magic Ylvain wove. I think what you must do, Alyen, is meld with the darklings as you melded with the sylphs and the salamandars last night."

Alyen's eyebrows rose as her stomach plummeted. "You want me to—*become* a darkling?"

"Not quite," Faer Dinnán said. "Last night when you melded, you were both yourself and the element. It will be the same with the darklings. You will still be yourself, but you will also be part of their darkness. It will be a stronger, purer connection than anything you could conjure with blood and will alone. Once you are inside the darkness, you will be able to light it from within."

Alyen took a breath, her mind unsettled as a flurry of questions crowded in all at once. She willed herself to remain calm, as she'd trained to do as a ruler, and to address each one in turn, starting with the most pressing.

"If I do this, will I still need someone to act as an anchor?"

Sympathy flashed in the faerie king's eyes. "Yes. That part does not change. If anything, you may have more need than before."

The hope that had sprung briefly in Alyen's chest fell. "And we still have to go to Illya?"

Faer Dinnán nodded. "I think it best. Ylvain's fires burned out when her life ended, thus unleashing the darklings, but Illya is still the heart of her magic. I believe you will have an easier time connecting with the full darkling force from there than if we attempted it anywhere else."

"Then the only difference lies with me. In what I have to do."

"That is correct." Faer Dinnán sat, silently watching Alyen's face as her mind turned.

A turmoil of emotion coursed through her body. Hope that success seemed closer than before. Relief that she wouldn't have to attempt blood magic. Sorrow that it changed nothing for Aaron. But beneath it all was fear. Fear at what this new strategy implied, and a niggling concern that it may not actually work.

"There may be a problem," she said, finally. "When I melded with the air and the fire, I ... I filled myself up with them first. I don't really know how to describe it. With the salamandars, for instance, I took all my memories of every kind of fire and put them all inside me until I could almost feel the heat and the light living in my body. And that's what I used to meld with the salamandars. With the darklings, though ..." Her voice trailed off, doubtfully.

Faer Dinnán was watching her keenly. "Is it that you don't know what to fill yourself with, Alyen? Or is it that you're afraid of the filling itself?"

Alyen's stomach squirmed. If she was honest, she didn't want to look too closely at the question or its implications. But the stakes were too high for the luxury of ignoring it.

"Both, maybe. My memories of fire are many and mostly happy. Becoming part of the fire felt wonderful, but also natural, as if I had always been a part of it in some way.

"But what's the darklings' element? Evil? Fear? Malice? What memories I have of these things, I try to avoid. They remind me of my worst moments. My greatest mistakes. The parts of myself I don't want to admit are there. I don't want to believe I have that kind of darkness to draw on. And certainly not enough to become the darkness itself."

By the time she'd finished, Alyen felt her body quivering. These were things she'd never spoken aloud. Not to her parents, not to Lirianna, not even to Aaron. They were things she herself never looked at too closely. Saying them now left her feeling vulnerable and raw, anxious about how the faerie king would react. She rubbed her arms as though to ward off the nighttime chill, and felt a small glow of gratitude in her chest as several salamandars swirled closer, warming the air around her.

Faer Dinnán listened to her, curiosity tracing his features by the end. "You fear your own darkness, is that it?" he asked.

"I suppose so."

Faer Dinnán looked out at the dark moor for a bit before turning back to Alyen.

"Darkness is a part of nature, Alyen. It's a part of everything, just as much as is the light. The world does not sit in endless daytime, after all, and the night brings with it its own blessings."

"But the night isn't evil," Alyen said softly.

"You are Dúramair's Keeper," Faer Dinnán pressed. "The one tasked with minding the Scales of the Balance. What would there be to balance if only light existed? Or, if light was always meant to be far greater than dark? The Balance, Alyen, is called so for a reason. The existence of both light *and* dark is what is good and natural and needed."

Alyen swallowed, her eyes dropping to her hands in her lap. When she spoke, her voice trembled. "I know that darkness exists, but … it was always supposed to be something separate from me. *I* was supposed to be only light. I don't know how to accept myself any other way."

Faer Dinnán's eyes were full of something Alyen couldn't find a word for. He reached out and took her hand in both of his flickering ones.

"We all have both light and dark within us, Alyen. You, me, the elementals. Everyone. To reject your darkness is to reject a part of yourself and to cut yourself off from your full power. I think it was this, more than anything, that allowed you to meld last night. For the first time, you allowed yourself to act without rejecting your fear. Embracing your own darkness will be harder, yes. But I think, Keeper of Scales, that you have great courage. Keep in mind, without your darkness, you would have no way to connect to the darklings to heal them. It is not your light, Alyen, but your darkness that will allow you to save our world."

Something was happening in Alyen's chest. A heaviness she'd carried for a long time was lifting, the knots loosening. But she couldn't let them go completely. Not until she'd asked one last thing, the thing she'd dreaded the answer to ever since she'd split the earth apart at Norhelm.

"And if I accept my darkness—if I accept it as part of myself—that doesn't make me like Ylvain?"

Faer Dinnán's hands tightened around hers and he shook his head. "No, Alyen. It does not."

Without warning, or knowing she was going to, Alyen burst into tears.

Faer Dinnán said nothing as Alyen wept. Wept for the person she'd been and lost. Wept for the person she'd become instead, a person she didn't always recognize, whose shoulders were too heavy and whose heart felt too full. She cried until her tears were spent, and eventually Alyen drew her hand away from the faerie king's grasp so she could dry her face on her sleeve.

"I'm sorry," she said. "I think … I'm just relieved."

"No apology is necessary, Alyen. Human emotions are powerful things." He watched silently for a moment as Alyen collected herself, then continued. "If ever you are in doubt, you need only remember the Balance. Ylvain had no balance within her. She gave herself over to her darkness and was consumed by it, thereby making herself easy prey for evil. To use one's shadow side as a tool in service of the good as you shall do, however, is completely different. It's a matter of mastering the balance of light and dark within, of ensuring that you remain in control and can direct both light and dark to fulfill a noble purpose. Incidentally, this is what we must train for now—assuming you agree to this new plan."

Alyen took a breath and exhaled. She pushed the hair away from her face and nodded. "Yes. I agree. How do we start? Do I have to practice connecting to the darklings?"

Faer Dinnán stood, offering his hand for Alyen to join him. "No. I think we will have only one chance to truly connect with the darklings. As soon as they feel your presence, they'll consider you a threat. They will likely attack, and if you're unable to heal them, they will not rest until they've conquered you. Therefore, we must save our efforts until we reach Illya.

"Instead, we shall continue to connect with other elementals in order to build stamina and familiarity with the process, and we will soon begin to practice with Aaron as your anchor. But there is one other thing we can try which may help you. Let me first ask: when the darklings are near, are you able to feel them?"

"Yes." They were walking now, the salamandars swirling around them so they remained within a globe of golden light. "I feel malice, rage … and something else. Evil, I suppose you would call it. Like a sickness in the Balance."

They had reached the top of a small rise in the moor, and Faer Dinnán stopped. "And these things you detect—they make you afraid, correct?"

"Yes."

"Then I think we shall also practice feeling the darklings' presence without connecting to them, so you may learn to master the fear of standing within their storm."

The faerie king gestured out across the moor, and the salamandars split apart, leaving Alyen a clear view of the dark expanse of land before her. She caught her breath as she recognized a deeper concentration of darkness that blotted out the stars, lit by occasional flashes of green-tinged lightning.

"Another storm?" Alyen asked.

"They are growing more frequent," Faer Dinnán confirmed. "This one won't come our way, but I believe you'll be able to reach them with your mind."

Alyen felt herself already bracing for the jolt she knew would come as soon as she felt the darklings' sinister presence. She tried to instruct her muscles to relax. "What shall I do?"

"Simply reach your mind out to them until you are close enough to feel the darkness they carry. Once you feel the fear, the malice—the evil—simply sit with it without trying to push it or your own feelings away. See if you can grow accustomed to holding yourself still amidst the storm."

Alyen nodded and took a breath. She shook out her arms, then faced the darkness and closed her eyes.

Her mind stretched out across the moor. She felt nothing out of the ordinary but her own apprehension at what she knew was to come. Then she felt it: the prickle of unease that grew into dread, the sickly feeling of rot and disease, then finally the hissing sensation of malice emanating from the darklings that dwelt in the heart of the storm.

She stopped pushing outward, concentrating on holding her own in the face of the chaos before her.

It wasn't easy. Or pleasant. She sensed the darklings stirring restlessly as they felt her presence, their desire to attack and destroy crashing around her like a wave. She felt her own fear rise in response, the familiar urge to flee at all costs. Yet she held herself still, not banishing the fear, but refusing to act upon it.

"Come back, Alyen. It is enough."

Alyen heard Faer Dinnán's voice, felt his hand on her arm, and finally she allowed her mind to retreat across the moor. She came to herself and opened her eyes, relief flooding through her. Sweat was beading on her forehead, and her limbs trembled.

Faer Dinnán's hand remained on her arm, steadying her. "Are you well, Alyen?" he asked, concern flickering in his eyes.

"I—I don't know. I think so," she replied, massaging her heart. She felt shaken, and suddenly wanted desperately to return to the campfire and her bedroll to sleep.

The faerie king's eyes darted across her face, and he nodded. "You need to rest. I'll walk you back to your fire."

"No," Alyen said, thinking of Aaron's reaction should Faer Dinnán show up in their camp. "I'm fine. I can go myself."

Faer Dinnán nodded again, dropping his hand from her arm. "You did well, tonight, Keeper of Scales. Rest easily."

Alyen smiled weakly, and turned her steps toward their fire, salamandars lighting her way as a rumble of thunder accompanied flashes of sickly green in the distance.

14

FALSE MEMORY

lyen reached the edge of their camp, the salamandars vanishing as she approached a watchful Brother Hugh. He cocked his head to one side as she neared the edge of the firelight, his brow crinkling.

"I say, Alyen, are you all right? You look a bit ill."

Alyen gave him a wan smile "I'm fine, Brother Hugh. Just tired is all."

"Well, do have a good night, my dear. If you should need anything, I'll be here, watching." His chest puffed out a bit.

"Thank you," Alyen said, trying not to smile too much at the former monk's pride in his new position. "Get some rest, yourself."

She left Brother Hugh peering seriously at the moor and sank gratefully onto her bedroll. Nah'dar was already asleep on the other side of the fire. Aaron's blankets were empty, the Slayer nowhere to be seen.

The warmth from the fire was comforting, and despite her

exhaustion, Alyen felt too unsettled to sleep right away. She held her hands out to the flames, savoring the heat, and tried to calm the fluttering in her chest and stomach.

"Can't sleep?" Aaron's voice asked behind her, and Alyen jumped.

"Saints, Aaron, don't creep up on me like that," she said, her voice sharper than she'd intended.

Aaron moved around her to the fireside and studied her face. "Sorry. Can I sit?"

Alyen nodded, and Aaron lowered himself onto the ground next to her. His eyes traced her face again. "What happened?"

Alyen shook her head, running a hand through her hair. "Nothing. Just getting used to dealing with darklings."

Aaron nodded, but didn't reply immediately. He sat watching the fire, the flames throwing flickers of orange and gold across his face. Suddenly he spoke, his eyes still fixed on the fire.

"I wish it wasn't so hard for you."

The words surprised Alyen. She shrugged, not knowing how to reply. "It's not so bad. Not really."

Aaron looked over at her, skepticism written across his features. "I know you well enough to know when you're upset, Alyen."

There didn't seem to be a good answer to that either, so Alyen said nothing.

Aaron considered another moment, then reached for a blanket and draped it over Alyen's shoulders. His face bore no expression, but his touch was gentle. Alyen's breath caught on the lump that rose in her throat, but she swallowed it and regained her composure.

"Why are you being so nice to me?" she asked.

Aaron chewed on the inside of one cheek while he contemplated the fire again, then turned to her. "I'm angry with you, Alyen. And confused." His brow crinkled as if he was struggling to hold on to a thought just out of reach. "Sometimes it feels like I can't even remember clearly how we got to this point. Everything was wonderful, and then it just … *wasn't.* I don't understand what you did or why, and at this point I'm not even sure I want to. But we're the Trianid. We have work to do. And we have to at least be able to talk to each other in order to do it. So, I'm trying. I'm still angry, but I'm doing my best. And maybe someday, if I try long enough, I won't be so angry anymore."

There were a million things Alyen wanted to say. And she knew she could say none of them. She lowered her eyes so Aaron wouldn't see the secrets they held and said the closest thing to the truth she could. "I hope you can forgive me someday, Aaron. I don't want to do this as enemies. I'm honestly not sure I can."

There was a pause, then Aaron's hand covered one of her own. "You won't have to. I may be angry, but I'm not your enemy. I'll do my part and help you through it. However I can."

Alyen looked up and her eyes met Aaron's hazel ones. The eyes that had always been open and honest with her. She curled her fingers around his and gave them a light squeeze. "Thank you."

For a moment they sat perfectly still, hands clasped, eyes locked, the only movement the flicker of firelight across their skin. Then Aaron dropped his gaze and released her hand. "You should get some rest. Do you need anything?"

Alyen shook her head, already feeling the emptiness move in as he withdrew.

"Well … I'll see you in the morning, then."

Alyen tried to smile. "Good night."

Aaron nodded, then moved to his own bedroll and lay down, his back to her.

Alyen sat a while longer, watching the salamandars swirling in the flames. The fire soothed her, and bit by bit she felt her body settle, releasing the unrest the darklings had left behind.

"I'll do my part." Those had been Aaron's words, and they sank like stones into Alyen's heart. She knew she should try to be hopeful. She supposed it was a good sign that Aaron had spoken to her at all. At least it seemed they had reached a tentative peace. And maybe, as he'd said, in time it wouldn't feel so strained. *Yes,* she told herself. *Progress has been made.*

But her heart remained heavy.

Finally, knowing morning would come all too soon, she lay down, burrowing into her bedroll. She hugged the blanket Aaron had left more tightly around her and let the flicker of the flames lull her to sleep.

The days passed, one blending into the next as they rode ever northward. Each day they pushed to cover as much ground as possible, and soon they had left the swells of the moor behind, following the road onto the flat grasslands of the Searing Plain. It was new terrain for Alyen as she'd never personally visited this part of her kingdom, and despite everything, she found she still enjoyed watching the spring scenery slip by as their horses' hooves thundered down the road.

Their relentless pace, however, took a toll. Days spent in the saddle with few breaks, followed by nights sleeping on the ground, soon left Alyen with a sore backside and a hunger for a night of sleep in a real bed. But she pushed such thoughts aside, concentrating instead on her preparations for Illya.

Her evenings were still spent with Faer Dinnán, learning to sit with the fear of the darklings without fighting or pulling away. It remained difficult and unsettling to say the least, but Alyen was gratified to notice that with time it didn't seem as insurmountable a feat as it once did. The time needed for her to regain her composure afterward shrank as well.

Her training wasn't always unpleasant either. As promised, Faer Dinnán also instructed her to practice melding with various groups of elementals. Whether it was from her practice with the darklings, or simply the fact that she became accustomed to the process, Alyen noticed that her meldings, too, became easier, the magic flowing more and more strongly within her. One night she melded with the tree elves, opening her eyes to find her feet shooting roots into the ground, branches stretching outward from her palms and fingertips, her hair bathed in a crown of leaves. Another time she melded with the moss sprites to find her body covered in soft, spongy greenery that smelled of cool shade and rich soil. She took every opportunity she could to meld once more with the sylphs, reveling in the weightless feeling of floating on the air, and the salamandars, who filled her body and blood with heat and crackling power.

Through it all, Faer Dinnán remained ever attentive to her well-being. He inquired often if she felt exhausted, if their work was causing her strain, and left ample time during their training sessions for rest and reflection. After several nights of this, Alyen realized she no longer felt the awestruck distance she once had in the presence of the faerie king, and the lashing anger that had flared in his presence since their meeting in the Keeper's cottage had mostly abated. They had settled into a comfortable camaraderie, and Alyen had even begun to think of him as a friend.

It was when these thoughts rose that Alyen reminded herself firmly that he was not human. He was a faerie, and Rowenna's words about him echoed in her mind: *"He doesn't follow the same moral code as humans do. He doesn't reason the same way we do. He doesn't necessarily consider the same things to be right or wrong as we do. To us, he can seem unpredictable."* And though Alyen wanted to trust the faerie king implicitly, she couldn't completely shake the feeling that he'd deceived her when he enchanted Aaron. Every so often, as she melded, a look would flash across his features that would make her feel deep in her belly that perhaps caution was still a good thing.

As far as she and Aaron were concerned? Thankfully, they seemed to be on speaking terms again. Things were so much improved, in fact, that Alyen found herself almost hurt at how much Aaron had seemed to recover from their split. Only the way he sparred with Nah'dar in the evenings belied the anger still brewing within him, and Alyen found herself grateful, once again, for the Captain of the Guard's presence. At least for now, Aaron had an outlet for his frustration, and if things went well at Illya ... Surely, once Aaron understood the full picture, everything could go back to the way it had been. And the tiny whispering voices that found their way into her mind, questioning whether she was sure Aaron would truly forgive her, were deftly silenced.

They were nearly halfway to Illya when Faer Dinnán surprised her with a change in routine. Alyen had just disconnected from her latest melding and, assuming they were finished for the night, was preparing to return to the fire, her mind already on her bedroll. But before she could turn to go, he stopped her.

"There is one more thing, Alyen."

Something in the faerie king's voice made Alyen feel suddenly wary. "Yes?"

Faer Dinnán's expression was inscrutable. "Tomorrow we begin training with the Slayer. You must bring Aaron with you, and I will teach you how to connect your minds so that he may anchor you as you endeavor to heal the darklings. But I must warn you now: there's a side effect to such a connection that could prove problematic to our plan."

Alyen's eyes narrowed. "And that is?"

"When such a connection is made," Faer Dinnán continued, stepping closer to Alyen, "the mind of each opens to the other. For a time, it's as if their minds become one, all barriers broken down. Memories are exchanged, and it becomes difficult for secrets to be kept."

Alyen's chin raised, understanding. "He'll see our talks, the Keeper's cottage ... He'll find out about the enchantment."

"He will. Unless you can keep it from him."

"How can I do that?"

"It's nearly impossible to attempt to withhold a memory. The act of trying to hide it brings it to mind, thereby exposing it to the connection. The better thing to do is to purposely bring forth memories you *wish* the other to see—

enough of them to occupy the connection for its duration, so your other memories never have a chance to be found. In this manner, we may use this memory exchange to our advantage."

"How so?"

Faer Dinnán's eyes took on a gleam Alyen hadn't seen before. "Aaron believes you left him for me, but he was given few details as to why."

The wariness in Alyen's stomach increased. "But that never really happened. I can't show him a memory that doesn't exist."

"True." Faer Dinnán moved forward and took Alyen's hands in his. His eyes were so intense they seemed almost to burn. "But we can make a new memory."

A chill went down Alyen's back, and she snatched her hands away. "No! Aaron may believe I've left him, but I haven't, and I won't betray him."

The familiar, amused curiosity flitted across the faerie king's face, and he inclined his head. "Your loyalty is admirable, Alyen, and it shall be as you wish. But we may still forge a memory together that, when seen through Aaron's eyes, will strengthen our cause."

"How?" Alyen's tone was suspicious.

Faer Dinnán held his faded hands out once more in invitation. "Will you trust me?"

Alyen hesitated, studying his face.

"I think you will like what I have to show you," he added.

Wondering if it was against her better judgement, Alyen took a breath, then stepped forward and took the faerie king's hands.

For a moment, nothing happened. Then, her hands grew

warm, and she felt a current of magic seeping into them as they rested in Faer Dinnán's grasp.

Suddenly, the world transformed.

It began with the stars. One moment they were twinkling as always, then they were growing, their shine intensifying until the night sky was a dazzling canopy of diamonds forged by fire and light.

Alyen's eyes grew wide as she gazed upward, transfixed.

"Look around you, Alyen," Faer Dinnán's voice whispered.

Alyen looked and felt her mouth open, speechless in astonishment. All of nature was aglow. The grass beneath her feet was a vibrant, silvery-green sheen. Each tree or shrub emitted a glow from within, the veins of each leaf shining as tiny threads of gold. Alyen looked to the stream and saw the water dancing with blue and silver light, its glow a river of moonlight and magic winding across the plain.

But most enthralling were the elementals. To Alyen, they'd always seemed to shimmer with their own, otherworldly sheen. Yet now each sylph, each salamandar, each splashing undine seemed to shine like its own sun. Even the gnomes and the tree elves glowed, the sparks of their lives radiating outward, each a precious jewel set in the fabric of the world.

Alyen felt rather than saw the faerie king's magic reach out to his elementals. Suddenly they were surrounded, shining spirits of nature filling the air and the ground around them. They swirled in a dance that seemed as old as the earth itself, joyously weaving the patterns of the Balance that were at once both ancient and new. Vibrant and alive with magic and light, the world took Alyen's breath away, and she felt tears sting the corners of her eyes.

"What is this?" she felt herself whisper.

Faer Dinnán's head leaned close, his voice in her ear like a breath of wind. "This is the truth of the world, Alyen. The truth no human eyes can see alone. It is how you would see the world if you were my queen."

Alyen looked up and her eyes were caught by Faer Dinnán's. Eyes that were both young and ancient in a face both whimsical and wise. Eyes that held her with an expression that was at once wanting and hopeful and sad. She closed her eyes just for a moment, trying to harness her thoughts, her lips parting in a vain attempt to find words for the sensations racing through her.

Then she opened them, and Faer Dinnán was gone.

The world looked as it always had.

The elementals had resumed their usual activities, with no trace of their cosmic dance.

Alyen felt empty and absently massaged her chest above her heart, trying to determine whether she'd just been given a great blessing or a cruel curse.

Then, as her head cleared, she remembered.

What she'd been given was a memory.

One that would act as a knife to Aaron's heart.

15

THE LAKE OF LEORA

By the following afternoon, they'd reached the Lake of Leora, the horses cantering easily along the road that followed the curve of the shore. Crystal blue water sparkled in the sunlight, and Alyen watched, delighted, as undines swirled with sunlight salamandars across the surface of the lake. With the sun warm on their skin, clear skies, and a fresh breeze blowing off the water, it was easy to forget the threat of a dying world.

They passed by a couple villages, but nothing large enough to support the need for an inn; the larger lake towns stood on the eastern side of the water. As late afternoon approached and they reached the northern shore, Nah'dar reigned in his stallion, signaling to the others to halt.

"We have pushed the horses for many days now. I suggest we stop early today and let them recover. There are no inns ahead for the next few hours, so we may as well take advantage of the lake and camp here."

Everyone agreed, and though she knew haste was critical, Alyen was glad for the change of pace. The horses weren't the only ones in need of a rest.

Alyen dismounted, glancing in Aaron's direction as she chewed her lip. She hadn't told him yet that today was the day he was supposed to begin training with her. She wasn't exactly looking forward to spending time with Aaron and Faer Dinnán together and didn't expect much enthusiasm from Aaron either, despite the surface improvements in their relationship. Perhaps she'd wait until after dinner to speak with him about it, after he'd expended some energy sparring with Nah'dar. But as soon as she'd thought it, a flicker caught her eye, and she looked up to see Faer Dinnán standing at the edge of the lake as though he was waiting for her. He raised one translucent arm in both a greeting and a summons.

Alyen's eyebrows rose in surprise. The faerie king didn't usually appear until nightfall. She sighed inwardly and nodded her acknowledgement, then turned to find Aaron.

Aaron was nearly done tending to Soran, and Alyen joined him, rubbing the chestnut stallion's nose as the horse huffed in greeting.

"Aaron," she began, trying to find a way to phrase her words in a way that didn't sound like he was being ordered around by the faerie king. "Faer Dinnán wants to train early today. He says it's time for us to start practicing together so we'll be ready for the anchoring."

Aaron didn't look up from the saddlebags he was unbuckling. "You want me to come train with you now?"

"Yes. If that's all right. I know you usually spar with Nah'dar."

Aaron straightened and met her eyes, his expression

closed-off. "All right." He twisted around to shout their plan to Nah'dar and Brother Hugh, then turned back to Alyen. "Let's go, then."

There didn't seem to be anything else to say, so Alyen nodded and headed for the lakeshore, Aaron following behind.

They walked to the edge of the grass, then half-walked, half-slid down a bank and onto the sandy shore. Faer Dinnán was waiting for them.

"Thank you for joining us, Slayer," the faerie king began, his eyes flickering over Aaron's face. "I'm grateful for your willingness to participate in such an important capacity."

Aaron's mouth was thin, but he nodded curtly. "What should I do?"

One of Faer Dinnán's eyebrows quirked upward briefly, but he followed Aaron's lead, getting straight to the point.

"As you know, Slayer, it will be your job to join your mind with Alyen's using the singing speech. In this way you will aid her efforts with your own power, anchor her mind to reality, and act as a safeguard to pull her back should she be unable to return by her own powers alone. This connection must be practiced in order to strengthen it before it is used in our attempt to turn the darklings' force. However, the new powers that Alyen has discovered through the course of our work are … arresting, when seen in action. I think it wise for you to witness it first without being connected to her, so you're prepared for what is to come when you do attempt to connect. I wouldn't wish our efforts to be thwarted by surprise."

"Very well." Aaron folded his arms across his chest and turned to Alyen expectantly.

Alyen gulped. She hadn't been prepared to be put on the

spot. Until now, she'd only ever melded in front of Faer Dinnán—and Nah'dar, though that was from a distance and she hadn't known he was watching.

Faer Dinnán saw her hesitation. "You have yet to meld with the undines, Alyen. Perhaps here at the lake is a good opportunity."

Alyen nodded and turned to the lake, closing her eyes, attempting to shut out anything but herself, the water, and the magic of both. Her heart thumped in her chest—nerves at essentially being asked to put on a performance—but she didn't push the feeling aside. Instead, she gave her fear its customary nod of acknowledgement, then turned her focus to the water.

She filled her mind with memories of cleansing rain, of soft snowfall, of babbling brooks and crashing waves. She thought of warm baths soaking exquisitely into her stiff limbs after a day spent in the chilly autumn forest. She remembered the fountain at Monstar, filled with silvery undines who dove and splashed as she and Lirianna trailed their fingers through the water on hot summer evenings. She remembered the undine who'd caught a tear from her cheek that terrible night in Sheanen Crann when Ylvain's henchman had tried to kill her.

Alyen filled her mind and body with every memory and essence of water she could think of. Then, feeling she could contain it no longer, she spoke in the singing speech. "Undines in the waves of sea, snow, and river, come to me. Join your magic to my own, let water shape me, mind and bone."

She released.

The now-familiar emptiness surrounded her, a moment she'd come to love almost as much as the melding itself, for in the emptiness, she found peace. Then came the tiny sparks of water magic, undines from all over the kingdom latching onto her essence until she was built anew, still herself but infused with the power of ocean, rain, dew, and snow.

"Saints, Alyen." It was Aaron's voice, and the tone of it made Alyen open her eyes and look down at her altered body.

Her limbs, graceful and fluid as the sea, were covered in shimmering scales, flashing blue, purple, and green in the sunlight. A million shining raindrops covered her body, each as radiant as a silver star. Tiny crystals of dew scattered throughout her hair, and tiny snowflakes trickled from her fingertips only to melt instantly in the warm spring air.

Aaron's arms had fallen from his chest, his shuttered demeanor abandoned. He looked at her as if she had fallen from the sky, his expression part shock, part awe, and part something Alyen knew would break her heart if she looked at it too closely. Instead, she looked to Faer Dinnán, meeting his gaze. His amazement had tapered the more he'd seen her meld, but now his expression showed something new, making Alyen's stomach flip. Was it pride? Or was there a hunger in his eyes?

Before she could react, the faerie king broke off his gaze, and whatever had been there was gone. "So you see, Slayer. This is the magic Alyen will be working at Illya. But instead of melding with the undines, she will meld with the darklings."

Aaron's brow furrowed, though his eyes never left Alyen. "Is that safe?"

"You will ensure it is," came Faer Dinnán's blunt reply, and Alyen could swear she heard the hint of an edge to his voice. Perhaps Aaron heard it as well, for he finally broke his gaze from Alyen and met the faerie king's eyes.

"I've always protected Alyen, and I always will. It's my duty as Slayer." This time, there was no mistaking the hardness in Aaron's tone.

A hint of a smile flickered across Faer Dinnán's features and he inclined his head. "So you have." He turned to Alyen. "In that case, Alyen, perhaps it's time you left the undines so we may practice the connection with your protector."

Alyen closed her eyes gratefully, her heart thumping once more. The tension was making her uneasy. She understood it coming from Aaron, but hadn't expected it from Faer Dinnán. Why was he needling Aaron, and to what end? She already felt queasy at the task to come. Unbidden, the memory Faer Dinnán had made with her the previous night bloomed in her mind's eye. Alyen resolutely pushed it away.

She disconnected from the undines and opened her eyes, glancing down to confirm that she was once again in purely human form. Before either Aaron or Faer Dinnán could say anything, she strode to Aaron's side and turned to face the faerie king. "So, how does this work?"

"It's fairly simple," Faer Dinnán said. "As the anchor, the Slayer must forge the connection by asking the elemental world to connect your minds using the singing speech. If successful, Aaron's mind will connect to yours first, and Alyen, you will witness visions of Aaron's past. Moments later your mind will connect to Aaron's and your own memories will be visible to him."

For a moment, Faer Dinnán's eyes bored into hers and she knew he was reminding her of the one part of his plan that could not be spoken aloud in Aaron's presence. Alyen kept her face impassive.

"Alyen will see my memories?" Aaron said, his brow wrinkling. "All of them?"

"Not all," Faer Dinnán said, and Alyen wondered if there was a hint of amusement in his voice. "She will see only what reaches her for the duration of the connection. Will that be a problem?"

Aaron hesitated only a second. "No. It won't."

"Very well, then, let us begin," said Faer Dinnán.

Alyen didn't miss the fact that he hadn't told Aaron he could control which memories reached her. Her stomach squirmed with guilt, but she kept her lips sealed. If Aaron knew he could control the flow of memories, he'd know she could as well, and that could lead to problems if things didn't go as she hoped.

Alyen and Aaron turned to each other, their eyes locking. Alyen wondered fleetingly if he felt as nervous as she did. If he did, his expression didn't show it.

Then again, perhaps Aaron didn't have anything to hide.

"It will help in this first attempt if your hands are joined," Faer Dinnán suggested.

Aaron's expression didn't change, but after only a second's hesitation, he held out his hands, and Alyen rested hers gently on top. His fingers closed around hers, his palms warm and hardened by swordplay. Alyen felt her own fingers squeeze his in response and hoped they were steadier than she felt.

It was the closest they'd been since the split, and immediately, memories of the Keeper's cottage swam into Alyen's mind. *No*, she told herself firmly, and she pushed the memories away.

"You may begin, Slayer," Faer Dinnán instructed.

Aaron's throat bobbed once, then he spoke in the singing

speech, his words halting, but clear. "Elementals of the land ... rivers, mountains ... trees and sand ... join my mind with Alyen's ... own, so I may bring her safely home."

Alyen had no time to react to Aaron's words. There was a sudden rise and rush of wind as spray shot from the lake and rained down upon them in crystalline droplets. Alyen felt a wave of vertigo as the earth seemed to roll beneath her, and she felt her head jerk backward as something collided inside her head. She would have fallen, but Aaron's hands tightened their grip, his arms steadying her. Slowly she righted herself, finding Aaron's face once more. Then her eyes grew wide as within her own mind, images that could only be memories from Aaron's past began flashing one after another, even as her gaze remained locked on the Slayer's eyes.

He was a tiny child, sitting on a dock, his bare, dirty feet swinging freely as a woman with a voice he loved called for him to come back inside to eat.

He was training with Morten, his first lesson with a sword, frustrated at his small frame's lack of strength, yet swelling with pride at his mentor's approval.

He was sitting with Morten on the cliffs of Brann Dala under a fiery sky, waiting for the time when the sun would set and the phoenixes would begin to burn.

He was at Monstar Abbey, watching Alyen across the gardens as she laughed with Lirianna. He watched the way the sun hit her hair, how she brushed it away from her face with the back of her hand, leaving a smudge of dirt across her forehead. She turned to him, smiling, and his stomach dropped, a feeling that was almost pain stretching across his chest.

He was riding with Alyen up to the Keeper's cottage,

watching her face as she took in her new home for the first time, the way her eyes widened, her lips parting in surprise.

Alyen's wits snapped to attention. She knew where these memories were leading. At the same time, she felt a tug in her own mind and knew that within seconds, her memories would be flashing before Aaron's vision as well. It was time to take precautions.

Aaron's past continued to flash before her, but she turned her concentration to her own memories, carefully ushering the ones she selected down the invisible thread that connected their minds. She had promised herself that she would never use the memory she'd created with Faer Dinnán—not unless it was truly necessary. If it was true that she could control what was shared, then any other memory she picked would do.

She focused on her memories of Castle Dúr. That was safe enough territory. She'd been a child and Aaron had rarely been there. Besides, if she was honest, Alyen was eager for Aaron to see that part of her life and who she had been when she was living it.

She sent memories of the stables, listening to Garret tell stories while they rubbed ointment into leather saddles, rain pattering on the roof above.

She was in the study during tutoring with Professor Glibb. He'd found the sketches she'd made of flowers and trees on the papers she was supposed to be studying, his nose twitching in annoyance as she answered each of his questions correctly despite her artistic endeavors.

She was sitting in the throne room, listening to a messenger relay news from the Eastern Kingdoms, her parents nodding in approval at the questions she posed.

She was riding Lusa across the moor, feeling the strange

pull from the forest drawing nearer: the Royal Wood on the first day she'd discovered her Sight.

The memories flowed out of Alyen's mind, and once she was confident she'd sent enough of them, she chanced a look at Aaron. His eyes locked on hers with an expression she couldn't read. Was it curiosity? Surprise? Or hurt that he wasn't present in the memories he saw?

But she didn't have time to ponder, for at that moment, Faer Dinnán's voice cut across the stream of memories they shared.

"Your connection is complete. Alyen, it's time to practice with the darklings as we have been doing. Aaron, use the connection to add your own energy to Alyen's. In this way you can steady her, but be ready to pull her back to you should the need arise."

Aaron's hands tightened on Alyen's briefly, and he nodded. "I'm ready."

Alyen gave him a quick smile, then closed her eyes and stretched her mind outward, seeking the telltale unrest of the darklings' swarm.

It didn't take long to find it. In fact, her mind collided with it almost immediately. They were close, she realized as fear rose in her. Too close for comfort. She took a shaky breath, trying to summon the resolve to sit within the storm without fighting it.

"I'm here, Alyen." It was Aaron's voice, sounding in her mind through their connection without the use of a hearing stone. At the same time, she felt a surge of warmth envelop her, filled with steadiness, strength, and something that was purely Aaron. Like a balm, it soothed her fluttering heart, and

she felt herself grounded and still as the darklings swirled around them.

This was wonderful. To feel so strong in the presence of such darkness. To know that she wasn't alone, that together they could face anything and emerge victorious. Her fear was still there, but far away, as though sensing it from the other end of a tunnel. Something within Alyen flared, and she felt Aaron's presence surge in response.

She knew immediately that something had gone wrong. The chaos of the darklings, usually a swirling mass of unfocussed rage and malevolence, suddenly stilled. As one, she felt the darklings' attention snap in their direction. A howl of rage and malice rose on a screaming wind, then the mass of evil that was the darklings surged forward in a rush of fury.

"Break off!" came Faer Dinnán's sharp command. Alyen's and Aaron's eyes flew open, their minds rushing back to them as their connection severed. Their hands broke apart as they spun around to look across the lake.

The darkling storm loomed over the water on the opposite shore in a vengeful tower of blackness and green lightning.

It was coming for them.

16

THE STORM

"Run," Faer Dinnán's voice breathed in Alyen's ear, then louder. "Run, and find shelter! I'll try to deflect the storm."

They needed no second warning. Alyen and Aaron fled the shore, scrambling up the bank, then raced across the grassy plain to where Nah'dar and Brother Hugh were setting up camp. Brother Hugh was already stuffing blankets and pans back into saddle bags as Nah'dar did his best to keep the horses under control.

"We need to find shelter! Now!" Aaron called over the howl of the wind.

"We passed a farm not far back," Nah'dar shouted. "Follow me!"

They mounted in haste, the wind whipping their clothes and hair as the first stinging raindrops slashed at their cheeks. Hooves pounded the plain beneath them, yet Alyen could hear nothing but the scream of a wind devoid of sylphs, filled with something much darker.

Minutes passed that felt like hours as they raced ahead of the storm. The wind grew colder and the rain fell fast and hard. Alyen chanced a glance behind them and her heart leapt to her throat as she realized the darklings were gaining on them. Any moment they would reach the shore they'd just left and they'd have only a few minutes before it was upon them.

"We have to hurry!" she screamed to Nah'dar at the front.

Nah'dar lifted his arm in response. Squinting through the pelting rain, she saw ahead a structure she assumed was the farmhouse he had spotted earlier. It was small, but looked to be made of stone, which was reassuring. A barn stood next to it, also stone, and Alyen prayed it would be large enough for all four of their horses along with whatever animals the farm's owners might keep.

A crash of thunder sounded, nearly directly overhead as they lurched to a halt in the farmyard. Alyen nearly tumbled out of Lusa's saddle, then Nah'dar was there taking the reins from her frozen fingers. "Go!" he commanded, gesturing toward the farmhouse. "Seek shelter inside with Aaron, and Brother Hugh and I will see to the horses."

Alyen needed no further urging. She and Aaron sprinted the short distance to the door and pounded on it with their fists.

It didn't open. Nor did they hear any voices call from within, though Alyen doubted whether they would be able to hear anything above the roar of the storm.

Alyen and Aaron exchanged a wide-eyed glance, then Aaron looked back up at the storm. It had arrived, and as they watched, the cover of the well in the farmyard ripped away in the wind, hurtling into the barn and smashing into a thousand splinters.

Aaron's mouth set, and he opened the door, pulling Alyen inside behind him.

Together, they pushed the door closed again, straining against the wind until it latched and Aaron secured it with the bolt. They turned around to take in their surroundings and Alyen's eyebrows immediately rose.

It was a small, one-room house. Against one wall was a bed, currently occupied by a man, his breath fast and shallow, a bloody gash trickling scarlet streaks down his face. A woman, heavily pregnant, knelt next to him, her eyes wide as she stared at the two strangers who'd just burst into her home. In one hand she held a bloody cloth. Her other arm circled protectively around a young girl, her hair hanging in wet strings. The girl stared at Alyen with teary eyes while her arm clutched a small, dirty doll to her chest.

Before anything could be said, there was a pounding at the door. Aaron turned and opened it for Nah'dar and Brother Hugh, both soaking wet but safe, the saddlebags clasped in their arms. The door was latched and bolted once more, then Alyen crossed the room swiftly, kneeling next to the woman.

"What happened?" she asked, taking the cloth from the woman's hand and pressing it to the man's wound.

"It was a beam from the roof of the barn," the woman said, her voice trembling. "The storm came up so fast, and it blew it clean off, straight into my husband. Who are you?"

"My name is Alyen. I'm the Keeper of Scales. I'm sorry we've rushed in on you. The storm caught us off-guard, too."

The woman stared at Alyen, the hand that once held the

cloth now fidgeting at the neckline of her dress. "The princess? Here, in my house?"

"The Keeper of Scales," Alyen said gently. "And it's a good thing, too. This is a nasty wound."

Alyen glanced at the girl whose watery eyes seemed far too large for her face. Her lips trembled as she looked down at her father. The girl saw Alyen watching her and pressed closer to her mother's side.

Alyen gave the girl a small smile, her hands still pressing the cloth to the man's wound. "Hello. What's your name?"

The girl continued to stare for a moment, then whispered, "Annith."

"Annith, your father's going to be all right. I know how to help him, and I promise he'll be fine."

The girl said nothing, so Alyen tried again. "I'm going to need a helper, though. Would you like to help me?"

The girl chewed on her bottom lip, then looked up into her mother's face. The woman murmured her consent, and the girl looked back at Alyen and nodded.

"Wonderful." Alyen gave Annith what she hoped was a warm and reassuring smile. "The first thing I'll need are two bowls. The biggest ones you have. Can you find them for me?"

The girl scampered away, and Alyen turned to the woman. "Boiling water as well, please."

The woman nodded and rose to put a kettle over the fire. Alyen looked over to the door where her three companions stood, looking wet and uncertain. "Could someone bring me my saddlebag? And you may as well sit. This will take a while."

Aaron brought Alyen her saddlebag, and introductions were made. The woman, whose name was Maera, looked thoroughly flustered at the presence of two members of the Trianid along with the Captain of the Guard in her home, but Brother Hugh soon had her seated at the table with a cup of water, insisting that anyone in her condition should be the one waited upon, regardless of rank or title.

Alyen checked the man's wound. The bleeding hadn't stopped completely, but it had slowed considerably. She lay her other hand on the man's arm. "Can you hear me?" she asked quietly.

His eyes fluttered open and he tried to nod, but winced at the movement and shut his eyes once more.

"It's all right, you don't have to move," Alyen said, relieved to find the man conscious and apparently of sound mind. "Can you tell me your name?"

"Coram," the man whispered.

"Coram. I'll tend to your wound and give you something for the pain. You'll feel better soon."

When the kettle had boiled, Aaron brought it to Alyen, filling the bowls Annith had delivered with the steaming water. He glanced at the man whose eyes remained closed. "Will he really be all right?" he asked in a low voice.

Alyen nodded. "It's a bad cut and it'll need stitching, but I don't think the damage is any worse than that."

Outside, the wind howled, rattling the shutters and the doors. But despite its small size, the house stood firm, and Alyen wondered if Faer Dinnán was somehow shielding them from the worst of the gale.

"What are you going to do?" It was Annith, looking at Alyen with a small, serious face.

"I'm going to fix the cut on your father's head," Alyen said, making her voice sound as light as possible.

"Are you going to do it with the faeries?"

"They're going to help, yes."

"Can I watch?"

"Well, it's up to your mother," Alyen said. She looked up to address Maera, who was watching with an anxious expression. "I'll have to sew the wound shut, but it won't hurt. I have a cream that will numb the pain."

"Can I watch, Mama?" the girl asked. "I want to see her sew Papa's head."

The woman held out her arms. "You can watch from my lap. We mustn't get in the way of the faeries helping Papa, right?"

Annith scrambled up onto her mother's lap and perched on her knee, somehow squeezing around the bulge of her future sibling.

Alyen checked the wound once more. The bleeding had stopped. She wet the cloth in one of the bowls and gently cleansed the blood from the man's face and around the cut. Once it was clean, it didn't look nearly so bad.

Alyen rummaged in her bag until she found the jar of cream she was looking for. She extracted a small amount and rubbed it gently into the skin around the cut. Already she felt its cool tingle on her own fingers, boosted by the elementals when she'd made it after the Battle of the Second Slayer. She quickly rinsed her hand off before the numbness could set in. She'd need her hands fully functional for the task ahead.

Alyen fished in her bag once more until she pulled out a small leather case containing the fine needles and thread used only for stitching wounds. She swiftly threaded one of the needles, then looked up. "Might I borrow a candle?"

"Of course," Maera replied, her gaze going to a candlestick on the table. Brother Hugh brought it to Alyen, and she held it in front of her, glancing quickly at the girl watching expectantly from her mother's lap.

Magic really wasn't necessary for anything Alyen had to do. The elementals had already done their part when she'd harvested the herbs for her medicines and teas. But the girl was watching so intently. She deserved to see something special.

Alyen held the candlestick in front of her, ensuring the girl had a clear view. Then she spoke, quietly but clearly, in the singing speech.

"Spirits of the fiery flame, lend to me your light again. Purify my tools for healing, let this wound close, cleanly sealing."

Alyen saw the salamandar swirl before her, dancing gracefully on the tip of the candle's blackened wick. But she knew that from Annith's perspective, the candle had just magically lit itself.

The girl gasped, her eyes flying wide. "Mama! Mama, did you see?"

The woman nodded, her fingertips pressed to her lips, and Alyen turned away to hide her grin.

She took up her needle and passed it through the candle flame a few times as Rowenna had taught her. Boiling water could have done the same thing, but the bowls had cooled and besides, it had been worth seeing Annith's reaction. In any case, she'd need a light to see by with the storm making the stone room dark and shadowy.

Alyen turned to her companions. "Will someone hold the candle for me?"

She expected Brother Hugh to come, but it was Aaron

who rose and took the candle from her. He held it near the injured man's head, careful not to drip the wax. "Is this good?"

Alyen nodded and gave Aaron a small smile, trying to ignore the memories that rose at seeing the firelight flicker across his features.

She looked down at the wound, needle ready. Coram's eyes were open now, and she could detect a hint of apprehension in them. She pressed her finger gently on the skin surrounding the cut. "Can you feel this?" she asked.

The man swallowed. "No," he answered, his voice hoarse.

"Good. Then you won't feel this either."

Alyen took up her needle and began to stitch, working carefully to make the mend as seamless as she could. Luckily, it was a fairly clean cut, and she doubted it would leave much of a scar once it had healed. For several minutes she worked in silence, fully engrossed in her work, no longer aware of the people watching her, or of the storm howling around them.

When she finally finished, she trimmed off the thread and sat back, taking in a full breath. She looked up and caught Aaron watching her face. His eyes were unreadable, but in the candlelight they glowed golden, making her breath catch. Was seeing her face in the candlelight making him remember the Keeper's cottage as well?

She quickly looked down and busied herself by extracting another jar from her bag, this time a cream to speed the healing of wounds, and spread some over the cut. "And we're finished," she said. She reached up to take the candle from Aaron, meeting his eyes only briefly. Then she whispered, "My thanks for lending me your light. Go now and enjoy the night."

At once, the candle extinguished, and Annith squealed in her mother's arms.

Alyen suppressed a chuckle and caught Maera's gaze. "Thank you," the woman said, gratitude lining her features.

"Of course," Alyen said, suddenly feeling uncharacteristically shy. She turned back to Coram whose face had regained some of its color. "Do you think you can sit up?"

The man nodded, and Alyen and Aaron helped him rise into a sitting position, propped up by pillows. "Thank you," he said to Alyen. "I didn't think it possible to have your head sewn up without feeling a thing."

Alyen smiled. "I'll make you a tea for when the feeling comes back. It'll likely be sore for several days, so I'll leave some with you. In the meantime, you should try to eat something." She turned to Maera. "I know we've dropped in on you unexpectedly, so please don't worry about feeding us. We have plenty of food to share, and Brother Hugh is a fantastic c—" Alyen stopped speaking as she caught Brother Hugh's expression. He was staring intently up at the rafters, his eyes a bit too wide and oblivious to the conversation. Alyen took the hint. "I'll be happy to cook for everyone," she finished. Brother Hugh beamed.

17

CONNECTION

The evening turned out better than Alyen could have planned. Within a couple of hours, she'd made a hearty stew with biscuits for her companions and hosts. Coram was sitting up now, alert, and sipping a pain-relieving tea, and she'd left a packet of it with his wife with instructions for its use. By the time the sounds of the storm were dying down and everyone had eaten their fill, the small room was filled with cozy, after-meal warmth. For the first time, the tension that had accompanied her presence among Dúramair's people had disappeared. It was a welcome change.

It wasn't lost on her that the events of the afternoon also marked the first time she'd worked as the Keeper of Scales. Not as an apprentice in Monstar, and not in some quest to save the world, but as the Keeper was *supposed* to work in normal times, healing and helping the people of her king-dom. A new feeling settled in her chest, spreading warmth through her stomach and strength through her limbs. It was happiness, yes, but a particular kind Alyen could only suppose came from finding true purpose, and knowing you'd fulfilled it well.

As Alyen was turning these thoughts over in her mind, Nah'dar rose to peer out one of the shuttered windows. "The storm has passed. We need not shelter any longer."

"Oh, please stay," Maera offered. "We can't provide much, but there's no inn for miles, and it's better than the wet ground."

Alyen glanced around at her companions, and, seeing no objection, nodded gratefully at their host. "Thank you. We would be honored."

Annith skipped over to Alyen and surprised her by reaching up her arms, one hand still clutching her doll. Alyen lifted her onto her lap. "Hello," she said.

"I saw you light the candle with the faeries," Annith said, her gaze direct.

Alyen smiled. "Did you like that?"

The girl nodded. "Do they always do what you tell them to do?"

"Not always," Alyen said. "I don't actually tell them to do things. I ask them, and most often they agree to help."

"Did you ask them like that when you broke the ground?"

The room went suddenly still.

"Annith," Maera whispered, tension lining her face once again. "I'm sorry, she shouldn't ask such things."

Alyen's smile faltered a moment, but she shook her head. "It's all right."

It had only been a matter of time. Sooner or later, someone she met was bound to bring up the creation of Alyen's Gorge, and the farther north they traveled, the more likely she was to be questioned. She looked down at the girl who looked back at her with questioning eyes.

"Annith, you know how sometimes accidents happen, right?"

The girl nodded.

"Well, when I broke the ground, that was an accident. I didn't mean to do it. I would never do anything harmful on purpose, and neither would the faeries."

"So, it wasn't your fault?" Annith asked.

Alyen's heart skipped and she swallowed. "It *was* my fault. I was still learning how to use the magic, and I hadn't practiced enough yet. I was trying to help keep people safe—people like you and your family—and it just didn't work the way I wanted it to. I'm really sorry it happened."

No one in the room moved, and Alyen was aware of Annith's parents listening keenly to her every word. Alyen wondered what they may have heard or said about her before, or if they'd known anyone who'd been lost.

For a moment there was silence, then suddenly Annith shrugged and turned her attention to fiddling with her doll. "It's all right. Everyone makes mistakes sometimes. I make them a *lot*."

A chuckle rippled through the room, dissipating some of the tension. Alyen blinked away the sting in her eyes and patted the girl's back. "Thank you, Annith. That means a lot to me."

Once again, the girl looked up into Alyen's face. "If you're going to stay here tonight, can I sleep next to you?"

"That's for your mother to decide."

Alyen glanced up at Maera and the woman smiled. "Of course."

Aaron had been studying Alyen's face throughout the exchange. "If we're going to stay the night," he said, "I should check on the horses. Alyen, will you help me?"

Their eyes locked for a moment, and Alyen recognized the unspoken words behind Aaron's gaze. "Of course," she said. She gently lifted Annith off her lap and followed Aaron out the door.

Once outside, Alyen breathed deeply, drawing in the cool night air of the plain after a storm. She looked around the farmyard, surprised at how well everything had held up. A few fenceposts had fallen, some thatching had blown astray, and the grass had been flattened over the drenched earth, but there had been no serious damage. Not even Castle Dúr had fared so well in the wake of a darkling storm. Perhaps Faer Dinnán had succeeded in protecting them after all.

Aaron waited until they were halfway to the barn to speak. "That must have been difficult. Are you all right?"

"I'm fine," Alyen replied, surprised at how fine she actually felt.

Aaron looked at her skeptically. "Really?"

"No, really, I am. I guess ..." They stopped in front of the barn and Alyen looked back at the house, searching for the right words. "I always dreaded having to talk about Norhelm with people, and I still do. Especially those who really suffered because of it. But I guess I never really understood how hard it was going to be for people to accept me as the Keeper in any case. Norhelm was a huge mistake that I have to answer for, but even if it had never happened, I don't think I was going to be welcomed with open arms. At least tonight I felt like I did something about it. Maybe now that I've shown these people who I really am, they'll tell their friends, and word will spread. The more times I do my work well … who knows? Maybe someday I won't be seen as a princess or a monster. Just a Keeper. Hopefully a decent one."

Aaron gave Alyen one of his half-smiles—the ones she'd missed since the Keeper's cottage—and her stomach flipped. "You're more than decent, Alyen. You did well in there."

Alyen shrugged. "Brother Hugh thinks it will help people get used to me if they see me do regular work like cooking."

"Does he?" Aaron's eyebrows lifted. "I suppose it can't hurt, but I'm not sure acting like someone you're not is the answer. I think it's your healing work that will win people over. Watching you do it …" He shook his head and looked off at the plain before turning back. When he met Alyen's eyes again, his gaze was softer. "It's like watching someone do what they were born to do. What they love doing. What they're best at. It has its own kind of magic, and it's not flashy, but it's powerful. Anyone who watches you wouldn't have any doubt you were meant to be the Keeper."

Alyen felt herself melt under his words. She knew she should look away. Aaron's gaze was getting too intense, and if things kept going as they were …

"Keeper of Scales."

Alyen started and Aaron spun around at the words that were more air than voice. Faer Dinnán stood before them, swaying like the grasses on the plain, his face drawn and haggard.

All four of his limbs were mottled with translucence.

"Faer Dinnán," Alyen breathed as Aaron's brows drew together. "What happened to you?"

Faer Dinnán looked at Alyen, exhaustion etched into his features. But his eyes held more than weariness; sadness and longing seemed to fall from his face like leaves from a tree in autumn.

"I held back the storm. I didn't wish harm to befall you. Or your companions," he added with a nod to Aaron. "It has exhausted me more than I thought it would."

"You didn't need to do that," Alyen said, unsure why her cheeks felt suddenly flushed. "We would have been all right."

Faer Dinnán gave Alyen a direct look, then flicked his eyes over to Aaron. "I don't think you two realize what has happened."

"Happened?" Aaron echoed, his eyes narrowing. "What happened?"

"It was no coincidence that the storm rose when you and Alyen approached the darkling swarm while connected. Your connection acted as a beacon, one that threatened everything the darklings thrive on. I hadn't counted on such strength from your union."

Faer Dinnán swayed alarmingly, and Alyen stepped quickly toward him. "What do you need? Can I do something for you?" Her hand reached out but faltered, unsure whether to touch the faerie king's faded form.

Faer Dinnán shook his head. "Nothing can be done. Not until you reach Illya. But I fear if I continue without resting first, I may not make it so far."

"Rest, then," Alyen said. "There's time yet before we get there."

"I won't see you for a few days," Faer Dinnán agreed. "Hopefully I'll regain some strength so I may be able to assist you—both of you." He looked once more at Aaron.

"We'll be ready when we get to Illya," Aaron assured him, and there was none of the sharpness in his tone that Alyen had heard on the lakeshore. "Will it be safe for us to practice just our connection again? Without approaching the darkling power at the same time?"

Faer Dinnán regarded Aaron, his face serious. "I believe so, Slayer. Keep your minds well away from the darklings, but practice, and keep your powers honed. We … I … will need you both to be strong."

Alyen gave the faerie king an encouraging smile. "Save your strength. We'll all be ready soon."

Faer Dinnán looked to Alyen, his eyes flashing for a moment, then nodded, dropping his gaze, and turned once more to Aaron. "Keep her safe, Slayer," he said. "I leave her protection in your hands."

And before Aaron could reply, he had gone.

Alyen felt her brow furrow as she turned back to Aaron, her assured demeanor falling away. "Aaron, I'm worried about him. He didn't look good." She rubbed her arms as a sudden chill spread through her limbs.

If Aaron bristled at her show of concern for the faerie king, he didn't show it. Instead, he reached up and unclasped his cloak. He draped it over her shoulders, his hands lingering on her arms a moment as the corners of her mouth lifted in gratitude. "It's Faer Dinnán. He'll be all right."

"Will he, though? What if we run out of time? We're still days away from Illya."

"We're getting there as fast as we possibly can. And if he rests, he'll regain some strength and buy us some time. The best thing we can do is to make ourselves as strong as we can so when we get to Illya, we're ready."

Alyen nodded glumly. She knew Aaron was right but was unable to banish the worry gnawing at her stomach.

"I liked seeing you that way." Aaron's voice was soft.

Alyen frowned. "What?"

"In your memories. When we were connected. I liked seeing who you were before all this."

"Oh," Alyen breathed, wishing with all her heart that she hadn't had to curate so strictly what he'd seen. How strong would the connection have been if it had just been able to flow organically without her control? She swallowed. "Thank you, I guess. It feels like another lifetime ago."

"You would have made a good ruler."

Alyen grinned almost sadly. "Maybe." She looked up at Aaron tentatively. "I liked … I liked seeing you with your mother."

Aaron's throat bobbed and he nodded, quiet for a moment. "She would have liked you," he said finally.

Without thinking, Alyen reached out and put her hand on Aaron's arm. He looked down at it for a moment, then lifted his eyes once more to Alyen's. "What did it feel like for you when we were connected?"

"It felt good. I felt strong—invincible almost. Like the darklings and all their evil couldn't touch me as long as you were there with me."

Aaron nodded, his eyes still fixed on hers. Alyen suddenly realized how close they were standing, and her breath quickened.

"Let's try it again," Aaron said.

"What, now?"

"Why not? We need to practice. Easier to do it here than while we're traveling."

Eagerness laced Aaron's words, and Alyen understood why. The same feeling raced through her own veins—a yearning to feel the connection again and the power that came with it. But it was more than that, too. She wanted to see Aaron again—his life, his memories. She wanted to feel closer to him than any other person in the world again. She wanted to see herself through his eyes again.

Alyen wet her lips. "Do you think the darklings are far enough away?"

Aaron nodded, glancing at the sky. "The storm's gone, and besides, we won't be going near them. This time it'll just be for us."

Alyen swallowed as her stomach flipped. "All right."

Aaron took her hands in his and began his singing speech, but Alyen didn't listen. Pulse racing, she sifted frantically through her memories, selecting what was safe to show him and hiding what he mustn't see.

She was only partly finished when the force of connection hit her. Wind rose and whipped around them, and once again, she felt Aaron's arms steadying her until the farmyard settled and their connection stabilized. Regaining her balance, her hands grasping Aaron's, she looked up into his eyes.

At once the memories flowed toward her.

They were huddled together in the darkness before dawn, poring over the book containing the prophecy in old Nethermairian—the missing clue that gave them hope of victory against Ylvain and her army. Aaron looked at her, taking in the excitement shining through the lines of exhaustion etching her face, his lips pressing briefly against hers in celebration.

They were standing atop the battlements of Castle Dúr watching Ylvain's army of morkshai crawl toward them across the moor. Sadness weighted his heart like a stone as he looked at her, knowing that the battle to come would likely erase the future they could have shared.

He was surrounded by darkness, squinting upward at a sliver of light, feeling himself being drawn up toward it, then breaking free into the starlight. Relief washed over him, then joy as his eyes landed on her, her face tearstained but smiling.

The memories continued, each one a moment they'd shared together. Alyen felt herself pulled into the flow of images and started as she suddenly felt the tug of memories from her own mind flowing toward Aaron. She scrambled, trying to control the part of her mind Aaron would see, but she was distracted. She snatched for memories she knew would be harmless; scenes from Monstar seemed safe enough.

She was practicing with the elementals in the forest surrounding the abbey.

She was listening to Lirianna practice her harp while she flipped through books from the library, snow falling in drifts out the window.

She and Lirianna were sitting in their basin on the battlements, watching Aaron train in the courtyard below. She was annoyed, noticing the younger nuns trying to catch his attention as they passed by all too frequently with their chores ...

The memory slipped out before Alyen could stop it and she heard Aaron's breath inhale sharply. Alyen refocused on his eyes and saw them burning as they bored into her own. He'd seen it—felt the jealousy that rose in her chest watching the other sisters flirt as she looked on.

Curses.

She needed to send something else, a memory to counteract the one that had slipped out. It wasn't as if she'd let him know about the enchantment directly, but contradicting it with memories of being together and the feelings that went with them couldn't be good either. She strained to focus, but a sudden rush of Aaron's memories suddenly collided with her mind, taking her breath away.

They were together in an empty corridor of Castle Dúr, making use of the moment alone to steal a kiss or three before meeting everyone for dinner.

They were riding together over the moor, wind rushing through their hair, Alyen's head tipped back in laughter, her cheeks tinted red with the late winter chill.

They were finishing their midday meal in the forest on their way to the Keeper's cottage, and Aaron reached over, pulling Alyen onto his lap ...

Alyen felt the surge that flared through their connection as her shared memory of that day in Sheanen Crann collided with Aaron's. She was dimly aware that they were standing much closer now, their torsos brushing against each other, faces only inches apart. Alyen's mind raced as she frantically tried to regain control of the flood of memories rushing between them. She grasped for anything at all she could send —anything mundane or ordinary—but each time she tried, another memory of Aaron would spring to mind, rushing down their connection before she could think to stop it. And if she was entirely honest, she didn't want it to stop. The more memories came, the stronger the connection blazed and the more she hungered for them. From the look in Aaron's eyes, she knew he felt the same.

Now her memory of the afternoon they'd discovered the tunnel in the tool shed at Monstar sprang before her mind's eye. The way Aaron had touched her in the dark, the first moment he'd ever done so ... and before she could snatch it away, it had gone. She saw Aaron's eyes widen as it reached him, and now a new memory of his was unfolding before her vision.

They were in the Keeper's cottage, in the bedroom with the fire throwing an orange glow over her face. She was turning around, lifting her hair so Aaron could unfasten the buttons resting below the exposed skin at the back of her neck . . .

Panic reared in Alyen's stomach. They needed to break off. It was going too far—perhaps it had gone too far already. She felt Aaron's hand at the back of her head, saw his eyes drop to her mouth, felt her head tilt upward in response. In that moment she knew what she had to do—the only thing she had the strength to do in the seconds before she would lose all control and succumb to the wanting that pulsed between them.

She reached into her mind and latched onto the one memory that had the capacity to stop everything. The one she'd hoped Aaron would never see.

The memory slipped down the connection, blooming before both their eyes at once: Alyen, standing with Faer Dinnán on the night-darkened plain, the world shining and glorious around them. Her eyes gazing with wonder as he leaned in close and whispered in her ear, "This is the truth of the world, Alyen. The truth no human eyes can see alone. It is how you would see the world if you were to be my queen."

Aaron froze, his face an inch from hers. She saw his eyes widen, first in surprise, then shock. She watched as he pulled back, their connection faltering, then severing completely, the emptiness of his absence already seeping into her bones. She saw the emotions run across his features: confusion, realization, then a sadness as vast as the sea.

"So that's why," was all he said, his voice hollow.

"Aaron, I'm so sorry ..." Alyen began, tears already stinging her eyes as the emptiness spread within her.

Aaron lifted a hand. "No, don't," he said. He dropped his gaze, and stalked away toward the barn door.

"Aaron!" Alyen called, spinning toward him.

But Aaron threw up an arm without looking back. He said nothing more, but the message was clear. He entered the barn and shut the door loudly behind him.

Alyen wanted to follow him. But she knew she couldn't. The memory had done what it was designed to do, and all the heartache in the world couldn't justify fixing it.

Not until they were done with Illya.

A ragged sob escaped her lips and she stumbled away from the barn, out onto the plain, Aaron's cloak still clutched around her middle. She gazed through swimming eyes toward the darkening horizon, at the black cloud that stretched across the distant sky, still flashing green from within. And as if all the world could feel her pain, raindrops fell from the sky, carried to the ground in the cradling arms of undines.

18

PURITY OF SIGHT

Night had fallen, and Lirianna set down her shuttle, resting it gently on top of the threads stringing her loom. She was weary. Another full day of weaving had passed with little result. There had been no visions to indicate how things would turn out with the darklings, how the kingdom or the Balance would fare—or if and how Alyen and Aaron would reunite, assuming things did go well at Illya.

Lirianna rose from her seat and was just reaching for the door of her workroom when she felt her hearing stone warming its spot just above her heart. She pulled the silver chain out of her clothing and clasped the smooth stone in her hand.

"Lirianna?"

It was Aaron's voice, and Lirianna's eyes widened at the agitation in its tone.

"Aaron, what's wrong?"

Silence met her question. *"Aaron?"* she pressed, her worry increasing.

"Everyone's fine," Aaron's voice finally said. *"I just … it's late, I'm sorry. I'm not even sure what I was going to say."*

"Aaron." Lirianna's voice was gentle now. *"What happened?"*

There was a breath, then Aaron began to speak. For the next several minutes, Lirianna sat, listening with increasing dismay as Aaron recounted the events of the afternoon, how he had connected with Alyen, how it had triggered another darkling storm, how they'd taken shelter in a farmhouse while Faer Dinnán held the storm at bay, weakening himself dangerously. She heard how her friends had connected again, how the memories had flowed between them, and finally, how Aaron had seen Alyen with the faerie king in a world more magical than anything he'd seen before, and how Faer Dinnán had offered it all to her, the chance to be his faerie queen.

"It's over, Lirianna," Aaron said when he'd finished. *"I never truly believed it until tonight, but I understand now. She's not coming back. There's no reason to."*

"Don't say that, Aaron," Lirianna said, her mind racing to find something to say. *"Things could change …"*

Lirianna could sense Aaron shaking his head. *"You don't understand, Lirianna. You didn't see what I saw. Sure, we were good together, but Faer Dinnán? He can offer Alyen everything I can't. He can give her an entire world filled with magic and power and a chance to be queen again. Like she was always meant to be."*

"Alyen was meant to be the Keeper, Aaron," Lirianna said firmly. *"You know that."*

"Maybe," Aaron said. *"But with Faer Dinnán she can be both."*

Silence stretched between them, Lirianna mentally kicking herself for her lack of anything helpful to say.

Finally, Aaron sighed. *"I guess I just wanted you to know that things might be a little awkward for a while. It might—it'll take me a while to get used to this. But it's getting late. You should get some sleep."*

Lirianna closed her eyes, frustration pulsing through her veins. She'd made a promise to Alyen, but … Drastic times called for drastic measures. *"Aaron, it might not be as bad as it looks. Just—just don't give up yet. All right?"*

There was a moment of hesitation, then, *"Goodnight, Lirianna,"* and her hearing stone went silent.

Curses.

Lirianna dropped her hearing stone back into her robes, her lips a thin line. This wasn't good news, and already she could feel the pull of her loom as the Balance shifted, sending unease crawling under her skin. She strode over to her weaving and sat, trying to summon the focus and calm she would need to see the threads of the future clearly. But her mind was distracted, thoughts racing between the disaster she feared was coming and solutions she had no way of acting upon.

What had Faer Dinnán been thinking? It was one thing to enchant Aaron until things were solved at Illya, but this sounded like a deliberate attempt to make the rift between Aaron and Alyen permanent. If what Aaron reported had truly happened, it made her wonder if Faer Dinnán's intentions really were purely in the service of restoring the Balance.

Something wasn't right. Try as she might, Lirianna couldn't shake the feeling that there was something they weren't seeing—that they were missing some piece of the puzzle, and an important one at that. They needed answers, and soon, or the Trianid would be at risk even if Alyen did succeed in turning the darklings.

With a determined set in her shoulders, she reached for her shuttle and closed her eyes.

Lirianna felt the familiar haze fall upon her mind as her hands started moving across the warp. Back and forth, her fingers guided the shuttle as her feet took up the rhythm of the treadles. *Treadle, shuttle, treadle, beater. Treadle, shuttle, treadle, beater.* In her mind's eye she saw the threads of the Balance wafting like spider silk through the air. But which should she grasp? She'd been seeking a vision about Aaron or Alyen or the Trianid for days … but maybe she'd been looking in the wrong place.

This time she focused on Faer Dinnán. Almost at once, the threads shifted, one glowing brighter than the rest, drifting closer to Lirianna's hand. She grasped it and immediately felt the tumbling sensation of falling into a vision. She waited for the vision to clear, knowing the disorientation would pass, and when it did, she found herself watching Alyen and Faer Dinnán standing together at night, hands clasped, surrounded by an unearthly glow. Alyen's face was rapt as she stared around her at what, Lirianna could only assume, was some elemental magic she couldn't see. Faer Dinnán's eyes, however, remained fixed on Alyen. He leaned over and whispered something in her ear, then Alyen's gaze turned to him, filled with wonder.

Lirianna's eyes narrowed. This wasn't a vision of the future. This had already happened. She was witnessing the creation of the memory that had just destroyed Aaron's hope of reuniting with Alyen. But why was she seeing it? Nothing could be done if it had already happened. So, what was the Balance showing her?

She studied the scene before her again, focusing in on the

faerie king. It was him, after all, she'd used as the center point for her vision. She took in his flickering form; if she was honest about it, he didn't look entirely healthy, even beyond his translucent limbs. His face looked somehow wan, his cheeks hollower than she remembered. She'd only seen him briefly before, but still, she'd always had the impression that Faer Dinnán exuded vitality, as if all of nature's life force was radiating from him. Now he seemed to have dimmed somehow, as if everything that used to shine out of him had fallen away, leaving more of a shadow than a glow.

Lirianna drew in a sharp breath as realization dawned. *Of course, why hadn't I thought of it before?* They'd all trusted Faer Dinnán so much, assuming his advice would always be in line with the Balance, that they'd never considered what might happen now that he was sick.

If Faer Dinnán and the elementals were part of each other, that meant the darklings were part of the faerie king as well. He'd never risk making a permanent rift in the Trianid for his own gain—not under normal circumstances. But the Balance was dying within him, slowly giving way to the chaos of the darklings. And perhaps his actions were following suit.

They needed to stop trusting Faer Dinnán's advice.

Lirianna's hands flew back and forth across her weaving, her mind racing. She'd warn Alyen, of course. Tell her not to agree to any more of Faer Dinnán's plans to drive Aaron away. She couldn't say anything directly to Aaron, much as she wanted to. She'd promised she wouldn't, and, though she hated to admit it, Alyen was probably right that it was the safest way to ensure their best chances of success with the darklings.

But something had to be done. Something had to give

Aaron back his hope, his faith that things with Alyen could eventually be restored. Lirianna's shuttle flashed back and forth as she strained to return to the threads of the Balance. If she grasped another thread, perhaps she could glean some indication of what could restore Aaron's trust? It wouldn't have to be big. Just some little hint that Alyen still cared for him more than she was letting on. That couldn't hurt, could it?

The minutes passed, but try as she might, the threads remained hidden, the future closed to her eyes. Feeling weariness settling in her bones, Lirianna's movements slowed until her hands rested, still upon her weaving, and she opened her eyes.

Her breath caught, and for a full minute, she simply stared down at her hands.

They were glowing.

From her fingers, golden light trailed into the threads of her weaving, making the fabric shimmer.

Lirianna snatched her hands away, clenching her fingers into fists. The glowing dimmed, and slowly the shimmer faded from the fabric stretched across her loom. Soon, her hands looked as they always did, as did her weaving. She stood and backed away from her work, her stomach in a cold knot.

She'd done something just now. Something she didn't understand. Something she wasn't sure she was supposed to do.

Lirianna left the room quickly, her hands fumbling with the key as she locked the door behind her. She strode through the weaving rooms and was soon winding through the abbey corridors, headed in the direction of Mother Brenwyn's study.

It wasn't too late yet, the abbess might still be there. If anyone would know what had just happened in her workroom, it would be the former Seer.

But as Lirianna approached the study, her feet slowed, and she hesitated. Light shone from beneath the door, indicating that her mentor was, indeed, still awake, but suddenly Lirianna wasn't so sure she wanted Mother Brenwyn to know what had happened.

Purity of Sight was the Seer's highest law. The ability to remain neutral, unbiased, and uninvolved with the workings of Destiny was the only thing that allowed the Seer to interpret her visions with accuracy. If she couldn't give trustworthy advice, she was useless at best—dangerous at worst. Did she really want to admit that she might have unwittingly tampered with a vision weaving? Especially if she wasn't sure?

Suddenly, the door before her opened, and Lirianna jumped.

"Lirianna? What are you doing here at this hour? Has something happened?"

Mother Brenwyn stood before her, the lamp in her hand spilling light into the corridor. Her brow was crinkled in concern.

"I …" Lirianna swallowed, and tried again. "I need to ask you a question."

Mother Brenwyn's eyes scanned Lirianna's face. The abbess nodded. "Come in and sit down."

Lirianna followed Mother Brenwyn back into her study and found a seat in one of the comfortable chairs. Mother Brenwyn didn't sit at her desk, but pulled a chair beside Lirianna. She looked at her pupil and waited expectantly.

Lirianna wet her dry lips, choosing her words carefully. "Did you ever … When you were weaving, did you ever notice anything … *odd* … about your hands?"

Mother Brenwyn's eyebrows rose. "Odd? Odd how?"

"I'm not sure. I just … I was weaving, and when I left the vision and opened my eyes, I thought I saw something unusual."

Mother Brenwyn was nodding, her face thoughtful. "Perhaps. As you know, it can take a few moments to reorient yourself after a vision. Especially a particularly vivid one. Sometimes it can take a while to settle back into the present. Blurred vision, tingling fingers—these are all normal."

Lirianna nodded, unsure as to whether this provided any answers or made her feel any better.

After a pause, Mother Brenwyn reached out and took one of Lirianna's hands in her own. "You've been working too hard, Lirianna. Barely eating, weaving until all hours of the night. I know you're worried. We all are. But wearing yourself out won't help anyone. It's not easy to spend so much time gazing into the heart of the Balance. Tired as you must be, I wouldn't be surprised at all if your eyes were playing tricks on you."

Lirianna forced a smile, nodding again. "I'm sure you're right. I'll make sure I get more rest from now on."

Mother Brenwyn gave Lirianna's hand a pat and released it. "See that you do. And if you still notice anything odd after you're more rested, come see me."

The two women rose and parted ways in the corridor, each heading for her own bed. In her haste, Lirianna had forgotten a lamp, and she breathed a sigh of relief once she'd entered her room and lit the candle next to her bed. The small flame sent a comforting glow throughout the space, banishing the dark and the gloom. Lirianna sank onto the edge of her bed, watching the flame flicker, her face serious.

It hadn't been exhaustion or a trick of the light. She knew it in her bones. Whatever had happened, it was magic. It had come from her, and it felt like it had been … *changing* her weaving. It didn't seem like Mother Brenwyn had ever experienced anything like it, and there was no one else to ask, no way to reach an explanation. But Lirianna didn't have to understand exactly what had happened to know that it came very close to the line a Seer must never cross.

She was the Seer of Strands. It was hers to watch the threads of the Balance and the weavings of Destiny with a cool head from a space apart. It was never her place to act or to fix things beyond delivering warnings to those who could. Other people had positions of action; she was meant to guide and serve as witness to them.

Lirianna sighed deeply, trying to ignore the heaviness that settled in her heart following this train of thought. She readied herself for bed, mustering what resolve she could. From now on, she would be cautious. She would set aside her personal feelings, live according to the Seer's law, and seek her visions only to observe and report as needed. It was the life she had freely chosen, in a role that was crucial and respected.

Lirianna slid beneath her quilts and blew out her candle. She closed her eyes to shut out the darkness that now filled her room; the shadows only served as a reminder of the larger darkness they were fighting. *In the end, all that matters is that we win,* Lirianna told herself. *In the end, it won't matter how it all came together, or how messy it got before it did. It'll only matter that light won.*

And with that, Lirianna turned over to sleep, trying to

ignore the tiny voice within her whispering that just maybe, those words weren't true.

19

A CHANGE OF PLANS

Alyen woke before the dawn as the first hints of gray light were filtering through the windows. She was the first to wake, and she lay motionless on her makeshift bed on the farmhouse floor, grateful for the moment of silence to herself.

Annith's small, soft form cuddled next to her, the child's warm back pressing against her side, her breath slow and deep. Alyen glanced down carefully and felt a swell of tenderness, seeing the doll still wedged under one of Annith's arms.

Alyen had never really thought about having children. She'd always assumed she would as it would be expected of her to produce Dúramair's next heir. But it was a duty that had seemed small compared to all she had to learn to rule the kingdom, so she'd never spent much time considering it.

It might have been different with Aaron. What would have happened if they'd stayed together? Would they have married? Started a family? Would Aaron have wanted children? She would have guessed yes.

Alyen's mouth turned up sadly as she imagined Aaron playing with a swarm of children—*their* children. Before she could dwell on it too long, she pushed the thought away. It was pointless to spend time imagining what might have been. Not when it looked so likely that such futures would never come to pass.

Aaron hadn't spoken to her since his retreat to the barn the day before. He'd finally come back in the house, but he hadn't so much as glanced at her. Nah'dar's eyes had narrowed as soon as he saw the expression on his fellow warrior's face, and he'd looked to Alyen, questioning. But she'd dropped her gaze, unable to tell him anything in the presence of so many others, and unwilling to think about what she might have done to her chances of ever reuniting with Aaron.

He'll understand when it's over, she told herself again. The thought sounded worn from overuse, but it was the only thing she could hope for now, so she grasped on to it like wreckage at sea, if only to stop herself from dreading the alternative.

Alyen's hearing stone radiated warmth against her chest. She fished out the chain, careful not to jostle Annith.

"Alyen?"

"Lirianna, it's early."

"I know, but we need to talk. It's about Faer Dinnán."

A fresh wave of concern rose in Alyen's chest. *"What about him? He tired himself out yesterday in a darkling storm. Did you see something? Is he all right?"*

"I heard about the storm and it's not that, but yes, I did see something. Alyen, I don't think you can trust him anymore."

Alyen frowned, Lirianna's words making her pause. *"What do you mean?"*

Lirianna sighed. *"Look, Aaron told me about the memory he saw of you and Faer Dinnán last night. He's completely destroyed, convinced you're never coming back to him. The whole thing didn't sit well, so I looked for a vision and saw the memory Aaron was talking about. I saw the way Faer Dinnán was talking to you, how he looked. Do you realize how sick he is?"*

"Yes, he's fading, but we knew that."

"It's more than that, Alyen. Maybe you don't see it because you're around him every day, but I'm not and I can tell you, he's changed a lot since we saw him at Castle Dúr. He's starting to look like one of the darklings."

"What? Faer Dinnán is a darkling?"

"No," Lirianna sounded impatient. *"But he's connected to them, isn't he? If they were elementals, they're a part of him, and the stronger they grow, the more of him they take over, right?"*

Alyen paused again, her mind working. *"I suppose so. I never thought of it like that. And you saw this in a vision?"*

"It's what the Balance showed me. Like I told you before: the worse things get for you and Aaron, the more everything feels wrong. Alyen, I don't think you should have shown Aaron that memory."

Alyen's heart sank into the cold pit of her stomach. *"But I did show it to him. It's done. And none of this changes the fact that we need Aaron to anchor me at Illya. We can't be together for that."*

"Are you sure about that?"

"That didn't just come from Faer Dinnán, Lirianna. It's in the Keeper's book."

Lirianna cursed, her voice uncharacteristically sharp, and Alyen's eyebrows rose. Her friend must be more strained than Alyen had realized. But why?

"Lirianna, is there something you haven't told me?"

"No. Just don't follow any more of Faer Dinnán's advice where Aaron is concerned. I don't know if he really wants you as his queen, or if it's just the darklings' influence, or both. But I know for a fact that the Balance wants you and Aaron together, so do whatever you must to make sure that can still happen."

"All right," Alyen agreed. *"And Lirianna, you'd tell me if there was something else going on, wouldn't you?"*

"Of course. You know I would."

"Good."

But Alyen hadn't missed the moment of hesitation that hung between them before her friend had answered.

❦

For the next two days, the group resumed their relentless pace, riding north and west, stopping only to water and refresh the horses before pressing on once more.

As they rode, Alyen wracked her brain for any way to bridge the chasm that yawned wider than ever between her and Aaron, but inspiration failed her at every turn. She couldn't deny the memory had happened, and she couldn't explain why it had been created to begin with. Not until after Illya, at least. And even if she *had* thought of something to say, Aaron was back to avoiding any kind of contact with her. In fact, he spoke very little to any of them. Even his sparring sessions with Nah'dar, though fiercer than ever, were mostly silent affairs.

Nor did Alyen see or hear from Faer Dinnán. She found herself scouring the landscape as they rode, or peering into the darkness from her seat at the campfire, looking for the telltale glow from the plains that would signal his presence. But the land remained empty and the night dark.

Lirianna's warning about the faerie king still echoed in Alyen's mind. Whether or not he truly wanted her as his queen was yet another thing to be sorted out after Illya, but Faer Dinnán's continued absence left an unsettled feeling in her stomach. She supposed the relatively clear skies were a good sign; if the faerie king succumbed, she assumed there would be nothing to stop the darkling swarm from overtaking the kingdom and ripping it apart. Still, the need for haste pulled at her more than ever, and she felt her jaw clench any time they had to stop for food or rest.

On the third morning after the storm, the Searing Plain came to an abrupt stop. Alyen reigned in Lusa behind the others, frowning as she took in the terrain before them. Where the grasses ended, a vast expanse of sand and pebbles stretched before them, punctuated by larger rocks and boulders. The road ended in a wooden dock, and a splintering, weathered barge lay abandoned to one side.

The Eirys, one of the largest rivers in Dúramair, had disappeared.

"What happened?" Alyen asked, her eyes scanning the dry wasteland.

Aaron shifted around on Soran to face her. It was the first time he'd fully looked at her in days, and his expression was still stony, but when he spoke, his voice at least was gentle.

"It happened when the gorge was made. The Eirys is fed from Norhelm, and when the earth split, it cut right across the river. It flows into the gorge now, and this side dried up."

Alyen froze a moment, then nodded, willing her mind not to spiral into all the ramifications she knew the river's absence must have caused: less water for drinking and farming, no fish to catch, no need for ferrymen who must now find other work. Thankfully, Nah'dar's voice spared her the necessity of answering.

"We shall have to move slowly until we reach the other shore. There are too many rocks to risk a faster pace."

Alyen suppressed the sigh of impatience that rose in her throat. "Let's go, then." She nudged Lusa forward, irritably ignoring Aaron's eyes as they searched her face. She knew what they were looking for—signs of her crumpling under a fresh wave of guilt. But he wouldn't find it. She had no time for such luxuries.

"Brother Hugh," she called over her shoulder as the others moved to follow her. "A song might not go amiss to pass the time."

Brother Hugh beamed, and obliged at once with a tune Alyen was quite sure he was making up as he went about a fish who somehow granted a baker's wish to possess a magically refilling flour sack.

The Eirys was wide. Noon had come and gone by the time they reached the opposite shore. Alyen ached to resume their former pace and try to regain some of the time they'd lost, but they had to eat, as did the horses, so they were forced to stop again. When at last they were ready to continue, it was well into the afternoon. Alyen kicked Lusa into a hard gallop, hopeful they could at least make up some ground before nightfall.

But not even an hour later, a shout from Brother Hugh made her reign in Lusa hard, spinning around to see what the matter was.

Brother Hugh had stopped and dismounted a ways down

the road. Aaron and Nah'dar were already on the ground examining the hooves of the former monk's horse. Alyen cursed and trotted Lusa back, dreading what she would hear.

Aaron glanced up as she arrived. "Two shoes thrown, and I have no idea why. Garret had this one newly shod just a few weeks ago."

Alyen struggled to mask her annoyance. "Can we fix them?"

Aaron shook his head. "Not ourselves, not here. It would take hours just to find the shoes, assuming we could find them at all. And besides, we don't have the tools we need."

Alyen cursed under her breath again, fingers raking through the hair across the top of her head.

Nah'dar scanned the horizon, his eyes narrowed with unease. "It is not natural. Perhaps one shoe lost could be explained, but not two new shoes at once. I fear something else is at play."

Aaron rose, dusting off his clothes. "We're lucky it happened just here, though. We're not far from Hammel. There's a good inn there at the crossroads, and I know the innkeeper well. She may be able to do me a favor and get us in with a blacksmith quickly. Anywhere else and we'd likely have to wait days."

"There, you hear that, my fine friend?" Brother Hugh said, patting his horse with affection. "We'll have you back on the road in no time."

"All right. Let's go," Alyen said, hoping her voice didn't sound as snappish as she felt.

They rode slowly now, plodding at a snail's pace to prevent any more accidents before they reached Hammel. Brother Hugh kept up a steady stream of encouragement to his unlucky steed, and Nah'dar kept scanning their surroundings, the lines of his face and shoulders tense. Chafing at yet another delay, Alyen cast about for some source of distraction. Aaron had at least spoken to her today, but she had no patience for his iciness in her current mood, so she reached into her dress and pulled out her hearing stone.

"*Lirianna?*"

"*I'm here. How are you?*"

"*Frustrated. Brother Hugh's horse threw two brand new shoes, so we have to stop in Hammel for a blacksmith.*"

There was a long pause. "*The horse threw two shoes? Both at once?*"

"*Yes. Nah'dar thinks it's suspicious, too, but I don't sense any darklings or gremlins or anything. I guess it just happened.*"

"*I see.*" Lirianna's voice sounded distant and a faint note of distress lined her words.

"*Lirianna? Is everything all right?*"

"*I—I don't know. Alyen, I might have … I might have done something.*"

Alyen's brows drew together. "*What are you talking about? What happened?*"

"*I'm not sure. I was weaving and … never mind. I'll sort it out.*"

"*Lirianna, you know you can talk to me, don't you? Or Mother Brenwyn? Can she help?*"

"*I'm sure she can. Really, Alyen, it's all under control.*"

"*Are you certain? You don't sound certain.*"

"*Positive. No need to worry. Are you close to Hammel?*"

Alyen didn't like the breeziness in her friend's tone, but she couldn't force Lirianna to talk to her. "*I think so. We should be there before nightfall.*"

"*Then you'll get to enjoy an evening in a real bed for once. It'll prob-*"

ably be a good thing in the end. You don't want to arrive at Illya completely exhausted from the road."

Alyen thought it sounded like Lirianna was trying to convince herself more than Alyen of the detour's benefits, and tried to put her friend's mind at ease. *"I suppose you're right. A decent bed and a full night of sleep do sound good."*

"Well, then. Rest up, and let me know how it goes with the blacksmith, all right?"

"All right."

Alyen's stone went silent and she dropped it back beneath her dress, her face thoughtful.

It wasn't like Lirianna to be secretive and anxious. If something *had* gone awry with her weaving, certainly Mother Brenwyn could help sort it out. But then why hadn't Lirianna asked her already? And what could she possibly have done?

Alyen heaved another sigh, wishing Lirianna had been more forthright, and weary at the thought of yet another dilemma to bother her mind. Perhaps Lirianna was right after all, and the inn would provide some relaxation. She could certainly use it, and with Aaron, Lirianna, and Faer Dinnán all preoccupied with their own troubles, her outlets for distraction were becoming fewer by the day. Yes, perhaps a night at the inn was exactly what she needed.

But as she watched Nah'dar scan the horizon as Brother Hugh's horse hobbled along half-shod, she couldn't help but worry that the chances of a leisurely evening were slim.

20

WOOL AND ASH

Lirianna ran a hand over her face, her skin ashen. Thankfully, she was alone in her weaving room or it would have been impossible to hide her reaction from Mother Brenwyn and the other sisters. She drew in a shaky breath, willing her racing heart to ease.

Horses lose shoes, she told herself. *It happens all the time. It might not mean anything.*

But she knew, deep in her gut, that the words were lies.

She had done this. She had caused this mishap with whatever it was she had done with her glowing hands, leaking their shimmering light into her weaving. She didn't know if this new, strange magic was dangerous in and of itself, but if she was influencing the future with it … For a Seer, it would be unforgivable.

You don't know it was the magic, her mind snapped. *There's no proof it was your fault, and you can't fall to pieces every time something goes wrong just because you don't know why your hands did whatever they did.*

But this time, Lirianna's practicality couldn't silence the certainty that she was responsible.

I should have told Mother Brenwyn.

The thought had been circling in her head ever since she'd left the abbess's study, and now it rang in her mind, more insistent than ever. It wasn't too late, though. She could still tell her. Lirianna felt her body quail at the thought of admitting not only to breaking Purity of Sight less than a month after becoming Dúramair's Seer, but also having kept it a secret. Still, it was likely the wisest thing to do.

But to what end? her mind whispered. *Whatever you did, it's done now. You can't undo it. Besides, no one's hurt, and no one's in danger. If the worst that happens is a detour and two new horseshoes, is it really worth alarming everyone over it? There's enough strain to go around already. Do you really want to add to it just to ease your own conscience? Dúramair needs to trust in its Seer—especially a new one. Now isn't the time to plant the seeds of doubt.*

Lirianna shook her head and paced to the window. It was no use trying to convince herself that she was keeping the secret for noble purposes. She was terrified of admitting what she'd done—of what the repercussions might be—and she knew it.

But that didn't mean her arguments were wrong.

Her eyes strayed to her loom, the shuttle sitting on the threads as she'd left it two nights ago. She hadn't dared touch it since. That was the real problem to be addressed, she decided. The Trianid couldn't function with a Seer too afraid to weave.

Lirianna crossed the room to her loom and sat down, tracing the taut threads with tentative fingers. It was the only way out of the uncertainty, she realized. Even if she did confess everything to Mother Brenwyn, the first thing the abbess would likely have her do was weave and see if it happened again.

Biting down on her lip, Lirianna picked up the shuttle. The familiar weight of it, the smooth wood, and the soft wool, soothed her somewhat. *Start with something simple*, she thought. *Nothing dramatic, nothing important. Just see if it happens again.*

She closed her eyes and relaxed her mind, opening up to the threads of the Balance drifting in the space that was neither here nor there. *Show me the present. Show me what's happening here, in the gardens.*

The strands before her swayed, and one drifted forward, glowing in invitation. Lirianna grasped it, her hands and feet moving over the loom of their own accord.

She was looking down on the gardens. Several of the sisters were finishing their work after a day of spring planting, their faces dirt-smeared but happy. They talked easily, and the occasional peal of laughter echoed against the surrounding mountains as spades, rakes, and jars of seed were gathered to return to the tool shed before dinner.

Lirianna opened her eyes and glanced down. Her hands moved across the loom as they always had. No glow, no shimmering light leaking into the threads.

A shuddering sigh heaved from her chest as tears of relief sprang to Lirianna's eyes. Everything was back to normal, her weaving unaltered. Whatever had happened that night, it had been a fluke. There was no need to fear her visions or her loom. And no need to confess.

Lirianna wiped the back of her hand over her eyes as half

a laugh escaped her lips. Feeling suddenly much lighter, she tightened her fingers around her shuttle and closed her eyes once again, eager this time. It hadn't felt right, not weaving for the past two days, and now that she knew it was safe, she was itching for more.

Once again, she regarded the threads of the Balance, wondering where to cast her vision next. Not to Alyen or Aaron, much as she loved them, and not to the darklings or Illya. She needed a break from worry and tension. She wanted something comforting and pleasant, joyful even. Something like home.

Lirianna smiled and filled her mind with thoughts of Tiragel, of her family and their farm. The threads swirled, and she grasped one that glowed with gold and green. Suddenly she was looking out at the rolling hills of lush pasture, their farmhouse nestled in the valley.

It was a future vision, but barely. Everything Lirianna looked at had that certain indistinct haze of a scene that wasn't yet set in stone—of a reality that could still be altered. But it was clearly still springtime. There were two of her younger brothers, Owen and Will, heading toward the sheep pens, the telltale grins on their faces making it clear that some plan was underway—likely one her parents hadn't sanctioned.

Lirianna followed them, curious as to what they were up to this time. Apparently they were still inseparable, being born only one year apart, but Will was at least three inches taller than when she'd seen him last, and Owen was starting to show the smallest shadow of a beard along his smooth chin and upper lip. Lirianna felt a pang as she realized how much she'd missed, but she ignored it, intent on enjoying her time at home, if only in a vision.

The two boys followed the line of the pens until they came to the smallest one at the end. The one that was half hidden by the house. Lirianna's brows lifted as she saw what was inside: a massive black bull with two sharpened horns and angry red eyes. It was already agitated, its hooves pawing and nostrils blowing as it watched the two boys approach.

What are they up to? Lirianna wondered as a twinge of concern hitched in her chest. Her family had never owned a bull. Cattle were far more expensive than sheep, and her family's farm was small. Only now did she realize that Owen held a rope in his hands, and her trepidation grew as she saw her brothers climb the fence, swinging their legs over to drop down inside the pen with the bull.

The bull bellowed and tossed its head, hooves raking at the ground. The boys flinched, then laughed nervously as Owen lifted the rope, a loop already formed at the end.

Suddenly, a movement caught Lirianna's eye and her head snapped around. Little Seamus, her youngest sibling and only four years old, was running across the field, his small face eager as he made for the pen and his brothers. The older boys didn't see him, intent as they were on the increasingly angry bull.

No! Lirianna cried, but her voice made no sound, and she watched in horror as Seamus scrambled up the fence.

"Owen! Will!" the tiny boy called from the top and at last the two boys spun around at the sound.

But it was too late. The noise was the final straw for the bull, and with another bellow, it charged at the small figure perched on the pen. Seamus's eyes widened and, as he tried to scramble back down to safety, he fell into the pen, disappearing beneath the bull's hooves as the older boys shouted in vain.

Lirianna's entire being screamed. The sound of her keening echoed around her, and the vision seemed to falter as she willed the terrible scene to end, to change, to erase itself from existence. Without thinking, she flung her arms wide, and the fencing that formed the pen suddenly exploded outward as the vision flickered and dimmed. With a sickening lurch she felt herself slam back into the present, a wail issuing from her throat as tears streamed down her face. Her eyes snapped open, bulging as they took in the weaving before her.

Her hands were radiating, almost too bright to look at, and her entire loom shimmered as the light wove itself through the threads of her weaving.

With a cry, Lirianna hurled herself from her seat, staggering backward, her hands clutched to her chest. Her stomach lurched and she looked around wildly for a moment before racing to her private washroom where she crumpled over a basin as her body heaved.

"Lirianna?"

A shout from the weaving room, a flurry of movement, then Mother Brenwyn was there. Her steadying hands guided Lirianna to a chair and pressed a cool cloth to her forehead. There were orders for tea to be brought, the door closed, and finally silence fell, with only her mentor to witness her distress.

"Lirianna? What happened? Was it a vision?"

Lirianna raised her face, strands of fiery hair plastered to her wet cheeks. "Mother Brenwyn, I … I'm broken … I'm sorry, I … Seamus … my hands … broken …"

Lirianna's eyes trailed to her loom and Mother Brenwyn's

gaze followed. The abbess's eyes grew wide and Lirianna collapsed into more sobbing.

The threads of the warp remained strung along the loom, standing ready for the Seer to weave. But the weft—everything Lirianna had woven with her shuttle—had burned to ash.

21

THE HUNTSMAN'S DAUGHTER

The shadows were lengthening by the time they made it to Hammel—a settlement that was large for a village, though not quite a town. The roads they followed as they wound their way to Hammel's northern end were unpaved, though the bustle of people and the many storefronts gave it the air of a prospering center of growing trade rather than a sleepy country hamlet. Curious eyes lifted as they passed, though none stared for long as everyone hurried toward home with the approach of evening.

The inn to which Aaron led them was near the edge of Hammel, settled conveniently for travelers at a crossroads, yet near enough to the center that the locals wouldn't consider it too far out of their way for an evening pint. As they reined their horses to a halt, the inn door opened, and a loud burst of lively chatter and laughter spilled into the courtyard from within.

"Well, if it isn't the Second Slayer, back after what, more than a year? What took you so long?"

Alyen turned toward the voice and saw it came from a young woman, her arms folded across her chest. A sly grin flitted across her face as her dark eyes homed in on Aaron. Wispy curls of brown hair escaped from the clip that held it back. Her cheeks were lightly flushed, and a crisp apron was tied around a green dress that was sturdy yet finely made.

The way she was looking at Aaron sent a fire searing through Alyen's chest.

The way Aaron looked back made her heart plummet.

"Marietta," Aaron said with an easy smile. "I see you've kept the place in shape. Still think you should change the name, though."

"The Huntsman's Daughter has a good ring to it. And my father keeps me well supplied with meat at a more than fair price. Everyone knows my stew is the best in Dúramair."

"And so it is. It's good to see you again, Marietta."

Aaron and the young innkeeper clasped hands, and the pit in Alyen's stomach clenched as she watched them make eye contact, one fact quickly becoming crystal clear.

They had a history.

One Aaron had never mentioned to Alyen.

"I take it this Marietta is the Huntsman's Daughter. She's quite pretty, isn't she?" Brother Hugh said unhelpfully to no one in particular. "And quite successful, by the look of it."

Alyen's mood soured even further as she glanced around the premises. Though she hated to admit it, Brother Hugh was right. The stone walls were clean and well-maintained, the roof freshly thatched, and the sign above the door freshly painted. A large wooden stable stood to the side, boasting the establishment's popularity, and no fewer than four stable boys were headed their way to assist with the horses.

"Alyen," Aaron's voice jolted Alyen back to attention. She saw that everyone was looking her way, the innkeeper's eyes evaluating and not entirely friendly as they fixed on her.

"I was just introducing you to Marietta, owner of The Huntsman's Daughter. Marietta, this is Alyen of Dúr, the Keeper of Scales."

Alyen didn't miss the fact that he hadn't given Marietta's formal title and clenched her teeth at the familiarity it implied. She forced herself to smile.

"I'm very pleased to meet you, Marietta. I'm sure we'll be very comfortable here during our brief stay."

One of Marietta's eyebrows quirked up but she inclined her head respectfully, returning Alyen's false smile. "I'm sure the pleasure is mine, Keeper of Scales. I'm honored to host your company for as long as you choose." She turned to Aaron, lowering her voice, but not so much that Alyen couldn't still hear her.

"I'll have the Slayer's room made up for you. That is, unless you'd prefer your old room, which I'd understand completely." Alyen's throat constricted as Marietta lay a hand gently on Aaron's arm with a squeeze of sympathy.

"The Slayer's room will be fine," Aaron said, his smile sad. "It can't stay empty forever."

Marietta's eyes were intent. "Morten of Hammel was one of our own, and we grieve him with you. You'll let me know if there's anything I can do?"

"I will," Aaron assured her, and Alyen nearly growled at the understanding she saw pass between him and the innkeeper.

"Actually," Aaron continued, gesturing toward Brother Hugh and his mount, "we need a blacksmith, and in a hurry. One of our horses threw two shoes and I was hoping you could put in a word for us?"

"Poor darling," Marietta said in the direction of Brother Hugh's horse. "I'll send for the farrier straightaway. I'm sure I can get him here this evening, morning at the latest. He owes me a favor, considering how much business I've sent his way."

Marietta shouted some orders to the waiting stable boys, and they sprang to action, gathering reins and assisting with saddlebags. Alyen handed a coin to the young boy who led Lusa away to the stable, and when she turned back, Marietta was already leading Aaron through the inn door without so much as a backward glance to her other notable guests.

Her hand was still on Aaron's arm.

"My, my," Brother Hugh said, rocking back and forth on his feet. "It seems the Huntsman's Daughter is a bit of a huntress herself!"

Alyen chewed down on her tongue to prevent her from saying anything she might later regret. She glanced at Nah'-dar, but he only met her eyes in silence.

"Let's go eat," was all she said, and turned, seething, to enter The Huntsman's Daughter.

It was an uncomfortable meal for Alyen. The bustling inn had several villagers employed as servers in the large dining hall, but their table was waited on exclusively by Marietta, who seemed to find any excuse to linger and chat with Aaron. Alyen remained mostly silent, a swirl of emotions warring with her clamoring thoughts as she tried to regain her footing and return to sense.

It doesn't matter how you feel about Marietta or Aaron right now. You can't let your feelings show. If Aaron finds out you're jealous, he'll be confused, and you've worked too hard to complicate things now. Don't let one pushy innkeeper sabotage the work you have to do. Even if she is beautiful and confident and definitely *interested in Aaron. Even if something did happen between them. Whatever it was, it couldn't have been that significant. Aaron would have told you about it if it was. He would have mentioned her before.*

Wouldn't he?

Uncomfortable with the direction her thoughts were heading, Alyen decided to join the conversation. She tried to arrange her features in a pleasantly neutral expression, then interrupted Aaron's and Marietta's laughter, straining to keep the edge in her voice at bay.

"So, how long have you two known each other?"

"Oh, forever." Marietta waved a hand in the air, barely glancing at Alyen. "We practically grew up together, didn't we, Aaron? At least whenever you and Morten were in the area."

"It's true," Aaron confirmed. "Marietta might be my oldest friend. I think we met when I was eight—the first time Morten brought me north." He looked at Marietta with a grin. "I remember you'd just been stung by a bee and you were bawling your eyes out with your lip swollen out to here …" Aaron held out a hand in front of his face and Marietta swatted it playfully.

"It was not so bad, but curses, it stung. And you!" She pointed an accusatory finger at Aaron. "You were kind. Never teased me once. You even admitted to being frightened of bees, yourself."

"Actually, I'm older," Alyen blurted.

Aaron and Marietta broke off and looked at Alyen in surprise.

"What?" Aaron said.

Alyen swallowed, cursing inwardly. She hadn't meant to speak—where was her control? She usually had a better handle on herself. But the look Marietta was giving Aaron had made something rear up inside of her, and the words sprang out of her mouth before she could think. Now she'd have to tread carefully. She tried to smile, brushing her comment off with a shake of her head.

"I meant I was an older friend. Aaron met me on his way north with Morten that year. So, that would technically make *me* Aaron's oldest friend. But it doesn't matter. I was just … saying."

Her words were followed by a distinctly awkward pause.

"Well then," Marietta said, and Alyen didn't miss the way she widened her eyes briefly at Aaron. "To old friendships." She raised her tankard and the rest followed suit. Thankfully, Brother Hugh chose that exact moment to compliment Marietta on the food, and Alyen let out a breath of relief. She took a gulp from her own tankard, and when she lowered it, found Aaron's eyes on her, a strange expression on his face. Alyen's breath hitched, and she looked away quickly.

"Does anyone fancy a game of Quivers?" Marietta offered. "I have a silver coin says I can still beat you." She nudged Aaron's arm.

Aaron turned away from Alyen and smiled, though perhaps not as readily as before. "Sure, I'll play. Anyone else care to join?"

Alyen hesitated. She hated the thought of leaving the two

of them alone together, but her lack of control had already resulted in one close call too many. "No," she said reluctantly. "I think I'll turn in early. Thank you, Marietta, for your hospitality."

Marietta nodded politely, a small, triumphant smile playing about her lips. She, Aaron, and a seemingly oblivious Brother Hugh left for their game.

Alyen turned to retreat to her room, but found Nah'dar's eyes on her as he remained in his seat.

"You may put your worries to rest, sanahara. They will not be alone together tonight. I shall find a reason to keep them company until dawn if need be. Perhaps this will bring you some small measure of peace."

Alyen's eyes stung. She wanted to tell him not to trouble himself. That his rest was more important, that Aaron was free to make his own choices, that she was sure there was nothing to worry about in any case.

Instead, she laid a hand on his shoulder, her voice a whisper. "Thank you."

And with that, she left for her room and what sleep she could get.

The Keeper's room at The Huntsman's Daughter was lovely. Alyen practically snarled as she entered, her eyes taking in the comfortable bed, the view of the rolling grasslands, the welcoming hearth. She knew it wasn't fair—not to Marietta, whose success could hardly be considered a sin, and certainly not to Aaron—but snarling was easier than acknowledging the heart that was slowly breaking beneath her breastbone. She was just about to reach for one of the overstuffed pillows on her bed so she could succumb to her urge to scream into it when her room was filled with the now-familiar scent of forest rain. She whirled around to find Faer Dinnán standing before her.

Or rather what was left of him.

Alyen caught her breath at the sight of the faerie king, alarm briefly easing the pangs of jealousy and grief. No longer was the fading restricted to his limbs, but his entire form seemed mottled, with patches of him flickering between solidity and the translucence of a ghost.

"We must act," he said, direct as usual.

"What do you mean? It's been days, where have you been? You don't look well."

"I'm not well. But I'm still here, and we must act."

"When?"

"Tonight. Now."

"Now? What are we doing?"

"You must help me to close Alyen's Gorge."

Alyen's eyes flew wide. "Close—*what*?"

"It's our only chance. You and your companions are planning on traveling around it, correct?"

"Yes. It'll take a few days. Three or four at most."

"Too long. You don't have that much time. *I* don't have that much time."

"But to close it … I …"

Alyen's palms were slick with sweat, and she found herself trembling at the thought of what Faer Dinnán was asking her to do. Memories slammed into her mind, memories of standing on the cliffs of Norhelm, power surging through her body, taking over, ripping the earth apart.

Memories of the terrible day she'd realized the cost of her actions.

Faer Dinnán spoke, his voice gentler but firm. "I wouldn't ask without need. I hoped not to ask at all. But I'm fading too quickly, Alyen. I must hope it's not already too late."

Alyen strode to the window, gazing out at Hammel, the people navigating its winding streets, the faint glimmer of lights in the grasslands beyond marking the farms and villages glowing in the dusky twilight.

"What of the people? How do we keep them safe? I can't put anyone in danger. Not again."

Faer Dinnán joined Alyen at the window, his gaze mimicking her own. "It will be different this time, Alyen. Your powers have grown. You have grown. This time you will have me and my power with you. And Aaron to anchor you as well."

"Aaron?" Alyen looked at the faerie king. "He's coming, too?"

Faer Dinnán nodded. "We'll use all the power and precautions available to us to ensure this goes well, and it will be good practice for what must be done at Illya."

Alyen pushed away from the window and filled her lungs, trying to ignore her fear. "What should I do?"

Faer Dinnán's eyes were approving. "Get Aaron and meet me at the gorge. Make haste."

And he was gone.

For the space of a heartbeat, Alyen stood frozen in the middle of her room. Then, springing into motion, she wrenched open her door, preparing to bolt down the stairs to find Aaron.

To her surprise, he was already there in the corridor.

His brow lifted. "Alyen? What are you doing?"

"I was coming to find you."

"Why?" There was a look on his face that Alyen had no time to decipher.

"We need to leave now."

"Leave?"

Alyen forced herself to take a breath. "We need to go to the gorge. Faer Dinnán will meet us there and the three of us have to close it."

Whatever Aaron had expected her to say, it wasn't that. "Close the gorge? How?"

"Faer Dinnán is fading too fast for us to go around it. He and I are going to close it while you anchor me, just like we've practiced. But we have to leave now."

Aaron hesitated only a second. "Then let's go."

They clattered down the wooden stairs and erupted into the noisy dining hall, Alyen looking around for Nah'dar and Brother Hugh. She spotted them across the room, Brother Hugh apparently intent on finishing the game of Quivers with Marietta, who looked much less enthusiastic about it than she had when it had been Aaron she was playing against. Nah'dar, who was watching from a nearby table, caught Alyen's eye and rose quickly, sensing her haste. Alyen jerked her head toward the front door and exited with Aaron into the cool night air.

They were soon joined in the courtyard by Nah'dar, Brother Hugh, and Marietta, whose eyes were sharp once more.

"What has happened?" asked Nah'dar, his hand hovering near the hilt of his scimitar.

Alyen hesitated, unsure if it was wise to say anything in front of Marietta.

"Marietta can be trusted," Aaron said, noticing Alyen's reluctance. He glanced at the innkeeper who nodded in agreement.

Unwilling to waste any more time, Alyen explained as briefly as she could, already feeling the pull building from the darkness beyond Hammel. Marietta listened with narrowed eyes, and Nah'dar's face was stony, but by the time Alyen finished speaking, Brother Hugh was bouncing on the balls of his feet, smiling widely.

"Lovely!" the former monk exclaimed. "Won't it feel nice to put that to rights, Alyen? And we'll save time to boot!"

"You can't be serious, Aaron." It was Marietta, whose eyes were now boring into Aaron's, her face contorted in angry disbelief. "You trust her with this? After what she did?"

A mix of guilt and anger flooded through Alyen's chest, her cheeks growing hot as she prepared for a fight. But then she caught sight of Aaron's face and watched his shoulders broaden as he stepped forward. He looked at Marietta, his eyes burning, and spoke in a dangerously quiet voice. "I trust Alyen with my life, Marietta. She is our Keeper of Scales, and one of the Trianid of Dúramair."

Marietta seemed to shrink back, some of the fire leaving her eyes, but anger still laced her words as she looked to Alyen. "I meant no disrespect, Keeper, but the facts can't be ignored. Many of us in the northlands suffered tragedy when the gorge was made, and few will be quick to forget the memories of those lost. I'm sorry, but your horses are in my stable, and I have an inn full of those loyal to me and to our home who will make sure they stay there."

Alyen saw Aaron bristle and open his mouth to speak, but a light had ignited in her chest as she watched Aaron defend her, sending a wave of calm throughout her body. She stepped forward to place a hand on his arm.

"You're right, Marietta," Alyen said, registering with satisfaction the surprise that rose in the innkeeper's eyes. "No one can rightly expect you to give me your trust. I haven't earned it. When I made the gorge I was desperate and inexperienced. I was working alone and lost control. The power I harnessed and unleashed almost killed me. And that act has haunted me, day and night, ever since. It's right that you see me as a danger. You have a life and people to protect."

She paused, studying Marietta's reaction. When the other woman didn't speak, Alyen continued.

"But tonight, there's a greater danger. If we don't close the gorge, if we don't get to Illya on time, Faer Dinnán will perish and the world with him. There won't be anything left to protect. And this time I won't be alone. The faerie king himself has been training me for this moment, and he'll be with me, guiding my actions and adding his power to my own."

Alyen paused and swallowed before issuing her final plea. "You may not trust me, but you do trust Aaron, and that trust is well-placed. He has power of his own, and he'll be using it to anchor mine. You have my word—*our* word. Your home will be safe tonight."

For a weighty moment, Marietta held Alyen's gaze, then her eyes cut over to Aaron. "You can control her?"

"No. But I can help her. Add my strength so her magic is stable."

Marietta looked away, her face a mixture of disappointment and disdain. She shook her head in disgust. "Fine, then.

Be on your way." Without another word or glance, she stalked back into the inn.

"Well," Brother Hugh said, once the inn door had closed with a bang, his expression that of someone trying to pretend they weren't present. "Perhaps she'll feel better about things once Alyen and Aaron return victorious."

Nah'dar said nothing, but his expression indicated his doubt on that front.

"We need to go," Alyen said, urgency filling her once more. "Faer Dinnán is waiting."

"Shall I accompany you?" offered Nah'dar.

Alyen glanced back at the inn door. "No. If that's how people here feel about me and the gorge, I don't want Brother Hugh alone while we do what we have to do. Stay here and keep both of you safe. If things don't …" She closed her eyes a moment, then locked eyes with Nah'dar's. "Run if you have to."

Nah'dar nodded, and Alyen and Aaron turned and made quickly for the barn.

"Good luck!" Brother Hugh called after them, one arm waving in farewell.

They saddled their horses in silence, their hands moving quickly in the shadowy barn. By the time they emerged ready to ride, their companions had returned indoors, and Keeper and Slayer faced the dark grasslands alone.

22
ALYEN'S GORGE

They rode through the darkness, the moonlight lending just enough light to see among the grassy swells. The chill of the night wind on her skin both roused Alyen and cooled her head so that, by the time Aaron slowed Soran to a walk, she was focused and alert, if a bit nervous. She followed Aaron's lead, pulling Lusa to a halt, then turned to the faintly glowing speck that was Faer Dinnán in the distance. As they dismounted, she wondered briefly why Aaron had stopped so far away, then supposed it wasn't so odd considering the Slayer's dislike for the faerie king.

"Alyen." Aaron's voice stopped her and she turned to face him. It was hard to read his expression in the dark, but his voice sounded different. Softer, perhaps. She waited for him to continue.

"It was a couple of kisses behind the barn when I was fourteen. That's all."

"What?"

"Marietta and me. We were both really young, and it was the first time I'd kissed a girl. That's all that ever happened between us, and, honestly, it didn't mean much. I swear."

Alyen sniffed and looked away, her arms crossed over her chest. "Seems like it should have meant *something* if it was your first kiss." Her voice sounded sulky, even to her.

"Well ... it wasn't with you."

The words hung in the silence and Alyen didn't know what to say.

Aaron cleared his throat. "Later that year, Morten and I were at Castle Dúr, and I saw you, and ... that was it."

Alyen heard the shrug in his voice and sniffed again at the sting in her nose. He knew she'd been jealous. And her jealousy had given them a way to reconnect better than anything she could have concocted herself. More than anything at that moment, she wanted to say something that would fix everything for good. To collapse against his chest and cry, knowing everything would be all right again.

But she knew that if she spoke, her first words would be "I'm sorry." The rest would follow, and Dúramair would be doomed. It was safer to leave things between them as a tentative truce.

"Well," Aaron finally said, his voice heavy with defeat. "I just wanted you to know."

"Aaron," Alyen said quickly, before he could walk away. He waited, and she placed a tentative hand on his arm. "Thank you for telling me."

Aaron let out a breath that may have been relief. She sensed more than saw his answering nod, and together they led their horses toward Faer Dinnán's glow, Alyen feeling at once both lighter and utterly broken.

It was hard to make out the gorge in the darkness, and Alyen found herself intensely thankful that it was nighttime. The glint of moonlight on the ragged edge of a cliff before it plunged into an even deeper darkness was more evidence than she ever wanted to see from that day in Norhelm. Despite her determination to focus on the task at hand, she felt a tremor pass through her and she turned her head away.

"Are you all right?" Aaron whispered in her ear, and Alyen felt one of his hands warm on her back.

She nodded, glancing up at him. "I'm fine."

Aaron said nothing more, but his hand moved from her back into her palm, and Alyen clasped it gratefully.

Faer Dinnán stood a stone's throw from the edge of the gorge, his half-faded form flickering around the edges.

"Are you both ready?" he asked, his voice sounding more like a ragged whisper than the rustle of leaves it used to carry.

He's not strong enough for this, Alyen thought, her heart twisting with concern.

Aaron had already nodded his consent, and was closing his eyes to clear his mind, but Alyen stopped him with a squeeze on his hand.

"Wait."

Aaron and Faer Dinnán both looked at her, and Alyen knew they expected her to admit being too afraid to continue. She shook her head and addressed the faerie king.

"Let us do this, Faer Dinnán. Let me and Aaron close the gorge alone."

Faer Dinnán regarded Alyen for a silent moment, and for the first time, Alyen saw what Lirianna had been talking about. It wasn't just the fading of the faerie king's form. His face was gaunt, and his eyes held a dark gleam she'd never seen there before.

"Do you think this plan wise, Alyen? It is a great undertaking, and melding with the gnomes may take more courage from you than melding with the darklings."

It was true, and Alyen knew it. Already she could feel the fear clawing at her stomach as she considered what she was about to attempt, and what the cost had been the last time she'd tried such an act.

But she also knew she was right.

"It's the wisest plan we have," she said, encouraged by how steady her voice sounded. "We know my power is enough to do this—it's already done it once before."

"The controlled mending of a continent is far more difficult than accidentally ripping it apart."

Alyen's teeth grated at the faerie king's lack of faith. "But this time Aaron will be with me, and I know what I'm doing. You've taught me well, and I've learned to work around my fear. The foolish thing would be to risk taxing you any further. Everything we've done will be for nothing if you perish of exhaustion before we even reach Illya."

Faer Dinnán was silent again, and Alyen took the opportunity to push once more.

"If you don't believe I can do this, how can you still hope for victory with the darklings?"

Faer Dinnán's eyes flitted between Alyen and Aaron, resting briefly on the hands clasped between them. "Very well," he said at last. "But I shall remain here, ready to add what powers I still have should it become necessary."

Alyen knew it was the best she could hope for and nodded her thanks. She turned toward Aaron.

"You can do this," Aaron whispered, his eyes radiating a confidence that warmed her like the sun. "*We* can do this."

Alyen took his other hand and squeezed them both in reply. Then she bowed her head, closed her eyes, and addressed her fear.

"I see you. I know that now, more than ever, you want to take control, and that's perfectly understandable. But it's not your time, and I have work to do. Stay if you will, but leave me to my task."

The fear didn't leave, but its grip eased, and Alyen found her breath coming easier. Somewhere in her heart, a feeling bloomed—much like the feeling she had when stroking Lusa—and wrapped itself around her fear like a blanket.

Without Alyen knowing why, tears pricked at the corners of her eyes.

There wasn't time to sort it out, though. It was time to do the magic she knew she'd been most afraid to do, ever since she'd discovered her new power.

It was time to meld with the gnomes.

Alyen took a steadying breath, then filled her mind and body with earth. The soaring cliffs that housed Monstar Abbey, the protective presence of the Mountains of Geal, the strong stones that formed the walls of Castle Dúr, her childhood home. She felt her hands sink into cool, fertile soil, felt the spongy forest floor beneath her feet, felt the cool silence of mountain caves. She felt it build within her, then, with a silent plea for strength, she called to the gnomes in the singing speech.

"Gnomes of earth and rock and stone, of mountain peak, of tooth and bone, join your magic unto mine, and with our powers thus entwined, help me with an urgent task. Help me to redeem my past."

Magic gathered and pressed from all sides. She felt its weight, its vibration, felt her instinct to struggle against it. But she wasn't new to this. She knew what waited on the other side of the discomfort, and despite her fear, she knew how to get there.

Alyen let the magic continue to build around her until she felt her arms trembling as they braced against it. Then, knowing it was time to meld, she squeezed Aaron's hands … and released.

The familiar void surrounded her, dark and peaceful, a space beyond. One by one, the tiny lights that were the gnomes bloomed around her, a scattering of stars against the welcoming night.

Why had she been afraid? This was no different than melding with any other elemental. She felt the pull of the beings around her, sensed their eagerness to converge their powers with hers, felt their loving acceptance, the oneness of their existence and her own.

This wasn't a terrifying force to control. This was *right*. This was coming home.

The gnomes gathered to her, attaching themselves to her magic, the essence that was her. She felt herself reform, felt joy spread throughout her limbs, then slowly opened her eyes.

The first thing she saw was Aaron's gaze still upon her, his eyes holding something close to awe. She looked down at their hands, still clasped between them. Her skin had transformed to resemble craggy rock, cracked with age, and mottled with moss and dusty lichen.

Alyen looked back up at Aaron, a smile on her lips. "I'm ready."

Aaron nodded and drew in his breath, closing his eyes in

concentration. He began the singing speech, but once again, Alyen didn't listen, realizing that she hadn't yet safeguarded her memories. Quickly, she pushed all thoughts of Aaron aside and cast about for some part of her mind that was safe to share.

Her lessons with Rowenna. That would be harmless enough. And there were plenty of them to last as long as she needed.

As soon as she'd pulled the memories to the front of her mind, she felt the connection with Aaron ignite. The grasslands whispered in the swirl of wind that rushed around them, and the earth vibrated as the now-familiar shock rolled through her. At once Aaron's memories unfolded before her mind's eye.

Morten was teaching him the proper way to hold a knife, adjusting his small fingers to ensure his wrist remained fluid.

He was balancing atop a tree stump, large enough for only one foot to find purchase. His body jerked awkwardly, straining for balance as he tried to block Morten's advances with a makeshift sword.

He sat in what must be the Slayer's cottage, a fire blazing in the hearth and Morten's booming laugh filling the room as snow fell in drifts out the window.

Perfect. If Alyen was witnessing Aaron's memories of his own training, then it would seem all the more natural for Alyen's memories to mirror the same theme. She felt the tug in her mind and willingly sent her selected memories out to Aaron, secure in the knowledge that he would see nothing that would distract from the task before her.

"Aaron," Alyen sent her thought through their connection. *"I'm going to try to close the gorge now. Are you ready?"*

"I'm ready," came Aaron's reply. *"Go slowly, and be careful."*
"I will."

Letting her memories continue to slide toward Aaron, Alyen turned her focus to the gorge.

Melded as she was with the gnomes, she could feel every rock, every crevasse beneath her feet and stretching out across the land. She felt where the terrain suddenly gave way, felt the yawning chasm and the way it felt unnatural, each side yearning for the other. Her mind ran the course of the tear in the earth, from the plain at the foot of Norhelm to the edge of the Western Sea. Once she felt her mind was holding the gorge in its entirety, she reached out to the gnomes once more.

"I stand before the wounded ground, the tear I caused when I was bound too tightly to your earthly power—a desperate move in a fearful hour. Now I wish to right my wrong, to heal the earth, to make it strong as once it was. But as I do, I must protect my people too. Join with me to mend this rift, guide the earth to slowly drift, gentle as it eases back, softly as we seal the crack."

From deep below ground, an energy surged upward, filling Alyen's entire being, making her blood thrum in her veins. As she had once before in Norhelm, she felt the thrill of power, the fierce joy of invincibility—but this time she also felt herself recoil from the wave of magic as fear suddenly twisted again in her heart. On instinct, she glanced up at Aaron, excitement warring with doubt in her eyes.

"I'm here," came Aaron's steady reply. *"I won't let you lose control."*

A drumming sound, steady and strong, flooded Alyen's ears and vibrated through her bones. At first she thought it was the rhythm of the gnomes, the pulse of the earth imbued in the magic filling her. Then she realized it wasn't coming from the earth at all.

It was Aaron's heartbeat, carrying his power to join with hers. It grounded her, anchoring her to herself, to him, to the place where they stood, and it amplified their combined strength a thousandfold.

Alyen squeezed Aaron's hands in gratitude, knowing now, beyond a doubt, that she had the strength and control to do what must be done. Memories still flowing out of her, she closed her eyes, feeling the intensity of the power, and began.

In her mind, she saw the two sides of the chasm draw nearer to each other, saw the rent in the earth narrow ever so slowly, inch by inch. A tremble rose from the earth, and Alyen slowed her pace even further, feeling the rightness of the deed and the eagerness of the gnomes lending her their magic.

Alyen didn't know how long she stood coaxing the earth ever closer together. She didn't know when sweat beaded on her craggy brow or when it fell in rivulets down her face. She didn't see Faer Dinnán watching her, his face unreadable as power radiated from her altered body. She didn't even pay attention to Aaron's memories still flowing down their shared connection.

She saw only the gorge, felt only the power—hers, Aaron's, and the gnomes'— until at last she felt the sides of the gorge meet.

Joy surged through her, as the knowledge of what they'd accomplished settled into her bones. She opened her eyes, looking to Aaron in triumph, but paused at the look she found on his face.

Only then did she remember that he was still witnessing her memories of lessons spent with Rowenna. She turned her mind back to their connection, anxious to see which part of her training he was witnessing—and froze.

The memory unfolding before him was one she'd forgotten. One he shouldn't see, not now, not yet. She and Rowenna were sitting before the Keeper's cottage the night she'd learned to cast a protective circle, just hours before her mentor had died. Rowenna was telling Alyen that she and Aaron could never be together, not in the way she wanted, and Alyen's anger was rising. Now they were arguing, tears standing in Alyen's eyes.

Curses! No good would come of Aaron seeing this memory. He would see more than simple jealousy; he would see just how broken she'd felt at the thought of never being with him. It wouldn't just confuse him; emotions would stir in a way they shouldn't, not this close to Illya.

Alyen felt her mind yank back, their connection severing as her hands dropped from his. She caught another glimpse of Aaron's face, surprise melting into concern as he saw her stagger backward.

Exhaustion crashed over her. She had to disconnect from the gnomes, the magic was too much to sustain, but she was too tired to form thoughts let alone words. She turned, searching for Faer Dinnán, her face forming a plea as she felt herself sink to the ground. Darkness closed in on her, and she felt herself slipping into the deep void of unconsciousness.

As her eyes closed, she felt Faer Dinnán's magic wrap around her like a blanket, releasing her from the melding, returning her to her small, human form. She wanted to protest, tell him to save his magic, but she couldn't find the strength to fight and instead surrendered to oblivion.

23

THE HEALER

For a time, there was only darkness and motion. Alyen's eyes remained closed, yet she had the impression of hurried movements and urgent voices as though heard from a distance. She slipped in and out of consciousness, finding herself in one moment riding fast across the grasslands, her body held tightly against Aaron's, then darkness slipping down again, mercifully quiet, and empty.

She woke again to the shuffling of feet on a wood floor, doors slamming, firelight piercing through her closed eyelids. The voices were closer now, and she could start to make out snippets of conversation.

"… happened out there?"

"Saints, is she all right?"

"… need a healer."

"I'll get my aunt. She's the best …"

"Hurry, Marietta."

Alyen turned her head away from the noise, wishing it would stop. But the motion only alerted people that she was awake, and Aaron's voice turned to her.

"Alyen? Can you hear me? Can you speak?"

Alyen didn't respond, hoping she would be left alone if she was silent. Perhaps it worked because she was being carried somewhere, away from the chaos and the noise. The light was dimming and when Aaron spoke again, his voice was softer, gentle in her ears.

"Don't worry. Help is coming. You'll feel better soon."

A door creaked open, and she felt herself lowered carefully onto a bed. A blanket was drawn over her, blissfully warm, and she heard the sounds of a fire being started in the hearth.

Her mind was coming back to her now. Flashes of memories were coalescing, reminding her of what she had set out to do that night, but they stopped short of informing her of the outcome. A knot of fear formed in her stomach, and with effort she cleared her throat.

"Aaron?"

Her eyelids rose just enough to see Aaron spin around at the hearth. His face was awash with worry and she almost wanted to close her eyes again so she wouldn't have to see it. But she needed answers, and he needed to know she was strong enough to hear them.

"Did it work?" she croaked.

Aaron crossed the room swiftly and knelt by her bedside. His hands folded around one of hers, and his eyes met and held her own.

"Yes. It worked. You closed the gorge."

Alyen swallowed. "And did I … Did anything …" she couldn't bring herself to finish.

"No," Aaron shook his head quickly, and she could see it was the truth. "Nothing bad happened. Everyone is safe."

A sigh escaped Alyen's lips as her eyes closed in relief. She sank back into her pillow, tears she couldn't hold back leaking from the corners of her eyes. Aaron said nothing, his fingers gently caressing the back of her hand.

After a time, she ventured again. "And Faer Dinnán?"

"I don't know. He just … disappeared." Aaron's voice flattened only a fraction.

Alyen paused for a moment. "Well, he can't be too badly off. The world still exists, right?" She cracked her eyes open in Aaron's direction and attempted a weak grin.

Aaron let out half a chuckle, the smile he returned showing his relief. "You can't be that badly off yourself if you're making jokes."

Alyen smiled and gave his hand a squeeze.

Aaron held her gaze, and this time she didn't look away. Silence spread between them, making the air heavy with things unsaid.

He still cared for her. Even after all she'd put him through, he still loved her. She could see it in his face.

"Thank you. For taking care of me," she whispered.

He paused only a second. "I'll always take care of you."

She'd never seen his face so serious, or so conflicted.

Aaron glanced away to the hearth where the fire crackled. Alyen watched the emotions flicker over his face, knowing he was struggling between wanting to speak and wanting her to rest. When he finally did look back at her, his eyes were shining.

"Alyen," he began and looked down at her hand clasped in his, his fingers still working her skin. "Alyen, it was so good. I know you've moved on, and I know why you did, but … there are other times I could swear you still want to be with me as much as I want to be with you. Couldn't we go back to it? Try again? We were so good together."

He looked back up at her, and Alyen's breath almost caught at the look on his face.

She paused.

She was too tired to pretend any more. Too exhausted to keep guarding her memories, too sick of seeing the hurt in his eyes, too weary to keep up the lie. And in the end, had it even been worth it? If Aaron still wanted her back, then the enchantment hadn't erased his love for her; it had only broken the love they had shared. Would that really be enough to keep him safe?

She had powers now that no other Keeper had ever had—that no other *human* had ever had. Perhaps there *was* a different way to heal the darklings. One they could find together.

She almost said yes. She cleared her throat to speak, her lips parting to utter the words—but then she saw Aaron's face drain of color, his eyes dropping, his hands drawing away from hers.

The few moments she'd taken to consider, he'd taken as silent rejection.

At that moment, the door opened and Marietta entered, followed closely by a woman carrying a leather satchel and a basket. They stopped abruptly in the doorway, eyes darting from Aaron's stricken face to Alyen's hand still stretched toward him, clearly unsure as to whether they were interrupting something they shouldn't.

Aaron stood quickly. "I'll be downstairs," he mumbled, and left the room without another glance. Marietta's eyes flicked to Alyen briefly. She murmured a few words to the woman, then turned and followed Aaron out, shutting the door behind her.

The woman crossed the room in a quiet, businesslike way. She set her things down and pulled a chair next to the bed. She sat and gave Alyen a warm smile.

"Your Highness, my name is Eefa. I'm Marietta's aunt and I work as a healer in Hammel. I knew Rowenna, and it's an honor to meet the next Keeper of Scales."

Distressed at Aaron's abrupt departure and upset with Marietta and the healer for barging in before she could fix things, Alyen could bring herself only to nod.

If Eefa was offended, she didn't show it. "May I examine you, Keeper? You do seem pale, and I've brought some restorative herbs that may help."

Alyen softened somewhat. Eefa seemed kind, and the unfortunate timing of her arrival was hardly her fault. She nodded again and added, "Please, just call me Alyen."

Eefa smiled and began her work, feeling Alyen's pulse and forehead, inspecting her eyes and tongue. She turned to her basket and removed a stack of cloths along with some sprigs of herbs.

There was a knock on the door, and a young girl came in bearing a large, steaming kettle of water. Eefa rose and took the kettle from the girl, hanging it on a hook over the fire. The girl remained rooted to her spot, staring at Alyen with wide eyes.

Eefa noticed and clucked her tongue. "Off with you, now," she said, and ushered the girl back out the door.

The healer turned back to Alyen, and the corner her mouth twitched up. "My apologies. I imagine you're the talk of the town now. It's not often the Keeper of Scales reforms the earth just down the road."

Alyen's eyes lowered. "A bit more often than everyone would like, I'm sure."

Eefa's eyes studied Alyen's face, but she said nothing. Instead, she filled a bowl with steaming water from the kettle and set it near the bed before adding the herbs.

Alyen watched, interested despite her exhaustion. "Lavender. And Lemon Balm?"

Eefa nodded, soaking a cloth in the fragrant water and wringing it out before folding it and placing it gently on Alyen's brow. "I'm sure it won't be as potent as what you could supply, but it should alleviate the stress and help you rest. I don't think there's anything wrong with you that a good night of sleep couldn't cure."

Alyen smiled wanly, another wave of exhaustion overcoming her. She lay back, content to let the healer work in silence. But when Eefa next spoke, Alyen was surprised at the words.

"You know, being the Keeper of Scales ... it was my dream as a child. But I was never gifted with the Sight. And I was too close to Rowenna's age anyhow. I would still fantasize about it, though. Even tried to talk to the fairies in the fields a few times." The healer chuckled, shaking her head. "I must have looked ridiculous."

Alyen said nothing, and Eefa's eyes flicked up to Alyen's face before she continued.

"Seems like it might not always be as magical as I imagined, though. The weight of it … must be a lot to carry."

Alyen knew Eefa was giving her an opening. A chance to talk and vent and release. It was the mark of a good healer. But she didn't have the energy for it, and wasn't about to spill everything that made her vulnerable to Marietta's aunt in any case, so she merely whispered, "It can be."

Eefa nodded and continued her ministrations. After a pause she spoke again, her tone almost tentative. "If I were in your place, I think I'd want someone to talk to. Someone to ease the burden a bit. And Aaron … if you ask me, he seems keen to have the job."

She glanced at Alyen's face again, but Alyen had shut her eyes and didn't reply. *How much did they hear before coming in?* she wondered, feeling a stir of discomfort despite the coziness of the room.

"You know, we always wondered why Aaron never showed more interest in Marietta." Eefa's voice was light and conversational, but Alyen began to wonder where this speech was going.

"Marietta is strong, independent, funny, sharp as a whip. Pretty, too. She comes from a good family and runs a prestigious business she's built herself from the ground up. And the Saints know, she made it obvious that she was available and interested whenever Aaron was around. It seemed a sensible match. A good match for both of them."

None of this was making Alyen feel any better. She wished Eefa would just stop speaking. But the healer's voice changed, growing softer.

"Then yesterday your party arrived and we all saw how Aaron looked at you. We didn't wonder any more after that."

Alyen swallowed, willing her eyes not to sting.

Eefa had finished with her cloths and spread another blanket over Alyen. She stepped over to the hearth, pouring water and measuring out leaves for tea. She kept her eyes on her work as she spoke.

"The thing is, we all have people that make us feel a little more alive in the world, who brighten our days, spark our passions. And we all need people we know we can go to when the world feels too heavy, to ease the burden and help settle the soul. But if you find both of those in the same person? Someone who lights the fire and calms the storm? And if you both love each other at the same time? That's a rare and precious gift, Keeper. One not everyone gets in their lifetime. Forgive me if I'm out of place, but I'd be thinking more than twice before turning my back on that."

Her words sank into Alyen, and she didn't know what hurt more: the truth of them, or the fact that Eefa thought her so heartless.

But wait—what had she said? About both of them loving …?

"Why do you think I love Aaron?" she managed to croak out.

Eefa straightened to face Alyen, her expression compassionate. "Because we all saw how you looked at him, too."

Their eyes locked for a moment, then Eefa lowered her gaze to the tea in her hand. She crossed the room to place it on a chair near Alyen.

"Drink this, then sleep. You'll feel better after some real rest. If you need anything, I'll just be in the next room."

She lay a hand on Alyen's arm and patted gently, then left, the door closing with a soft click.

Alyen eyed the tea, but felt too tired to bother with sitting up to drink it. Instead, she closed her eyes, Eefa's words about fire and storm echoing in her mind until sleep mercifully took over.

24

THE HARPIES

There was a sound she didn't recognize, a sound that pulled her from her sleep. A sound that sent dread climbing into her throat before she was even fully awake.

Alyen's eyes fluttered open and she squinted, blinking into the shadowy room. Confusion lay on her like a fog. She'd slept long and deeply, she could tell, and the fire had all but burned out in the hearth. But it was too dark to be morning, and outside, a moaning carried by a restless wind circled the stone walls of the inn.

By the window, Aaron stood, looking out at the gloom with a worried scowl.

Alyen sat up and shuddered, struggling to orient herself more quickly. "What time is it?" she asked, causing Aaron to start.

"Just past dawn, I think," he replied, crossing over to her. "How do you feel?"

"I'm all right. Really, I am," she assured, noticing the skeptical expression that flashed over Aaron's features. "What's going on? Why is it dark?"

"I don't know," Aaron's voice was as uncertain as his words. "I was hoping you'd have an idea when you woke up."

Alyen swung her legs to the floor, ignoring Aaron's cautionary gesture, and strode to the window.

Gloom had settled over the grasslands and the nearby hills that led to the sea. The sky roiled with green-tinged clouds, and though it wasn't storming, Alyen felt the darkling presence like a malevolent weight blanketing the earth. The wind that carried the unearthly moaning whipped at the grass, circling as if waiting for someone to dare exit the inn.

"How long has this been going on?"

"A few hours. It started in the middle of the night." Aaron joined Alyen at the window. "It's the darklings isn't it?"

Alyen shook her head, straining to feel the earth and the elementals through the oppressive gloom.

"It is, but not like before. Something different is going on. Something ... *more*."

A suspicion was niggling at her mind—a possibility she didn't want to entertain. Alyen closed her eyes and sent her mind out further, grasping for any trace of magic other than the crackle of darkling power.

"Alyen, are you sure you should be using your magic? You're barely recovered—"

"Shh!" Alyen hissed, sharper than she intended. But she didn't have time for distractions.

Finally, she felt it. The magic was there, but it was faint. Now that she thought of it, even the darklings' power seemed subdued.

Alyen opened her eyes, her face white. "Aaron, I think the world is dying."

Fear lit behind Aaron's eyes. "What do you mean? Are you sure?"

"Not sure, no." Alyen said, her brow wrinkling with worry. "But everything feels weak and far away. Like *everything's* fading, not just Faer Dinnán."

"But Faer Dinnán—he didn't use his magic. We closed the gorge ourselves."

Alyen shook her head, her heart sinking. "He *did* use his magic. Not to close the gorge, but to save me at the end. I was too tired to disconnect from the gnomes, so he did it for me. It must have been just before he disappeared."

Aaron's troubled eyes scanned the scene out the window. "You think he overdid it?"

"It's possible. I don't really know how to explain nature's magic right now. It just *feels* like everything's dying. Aaron, what if we're too late?"

Now Aaron shook his head, peering up at the swirling clouds. Alyen knew he was grasping for any other explanation than the one he didn't want to be true. "Could just be the darklings, though, couldn't it? Like when they came at us after we connected by the Lake of Leora? We just did a pretty big thing with another connection. Maybe it attracted them again."

"Maybe," Alyen said doubtfully. "But look at it, Aaron. This isn't a violent storm coming after us like it did at the lake. This is just a blanket of darkling energy slowly devouring the world until everything dies *including* the darklings. And even if it *was* a darkling storm, that would mean Faer Dinnán is likely using up the rest of his power just trying to keep it at bay. We need to get to Illya. I think … I think we have to run."

Aaron turned back from the window and Alyen held his eyes, willing him to believe her.

She saw the moment it happened. The shift in his eyes, the grim set of his mouth. He nodded once. "Then we run."

Relief bubbled up briefly but was eclipsed by a new wave of urgency. "I'll gather our things. You find Nah'dar and Brother Hugh and tell them the plan. Is Brother Hugh's horse shod yet?"

"No."

"Then we'll have to go alone; Nah'dar should probably stay here with Brother Hugh. I don't think there's much he can do at Illya anyway. I'll meet you in the barn."

Aaron nodded and hurried out of the room.

Alyen moved quickly, gathering her things, and buckling her saddlebags before crossing the hall to Aaron's room and doing the same for him. Luckily, there was little to do as they'd had no time to properly unpack. Around the inn walls the moaning continued, and Alyen tried to focus on her task rather than letting her mind wander through questions she didn't know if she wanted answered. There was no use wondering if they were too late or what would happen at Illya or if there was any hope of success. They were going as fast as they could, and there was nothing more to be done.

Despite her haste, a calm certainty settled over Alyen as she worked, a deep knowing that the end of the journey was near. Now that the time had come, she found she was glad they were going alone. Brother Hugh and Nah'dar had been welcome companions, but something told her it was a journey she and Aaron had to finish together, on their own, as it was always meant to be.

Footsteps echoed in the corridor as Alyen was finishing, and Nah'dar entered the room.

"Nah'dar. Did Aaron find you?"

The captain nodded. "You are leaving then?"

"We have to. I just hope we aren't too late already."

"I do not like the idea of staying behind. You may find yourselves in need of defense."

"I'm not sure weapons can do much against the foes we're facing this time," Alyen said, a wry smile tugging at her mouth. "But even if it comes to that, we'll be all right. Aaron is the Second Slayer after all."

"A fair point."

Nah'dar hesitated, looking uncharacteristically uncomfortable.

Alyen paused in her work, studying the captain's face. "Nah'dar? Is there something else?"

Nah'dar met her gaze, his black eyes uncertain. "I have watched you and Aaron on this journey. I have seen the toll this quest has taken on both of you."

Alyen swallowed, waiting for him to continue.

"These things you do. The tasks you must complete. It is not my area of expertise, nor my place to give advice."

"Nah'dar, what is it?"

His eyes closed momentarily, and when they reopened, his voice was quiet. "I know what it is to have a life ruined by lies and magic. Do not let the same happen to you."

Silence filled the room for a moment, Alyen searching for words. Before she could find them, Nah'dar turned abruptly and left the room.

They had ridden for two days, barely stopping, pushing Lusa and Soran to the edge of exhaustion. The few times they did stop, they huddled in their cloaks, trying to get a few hours of sleep, but it was impossible. The sky remained dark and turbulent, green lightning flashed almost constantly, and the endless moaning of the wind sent perpetual chills running down Alyen's spine.

On the second day, the rain began, making rest even more unrealistic. Alyen couldn't remember ever being so wet for so long, but there was nothing to be done about it. They simply continued to push on through the soggy terrain, until at last the land sloped downward and Alyen caught the first whiff of the sea.

At what would have been dawn on the third day, Alyen and Aaron crested a bluff and reined in their horses to take in the scene before them.

The bluff sloped down to a rocky coastline where iron-gray waves slapped the shore. Beyond it stretched the sea, whose waters mirrored the turbulence of the sky above. A ways out, an island of obsidian rock rose from the waves, with a black tower spearing upward, menacing and cold.

Alyen and Aaron looked at each other, the ordeal before them seeming suddenly much more real now that they stood in sight of Illya.

"I guess we made it in time," Alyen said. "Won't be much longer now."

Aaron nodded. "Let's go down and see if we can find anyone. I see a few boats on the beach. Maybe we can borrow one."

They picked their way down to the pebbly shore, Lusa's and Soran's hooves sliding on the loose, sandy ground. Aaron had been right; a few rowboats sat, pulled up far enough to avoid the tide, and a scattering of fishing huts stood nestled against the bluff. But no smoke emerged from the chimneys, and the forlorn look of the structures accented by the occasional broken window quickly told them that the huts had been long abandoned.

Aaron shook his head. "Fishermen are a superstitious lot. I'm sure everyone left once Ylvain conjured Malscath and the tower was always surrounded by smoke."

"I don't think you'd really have to be superstitious to know something was wrong," Alyen agreed. "Do you think we can just take one of the boats, then?"

"I don't see why not. There's no one here, and we'll bring it back."

Alyen nodded, hoping they would, in fact, be bringing it back when all was said and done, and trying not to think of the alternative.

They found a place to tether Lusa and Soran where the bluff shielded them from the worst of the wind and rain. Alyen opened her saddlebag, icy fingers fumbling with the buckle, and retrieved her healing bag from within. She slung it over her shoulder, whispered a farewell to Lusa, and joined Aaron, who had inspected the rowboats and selected the one he deemed most seaworthy.

Together they dragged the boat to the water's edge, and Alyen climbed in. Aaron shoved it into the choppy sea before vaulting in himself and taking up the oars.

In silence they inched their way ever closer to the black isle, Aaron intent on the rhythm of his rowing, and Alyen trying to clear her mind in preparation for the events to come. The boat rocked uncomfortably in the restless water, and above them the wind continued to moan under a bleak and sickly sky.

As Castle Illya loomed closer, Aaron twisted around in the rowboat, craning his neck as he squinted toward the island. "Curses," he muttered.

"What?" Alyen asked.

Aaron turned back to her, his face dark. "Harpies. There's several of them waiting on the shore. I was afraid of this."

"What are harpies?" Alyen asked, recognizing the name, but recalling nothing about them. "Are they dangerous?"

"Very," Aaron said. "Harpies are more monsters than magical creatures, and they're a nasty lot. They congregate wherever there's been corruption or moral decay. Dark magic attracts them, so I'm sure they were drawn to whatever remnants of Ylvain's magic remain on the island."

"And what do they do?"

"They try to lure you in, seduce you with your innermost longings, dig into the places you carry your pain and offer you escape from them. Then, once they have you, they eat you."

"They *eat* you?"

"Yes." Aaron looked distracted. "Usually harpies only go after men, so you should be all right as long as you stay near me. I've learned how to mentally defend against them, but there haven't been harpies in Dúramair for a few generations at least, so I've never practiced with the real thing. I should be fine, but … if they get to me, Alyen, I might need you to slap me."

"Excuse me?"

"I'm serious. If I get taken in by them, you have to slap me out of it."

"Aaron, I'm not going to slap you!"

"You have to!" Aaron sounded angry now. "I'll need some kind of shock to break the illusion. A good slap in the face should work, and it's a lot better than being eaten. If I'm going to be there to anchor you, I need you to do this for me. Promise me!"

"All right!" Alyen said, raising her palms in surrender. "I promise, I'll slap you as necessary. Just—try not to need it."

Aaron made an indecipherable noise and rowed the remainder of the way in silence.

Alyen narrowed her eyes at the approaching beach, trying to see the harpies. She could detect some movement from what looked like several figures, but the rain was falling harder now, making it impossible to see any detail.

Soon the boat jerked as the bottom scraped against black, pebbly sand. Aaron leapt out and pulled the boat up onto the shore. He offered Alyen a hand, and as she stepped out of the boat, she heard his voice, low in her ear.

"We make straight for the tower. We don't stop, don't listen to what the harpies say, don't respond in any way. Once we're inside, we'll be fine."

"And if you get distracted?"

"Then you know what to do," Aaron said with a look.

Alyen nodded and turned with Aaron to face the black tower.

She immediately bristled.

Five women were approaching them, walking calmly but purposefully along the shoreline. All five were beautiful with long, lustrous hair that seemed to swirl artfully in the wind, unaffected by the rain.

They were also completely naked.

"Aaron!" Alyen hissed.

"I told you they try to tempt men," Aaron said, sounding defensive, a flush staining his wet cheeks. "Just follow the plan, all right?"

Alyen felt her lips purse, but she said nothing, and they headed briskly in the direction of the tower.

It didn't take long for the harpies to reach them. Alyen, following just behind Aaron, may as well have been invisible—none of the women gave her so much as a glance. But Aaron was soon surrounded, and one, who seemed to be the leader, started murmuring in his ear.

"Welcome, mortal. Where are you going? Why rush off so quickly? Stay here with us a while. We know a place that's warm and dry, a place where we can make you comfortable."

Bile rose in Alyen's throat, and she was gratified to see that Aaron's pace didn't falter once. He continued to stride toward the black tower, and Alyen followed, listening to the harpy's continued cajoling while her fellow seducers ran their fingers over Aaron's shoulders and down his arms.

"You are weary, Slayer. Your journey has been long. You sacrifice much in the name of duty, but has it brought you happiness? Has it brought you pleasure or peace? We can give you these things, if only you stay."

Alyen's teeth grated, her jaw clenched. She forced herself to keep her focus forward. The tower was close now. A few more steps and they would be inside.

But just as she began to think they'd make it without incident, the harpy leader suddenly turned and looked straight into Alyen's eyes, a wicked smile stretching over her face. Without breaking eye contact with Alyen, she leaned once more toward Aaron's ear.

"Loyalty," the harpy purred. "*You* showed loyalty to those you love, and where did it get you? Did those who benefited from your devotion show you loyalty in return? Did they value the love you offered so freely?"

To Alyen's horror, Aaron's steps slowed.

The harpy's smile widened.

"They didn't, did they? They threw it away without a second thought. Is that what you deserved? Is that all the devotion of Dúramair's Slayer is worth?"

Aaron stopped walking.

Alyen scrambled over the rocks, pushing caution aside as she shouldered her way past the circling harpies. Once she faced Aaron, she took his face between her hands, eyes boring into his unfocussed gaze. "Aaron! Don't listen to them! We're almost to the tower—we can make it!"

But Aaron's eyes remained hazy. The harpies cackled around her, a sound that didn't match their alluring appearance, and their leader swooped in once more, triumph gleaming in her eyes.

"Come with us, Slayer. Come see what it feels like when you are wanted. Admired. Adored." The harpy looked again at Alyen, her grin suddenly vicious. "Come see what it's like to *truly* be loved."

Aaron's head turned a fraction of an inch toward the harpy, and rage erupted in Alyen's gut. Her hand flew of its own accord, and a crack sounded as it connected …

With the harpy's face.

Chaos exploded. The harpies shrieked with fury, and at

once, their bodies transformed. No longer were she and Aaron surrounded by beautiful women, but grotesque, bird-like creatures with clawed feet, black wings, and human heads. Their faces contorted with bitterness and rage as their mouths yawned open to reveal rows of decaying, razor-sharp teeth. As one, all five leapt toward Alyen.

Aaron moved faster than Alyen thought possible. Eyes snapping to focus, he drew his sword. It flashed once, arcing gracefully, then sliced cleanly through the torso of the harpy leader, severing her body in two.

Black blood gushed over the rocks as the two halves of the harpy fell just inches from Alyen's feet. The shrieks of the remaining four harpies turned to wails. They launched themselves into the air on clumsy wings, flying into the rain and gloom until they disappeared over the sea.

Suddenly the beach was quiet once more, the only sound the lapping of waves, the raindrops hitting the rocks, and the distant moaning in the wind.

Alyen swallowed hard, trying not to look at the carnage at her feet. Instead, she turned to Aaron. He looked shaken, his face pale. A thick silence stretched between them.

Alyen knew he would feel the need to explain. Or perhaps he would expect an apology? But it wasn't a door they could open right now. They needed strength and focus for the task at hand, and dredging up everything from the last few weeks now would take time they didn't have.

Besides, if all went well, everything would be explained before the day was done.

Alyen brushed her hand against her thigh, feeling the need to cleanse the place it had touched the harpy's face. "Well," she said, trying to keep her voice matter-of-fact. "I guess that's done."

Aaron shook his head. "Alyen—"

"Don't, Aaron," she said, cutting him off. Then more gently, "Let's just do what we came to do. We can talk later—maybe on a sunny beach for a change?"

Aaron looked away, his throat bobbing once. He seemed to collect himself, and nodded. "All right. Let's do it."

Alyen longed to say something more, to wrap her arms around him, to make the haunted look leave his eyes.

Instead, she waited in the rain while Aaron cleaned his sword of the black harpy blood.

Then, sword sheathed, Aaron joined her, and together they entered the doors of Castle Illya.

25

CASTLE ILLYA

It was cold inside Castle Illya, and the kind of quiet that made the hairs on Alyen's arms rise. Thick obsidian walls blocked out all sound from the outside, and the only noise was the distant echo of water dripping on stone.

It was still. Too still. Alyen couldn't help but feel that the ghosts of evil things past watched her from the shadowy corners.

"What was this place?" Aaron asked, one hand hovering near the hilt of his sword. "Why was it built?"

"No one really knows for sure," Alyen replied. "It's called Castle Illya, but it's been just this tower for as long as history remembers. It's one of the oldest structures in Dúramair—maybe even older than Castle Dúr. Since it's so near to Nethermair, most scholars assume it was meant to be some kind of watchtower, but ..." She shrugged.

Aaron looked toward the ceiling far above them. "Doesn't feel much like a watchtower, does it?"

Alyen shook her head. "Even if that *was* the original intent, it's been stained by a dark history. Seems like every story of dark magic in the kingdom involves Illya in one way or another." Alyen rubbed her arms again as she looked around in distaste. "This place makes my skin crawl."

"Mine, too," Aaron agreed. He took a breath and nodded at the stairway that wound upward around the inside wall of the tower, leading to the top. "I assume we go up?"

"I suppose so."

Aaron drew his sword. "I'll go first, then."

Alyen gave him a thin smile and nodded, trying to ignore the way her stomach was suddenly fluttering with nerves.

They climbed the stairs slowly, in part because there was no railing to prevent a misstep resulting in a deadly plunge to the floor below. But even if there had been, the ominous weight of the place pressed about them in a way that would have made haste feel impossible.

Occasionally, they would pass a doorway leading into a room set in the tower wall. Some were empty, while others had chains embedded in the walls bearing dark stains that made Alyen's stomach churn.

One room seemed to be someone's sleeping quarters, and Alyen paused, peering inside. It was sparsely furnished with a hard bed and a single oil lamp. A few books and pieces of parchment lay scattered on an old, moldering table, along with some jars and a couple bowls and spoons. Was this where Ylvain had slept all those months as she'd conjured her magic, plotted with Malscath, and bred her hoard of morkshai? The thought of staying in this place for even one night seemed unbearable, let alone a year or more.

A cold feeling settled in Alyen's gut as she thought of the

woman she'd slain. Somehow seeing this place, this room, Ylvain's personal things, made her stomach twist in a way she knew wouldn't help her mind focus on what she'd come to do. She dropped her eyes from the room and hurried to catch up with Aaron.

For the rest of the climb, she kept her eyes on the stairs.

They reached the top of the staircase and emerged atop the tower through an opening near the battlements. Cold rain and the moaning wind immediately hit Alyen's face, but she found she was relieved to be outside the tower once again. She filled her lungs with the ocean air, free from the echoes of evil deeds, then took stock of her surroundings.

The tower top was an empty circle of obsidian rock. To one side stood what seemed to have been a brazier—presumably, the object with which Ylvain had conjured the darkling magic to begin with. But its fires had long since gone out, and the brazier now supported a shallow black basin filled with rainwater that rippled and quivered as raindrops hit its surface.

Aaron was staring downward, a scowl on his face. Alyen followed his gaze and saw the reason for his expression. A large circle filled with symbols and scripts in languages long forgotten had been roughly etched into the stone. The pattern held a kind of terrible beauty, its symmetry marred only by a single slash mark that ripped across the circle's edge from a point near the brazier.

"This was how she did it," Aaron said, anger lacing his words. "This is where she raised Malscath."

Alyen nodded, words escaping her. They'd never talked much about the deed that had earned Aaron the title of Second Slayer, or what it had been like being swallowed by the earth as he and his flaming sword burned out the heart of an ancient demon. But she could see on his face and the way his eyes burned that he carried a shadow from that day, and that seeing the place where his foe had risen had caused that shadow to stir.

Alyen moved to Aaron's side and slipped her hand into his. "It will also be the place where we end it, once and for all."

Aaron's eyes found hers and the fire that burned in them seemed to soften. "Are you ready?" he asked.

Alyen bit down on her cold lip, a wave of uncertainty rolling over her. She looked away, toward the sea.

"What is it?" Aaron asked.

Alyen shook her head. "I'm not really sure. I know what to do, and I know I have to do it. But I'm afraid to fail. And I suppose … I suppose I was counting on the fact that Faer Dinnán would be here to help. What if—" Alyen closed her eyes as a tremble entered her voice. "What if I can't do it on my own?"

There was a pause as cold rain continued to hit her face. Then warmth as she felt Aaron's fingers gently lifting her chin. She opened her eyes to meet his, the eyes she knew better than anyone's, the eyes that had always been open and honest, the eyes she'd filled with so much pain, but that loved her still.

"You were never going to do it alone, Alyen," Aaron said. "And *we* won't fail."

In his eyes, Alyen saw that Aaron truly believed his words.

At that moment, the sky changed. Dark clouds grew darker still, and the green tinge intensified. The moaning on the wind rose in both pitch and despair, and from deep below, the earth trembled, causing the sea to churn and crash against the shore.

Aaron's head snapped upward as Alyen's arms shot outward for balance.

"I think we're running out of time," Aaron said, his voice tense. "We need to do this now."

Alyen nodded, the urgency banishing all doubt and hesitation. She slung her healing bag off her shoulder, setting it against the battlements. It clinked as it landed, and Alyen paused, remembering something. Quickly, she knelt and opened the bag, fingers fumbling in her haste. She thrust her arm in, and pulled out the pestle and mortar Faer Dinnán had given her during the Ceremony of Three. Her fingers traced the carvings wrought by elemental skill and magic.

"Alyen?" Aaron's voice was urgent.

Alyen stood, leaving the pestle, but bringing the mortar with her. "I want to hold it," she explained in response to Aaron's questioning frown. "It was made by elementals and gifted by Faer Dinnán. Their magic is probably still contained within it. It might help to be able to feel healthy elemental magic while I try to turn the darklings." *And,* she added silently to herself, *it's the closest thing I'll get to feeling Faer Dinnán beside me.*

Aaron didn't protest. "Where do you want to stand?"

"Here is fine. I don't want to stand on any of *that*," she said, eyeing the etchings on the tower floor with distaste.

Alyen extended her hands, the mortar clasped between them. Aaron stood before her and wrapped his hands around her own.

On an impulse, Alyen looked up into Aaron's eyes. "Connect with me first this time."

Aaron's face flickered uncertainty. "Why?"

"I think," Alyen swallowed, unsure if it was intuition or

fear she was acting on and hoping desperately it was the former. "I don't want to meld with the darklings alone. It might be safer if we're already connected, so you can get me out if things go wrong. But maybe I'm just afraid ..." Her voice trailed off.

Aaron's face was thoughtful. "There's a risk," he noted. "The darklings will feel our connection, and we're as close to them as we can be. They might attack again."

"You're right. But if I'm melded with them, I don't think they will. I'll just have to be quick about it. What do you think?"

Aaron paused a moment, then nodded. "I think it's a good idea. We'll connect first. Are you ready?"

"Yes. Are you?"

Aaron nodded, took a breath, and began the singing speech.

Alyen wished she could listen fully; focus only on the connection they were forging. But she knew that, now more than ever, she must shield her mind before the memories started flowing. *It's the last time,* she told herself as she sifted through her mind. *After today, I'll never have to shield myself from him again.*

She chose the blandest memories she could conjure. Tutoring lessons with Professor Glibb. Reviewing treaties with her parents. Reading books that she'd found in Castle Dúr's library as Bridget tidied her room, preparing for the next day. Nothing that would distract, nothing that would interest, nothing that would pull Aaron's mind from the task of anchoring her to her true self and a world free of darklings.

She heard Aaron's voice stop, felt the wind and sea surge, felt the impact of the connection forming. She felt Aaron's hands tighten around hers as her fingers clutched the mortar. When Aaron's memories came, she was gratified to see that he'd apparently been thinking along the same lines. His memories were filled with flashes of Dúramair's most beautiful scenery, places he'd seen in his years of traveling the kingdom with Morten. She saw the depths of Sheanen Crann, canopy aflame with autumn color. She saw the red canyons of Brann Dala, the rugged peaks of the Mountains of Geal, the sparkling waters of the ocean at sunset.

He was remembering all the places he wanted them to save.

Alyen felt her memories string toward Aaron, and knew her time had come. She found Aaron's gaze one last time, her mind filling suddenly with so many things she wished she could say, not knowing if she'd get another chance.

But she pushed them deftly away, refusing to let Aaron glimpse anything beyond that part of her mind she reserved for shielding the rest of it and settled for taking in his rain-soaked face and eyes that burned with determination.

Aaron gave her a nod, and the side of his mouth lifted in the half-smile that was so rare these days. *"See you on the other side."*

Alyen's mouth twisted upward, and she nodded. *"On a sunny beach."*

Then, before she could think about the sadness lining Aaron's smile, she closed her eyes and reached for the darkling swarm.

Darkling magic hit her with a force like lightning. Fear reared within her chest, threatening to consume her before she'd even begun.

They knew.

The darklings knew she was there, felt her connection with Aaron, and she could feel their ire rising.

"Aaron!" her mind cried out in panic.

"I'm here," came his voice, steadying and calm. *"You've done this before, and you can do it again. I won't let you fall. Just do what you did last time at the gorge."*

Alyen drew a shaky breath, collecting herself amidst the swirl of chaos and fury. Fear raced like fire through her veins, but Alyen paused, forcing her focus to turn to her breath, her heart, the living rhythm within her that echoed the rhythm of the earth.

This was it. This was the time it mattered the most, the time she had to truly tame her fear more than ever before. She looked fear in the eye, and for the first time saw not an enemy, not an obstacle, but herself. The part of herself that was a protector, a guardian, a messenger. The part of her that loved herself so much, it would do whatever it took to keep her safe —even at the expense of her own happiness. As her fear quailed before the rising darkling storm, a feeling of tenderness spread through Alyen. She addressed her fear.

"I see them. I see the darklings, and you're right: we might not survive this. But we have to try. You've protected me through so much, and now I need you to let me work so I can try to save us all. But you can help. You can add your strength to mine, and together we can face the storm."

The fear eased, and Alyen felt it change. Where once her limbs had trembled, now fear solidified into strength. Doubt became determination, and panic sharpened into alertness, her senses humming, keen as any blade.

The darkling swarm churned, its fury building, and the tower trembled again.

"Hurry, Alyen," Aaron's voice urged.

"Don't worry, I'm ready," she replied, knowing deep within that this time, her power would be greater than ever before. Then, feeling the steadiness of her transformed fear and the power created by her magic bolstered by Aaron's, she filled her mind with darkness.

She remembered the darklings as she'd first seen them at the Ruins of Enlair. She felt their hands restraining her in the Royal Wood, watched as they ensnared Aaron at Ylvain's bidding. She felt the vengeful malice of their storm as it crashed over Castle Dúr, or raced toward her across the Searing Plain.

Alyen felt the turmoil build within her, but knew it wasn't enough. Not for what she needed to do, not if she wanted to become a part of the storm. She steeled herself once more, then continued to fill herself with darkness—this time from her own being.

She was in the Royal Wood, Scala burning in her hands as she thrust the blade into Ylvain's chest. She stood on the cliffs of Norhelm, rejoicing in the ecstasy of her own unharnessed power as the world cracked and thousands died. She saw herself in Sheanen Crann, screaming at Aaron after Nah'dar had killed her would-be assassin, shouting words chosen to strike pain where she knew it would hurt.

Memory by memory, Alyen filled herself, body and mind, with every mistake, every moment of weakness, envy, or shame, and swirled them together with the dread, malice, and rage the darklings brought. Darkness reared within her, a mighty force that swirled and strained, threatening to consume. She ignored the discomfort and her desire to flee. Instead, she reached for the singing speech.

"Darklings, spread throughout our land, birthed and

turned by evil's hand, add my powers to your might and make of me a part of night."

Darkness and fury pressed down on her. Sweat mingled with the rain on her face as she fought to brace against the crushing force of darkling magic. It built, ever stronger around her, a scream of triumph echoing in the wind as the swarm sensed victory was near. When at last she felt she could withstand no more … she released.

The void was cold this time. Whispers seemed to hiss around her in the restless dark, so different from the blissful peace she'd known when melding before. She waited for the sparks of light to ignite around her, but they didn't come. Instead, she sensed shadows gathering. Shadows that were gradually illuminated by the sickly green glow that emanated from the darkling storm. The shadows flocked to her, eager and triumphant, and Alyen winced as she felt them latching onto her limbs, her torso, her face. She felt her body changing, rippling and heaving in a transformation that felt wrong and broken. She opened her mouth to cry out, whether from pain or anguish she couldn't say.

Then suddenly she lurched, shivered, and everything stilled save for a roiling chaos that spun where her heart once was.

She opened her eyes.

Aaron still held his hands around hers, his face ashen. "Saints, Alyen," he breathed, taking in her altered form.

Alyen looked down. Her limbs had thinned, her skin had turned gray. Bony joints protruded and sharp nails scratched against the mortar still clutched between her hands. She turned her head and gazed down into the basin of rainwater beside her. Raven black hair and a gaunt, gray face stared back at her through eyes that had been flooded to black ink. The whites of her eyes were completely gone and she saw only malice gleaming from within the depths of their darkness.

Power surged through her. She was strong. So strong. Strong enough to wield the storm, to rule the world, to destroy everything in her path. Alyen watched her reflection as a slow, wicked smile spread across her face.

"Alyen." It was Aaron's voice in her mind, and Alyen's head snapped up at the sound.

Aaron's eyes were on hers. There was fear in them, but also determination. *"Alyen, you need to focus. You need to do what we came to do."*

"I don't want to," Alyen replied, feeling somehow distant from the surging power that pulsed through her. *"We feel good this way."*

Aaron's gaze intensified. *"But if you don't, you won't survive. The darklings won't survive. Nothing will be left."*

"I don't think that's true. The world is too big to die. Too powerful. I think it was all a lie."

"Alyen," Aaron said, his head shaking. *"I'll die, too. Does that mean anything to you?"*

From somewhere beneath the swirling vortex in her chest, Alyen felt a tug. It persisted, growing in strength and intensity, and she felt the darklings recoil from it with a hiss.

Curious, Alyen brought her attention closer to it, reaching out with her mind until it prodded the edge of whatever it was.

Her mind exploded.

A flood of images erupted before her vision, memories of her and Aaron, of every day they'd spent together, every time they'd held each other, every time they'd looked at each other and felt they were looking at home.

The tugging blazed and Alyen recognized it for what it was—the connection between her and Aaron that she'd almost forgotten when she transformed.

The swirling chaos in her chest faltered. Alyen's eyes flitted from image to image, her own memories bubbling up to the surface and joining them. The swirling was dwindling now, her mind becoming more and more her own. She looked back at Aaron, tears pooling in her eyes as she found his. Their connection surged, and the swirling evaporated, her heart beating steadily once more in tandem with the calming drum of Aaron's own heart. Alyen glanced back at her reflection.

She was still melded with the darklings. But her mind and her heart were her own.

"Thank you," her voice whispered in Aaron's mind.

The Slayer's eyes were filled with relief. *"Go, then. Turn the darklings back while there's still time."*

Alyen nodded, and closed her eyes.

There were so many of them. Hundreds of darklings—maybe thousands—all connected in a swarm of evil, and all latched onto her. Before, when her heart had swirled with that darkness, she had felt their triumphant glee at having joined with her. But they knew something had changed. She felt their magic transforming, turning back to rage and hatred, snarling at the bonds that connected them and trying to tug away.

She wouldn't be able to hold them forever, and if they broke free, they would attack.

Alyen licked her cold lips, unsure of what to do. She couldn't fight them, even if she hadn't promised Faer Dinnán she wouldn't. The faerie king had told her that she had to light the darklings from within, but she didn't *feel* like she was within them, even while connected to them.

That's the answer, then, she thought. *I have to find a way to get to the core of the darkling swarm.*

The darklings jerked again, and Alyen knew her time was running out. She exhaled, concentrating on gathering every ounce of her magic to her. She prodded at the mass of her and Aaron's combined power, testing its strength. It was a considerable force, but she wasn't sure it was enough to counter the entire darkling swarm.

Then she remembered: the mortar.

As soon as she thought of it, the mortar warmed in her hands. She felt the faerie magic emanating from it, carrying within it the power of sea and mountain, forest and plain, of every tree and every creature that wove together in the fabric of their world. The magic seeped from the mortar into her hands and entwined itself through the power woven of Aaron's magic and her own. She felt Aaron's hands tighten around hers as the combined magic blazed, encircling them in a sphere of light that made the darklings recoil, leaving the swarm momentarily open and vulnerable.

Knowing it was the best chance she would get, Alyen took a breath, and dove with her mind into the depths of the swarm.

26

THE SWARM

It felt like she was falling into endless darkness. Chaos snatched at her with eager fingers, but Alyen, bolstered by the magic she'd gathered, ignored it and continued onward toward the heart of the swarm. Around her she heard the echoing shriek of the darkling storm, the howls of rage and hate that cried out for destruction and death.

The center was near now, she could sense it, and as it approached, the darkling voices she heard around her began to change. Shrieks turned to wails, malice and anger turned inward and crumpled into something raw and true that the storm had been hiding beneath its rage.

A new hope kindled in Alyen's chest. Understanding bloomed in her mind and she pressed on, eager now, toward the approaching center.

These elementals-turned-darklings didn't truly want to destroy the world or wield power over it. They were mourning. Mourning the loss of their true selves, their identity, their purpose; the Balance they were once a part of.

The core of the darkling storm was not evil. It was grief. And in the absence of any way to assuage the sadness, grief had turned to despair, and despair to malice and hate.

When the grief around her became the only thing she could feel, Alyen stopped her descent, knowing she rested at the heart of the darkling swarm. This grief, unbearable though it was, was a good sign. It meant that here, at the very core of darkness, the darklings' true elemental spark still lived, if only to grieve its own fall.

If it was there, Alyen could find it.

If she could find it, she could show it a way out.

She was the Keeper of Scales. She was a healer, and this was a wound.

This was something she could fix.

Alyen reached deep into the grief that surrounded her. She found the spark, weak and dwindling, but still aflame.

"I understand," she whispered to the tiny glow. *"I know what it is to lose yourself. I know the pain of discovering you aren't who you thought you were, and far from who you want to be. But I also know that you can find yourself again and rise stronger than you were before. If you let me, I can show you the way."*

Arms extended, she reached out to the spark, and it sank into her hands like a sigh. Alyen gathered it to her, holding it tight against her chest.

"Come with me. I'll carry you out, back to the light where you belong. You don't have to stay like this anymore."

She felt the spark melt against her, trusting and exhausted. Then, enfolding them both in a shield of magic, she rose back upward into the storm.

Higher she rose, cradling the elemental spark. The wailing returned, changing once more to a shriek as they rose into the chaos that ripped at her even more viciously as she passed, sensing the precious cargo she carried.

Now the darkness ahead was lightening. The storm's edge was near. A few more seconds and they would be out. Alyen drew in her breath, preparing to break free into the open air.

But just when she thought they'd made it, a cry of victory ready on her lips, Alyen felt herself yanked backward, hard enough to drive the breath from her lungs. She gasped, clutching at the elemental spark she carried as she scrambled to orient herself. Around her the storm howled in defiance, unwilling to let her escape. She felt herself being dragged backward, back into the darkness and chaos.

"Aaron!" Alyen cried out. *"Aaron, help us!"*

"Alyen!" She heard his voice and looked up toward the patch of light she was slowly sinking away from. She saw Aaron's face at the opening, saw understanding light in his eyes as he realized what was happening. He thrust an arm into the storm, reaching for her, his fingertips just barely out of reach.

Alyen stretched an arm upward, the other one still clutching the elemental spark tight against her. She strained, summoning every ounce of strength and magic she could— hers, Aaron's, and faerie-given. Her descent stopped, but she couldn't raise herself up the last few inches to reach his hand.

From somewhere deep below, a tremble rose, shaking the world around them. Even from within the storm, Alyen felt the world sag and falter. Time was running out.

"Come on, Alyen! Reach!" Aaron's eyes burned into hers.

"I'm trying!" Once again, she strained with everything she possessed, but still, she didn't move.

Even with Aaron, even with her mortar, the magic wasn't enough.

No, she thought, dashing tears away with a shake of her head. *This can't be the end. Not when we're so close!*

There had to be some tiny ounce of magic somewhere, some bit of strength as yet untapped that would be just enough to nudge her up to Aaron's outstretched hand.

Then, from somewhere deep within her, a small voice whispered. *There is one more bit of magic left to use. And you know where it is.*

Alyen paused, knowing full well what her own mind was telling her. There was, indeed, one small part of her she'd set aside. One part she'd reserved for a different task.

It was the part that was shielding Aaron from her memories of the truth.

If she was to save the spark that trembled against her, if she was to break free of this storm and heal the wound that had turned nature against itself, she would need *all* her magic. She would have to reveal the betrayal she'd fought so long to conceal. The thing she thought would doom their quest to failure. The thing that would put Aaron in mortal danger.

But it was the only thing left to try.

Alyen closed her eyes momentarily, releasing a desperate plea to Béathan to keep Aaron safe. Then she dipped once more into her memories.

She found the morning she'd discovered the Keeper's book. She saw Faer Dinnán confirming that it was the only way to succeed, and Aaron's refusal to relinquish his memories.

She watched her heart break as she chose the unthinkable, felt the shock and rage upon discovering the lie she must now uphold.

She crumpled as she beheld the result of her betrayal in Aaron's eyes, and heard fear telling her she'd had no choice.

She gathered the memories to the edge of the connection that linked her mind with Aaron's. She looked up once more to Aaron and saw his expression shift to confusion as he took in the look on her face.

For one last moment, she held the memories tight.

Then, she let them go.

They flowed down the connection, spreading before Aaron's vision, a tapestry of light and motion. For a moment he froze, his eyes going wide, his face draining of color. Shock registered across his features, then slowly, as if some invisible force lifted, comprehension. He looked back at Alyen, and she saw his jaw set.

Once more he thrust his arm toward her. *Try again, Alyen. Come back to me. We can do this!"*

It would be her last chance, and Alyen knew it. For the final time, she gathered every ounce of her magic—this time holding nothing back—and with all the strength she possessed, hurled herself and the spark she carried upward.

Her fingers grazed Aaron's palm, and his hand closed tightly around hers. Through the roar of the storm that echoed in her ears, she heard Aaron's voice, shouting in the singing speech.

"I call on all of nature's power! Join me here on Illya's tower, help me save Alyen this hour!"

Magic surged. With a final shout, Aaron wrenched her from the clutches of the storm, and Alyen opened her eyes.

She still stood across from Aaron, both breathing hard, their hands clasped around the mortar.

But inside the mortar rested a tiny spark of light—dim and faltering, but alive.

"What do we do now?" Aaron asked.

Alyen tossed her head, trying to clear the rain from her vision. Battling the storm had taken more energy than she'd realized, and she was tired. But they weren't done yet, so she pushed the feeling aside.

"Just keep doing what you're doing," she said. *"If we can give them enough light, they should remember their own and heal themselves."*

Aaron nodded. *"Use my memories. The ones of Dúramair and all the places I've seen. Maybe it'll help them remember how they used to be."*

The earth heaved again. Alyen fought to regain her balance, afraid of spilling the spark from the mortar. This was the part she was least certain about. The part she wasn't sure how to do, despite what she'd told Aaron. Faer Dinnán hadn't gotten around to teaching her how to turn the darklings before he became too weak. Alyen glanced down once more at her altered form and gray skin, then set her shoulders and focused all her attention, all her magic, all the power she possessed, on the tiny light in the white stone mortar.

"Elementals of this spark, you who've suffered in the dark, taken from your truest selves, salamandars, undines, elves, sylphs and gnomes and garden sprites—it's time to turn once more to light. I'll shine for you to mark the path, to help you heal from evil's wrath. Together we can right this wrong and once more make the Balance strong."

Gently, so gently, Alyen pushed her magic toward the mortar in her hands. She pulled every memory she had of the elemental world, of the magic that laced through every facet of nature, and infused them into the light she sent toward the flickering spark. She added Aaron's memories—all the places the elementals had created, guarded, and called their home. She sent it all in a gentle but constant stream toward the mortar, praying to Béathan and all the Saints that it would work.

Nothing happened.

Alyen refused to look at Aaron, refused to acknowledge the doubt she would see there, knowing it would be mirrored in her own face. Silent now, she kept her eyes on the spark, willing it to grow, to heal, to transform.

Then slowly, as if it recognized the elemental magic held within, the mortar began to glow.

Aaron's hands tensed around hers. *"Look!"* he said, his voice hushed.

Alyen held her breath, not daring to move or make a sound. She continued to push her magic, her will, her love toward the mortar, and gradually the light intensified and spread. The spark itself began to grow, soon filling the entire mortar, then engulfing it and spreading outward, over their hands, their arms, their entire bodies.

Now the whole top of the tower was bathed in golden light. The wind died down, its moaning ceased, and the rain fell no more.

For a moment, all was silent, the world utterly still as if preserved in glass.

Then, magic exploded, and the world seemed to shatter.

Light speared from the tower top in all directions, piercing through the clouds until they evaporated, revealing a sky that was blue and filled with salamandar sunlight. The ocean no longer slapped in restless, iron-gray waves against the shore, but rolled playfully, guided by undines that splashed joyfully through the sea foam. Sylphs danced in the air, sending a warm breeze weaving through the strands of Alyen's hair.

It was then that Alyen realized her hair was no longer wet or black. The darklings' power she'd melded to was still there, but it had changed. No chaos or malice roiled within her, but the thrumming of nature's music sang in her veins.

Quickly she looked down at her arms and into the basin of clear water where her face was reflected. Characteristics of every type of elemental splashed across her features. Flames licked over her fish-scaled limbs. Half her face resembled a craggy boulder, while vines snaked over the other half. Her hair swirled in the air around her, and tree roots wound around her feet and ankles, grounding her to the tower's black rock.

She'd done it. The darklings had healed. And Alyen was now melded with all of nature.

Aaron's voice shouted in triumph. *"Alyen, it's over! You did it!"*

"We *did it,*" Alyen replied, the first true smile she'd felt in weeks breaking across her face. *"But it's not over. Not yet."*

Confusion flitted over Aaron's face. *"What do you mean? What's left to do?"*

Alyen looked around them at the battlements that encircled the top of the tower. She looked at the etchings on the floor that had risen a demon. She thought of the rooms below them, of the dark history they'd witnessed. She looked back to Aaron.

"It's Illya. I want to tear it down."

Aaron's brow rose, his eyes wide. *"You want to tear down the tower?"*

Alyen nodded. *"It's been a place of darkness for too long. I want to destroy it."*

"All right," Aaron said, his voice carrying doubt. He frowned, concern lighting in his eyes as they traveled over Alyen's melded body. *"Are you sure you want to do it now? You've already used so much magic. You could over-tire yourself."*

"No." Alyen was firm. *"It should be now. Now, when I have all of nature's magic in me."*

Doubt still flickered in Aaron's eyes.

"I'll be all right, Aaron," Alyen said, eyes warming as she looked at him, her greatest defender. *"I'll be all right because you're with me."*

Aaron hesitated only a moment before he nodded his agreement. *"Shouldn't we get off the tower first?"*

"We won't need to," Alyen replied. Ignoring the confusion that crossed Aaron's face, she closed her eyes once more.

"Elementals one and all, heed my words, my final call. There's one thing more I have to ask, one thing to complete this task. Help me to destroy this tower, this place of dark and evil power. Help me wipe it from our land, nevermore shall Illya stand."

The magic filling Alyen surged, and she felt her body tremble with near exhaustion. She'd have to be quick, but she wouldn't stop until the tower was gone. Feeling the host of elementals with her, she sent her mind and all her magic downward, down to the bottom of the tower, down farther still to the depths of the earth beneath the island. She found the heat that lived there and drew it upward, higher and higher until it reached the surface.

Then, she unleashed it on the black stones of Castle Illya.

Beside her, she heard Aaron draw in a sharp breath. *"Alyen, what's happening?"*

The tower was sinking, ever so slowly, carrying them down toward the shore below. Alyen opened her eyes and smiled at him. *"It's the tower. We're melting it."*

"You're *melting* the tower?" Aaron repeated, shock causing him to speak aloud.

Alyen laughed as they sank, farther and faster, the ground now quickly approaching. Dimly, Alyen realized she was still laughing. She didn't seem to be able to stop. In fact, her mind was somewhat removed, her body feeling farther and farther away.

"Alyen?" Aaron's voice was sharp with concern.

"Aaron …" Alyen said, her voice faltering.

The last thing she knew was Aaron's arms closing around her as they fell with the tower toward the ground.

27

FIRE AND STORM

The first thing Alyen registered was Aaron's voice calling her name. He sounded worried. That was too bad. She didn't want him to worry.

She moved her fingers experimentally, and found them dragging through rough, pebbly sand. She was on a beach, then. That's right, Illya's shore. But her head wasn't on the sand, it was on something softer. Her eyelids fluttered as they opened to find Aaron's face above hers, her head resting on his lap.

A ragged sound of relief issued from Aaron's throat. "Saints, Alyen. You have to stop doing this to me."

Alyen smiled weakly, only now registering the exhaustion in her body. "Sorry. I hope this was the last time."

They stayed that way a good while, Alyen regaining her bearings and strength while Aaron's fingers ran through her hair.

Finally, Alyen squinted up at Aaron again. "How did I unmeld? Did Faer Dinnán show up again?"

"No," Aaron said, a catch in his voice Alyen wasn't sure how to interpret. "No, I did it myself."

"*You* did it?"

Aaron nodded. "With the singing speech. I had to leap off the tower with you before we hit the melting point, and once we were clear, I asked the elementals to let you rest."

"Melting point …" Things were coming back into place in Alyen's memory. "That's right. I melted Castle Illya. *Did* I melt Castle Illya?"

Aaron's mouth twisted upward on one side. "See for yourself. Can you sit up yet?"

Aided by Aaron's steadying arms, Alyen hoisted herself into a sitting position and gazed across the island. Nothing remained of Castle Illya save for a hardened black sheet of obsidian that sloped down one side of the shore and emptied into the ocean.

"Well," Alyen said, impressed despite herself. "That's … interesting."

"Best part of it is, you've made a really great slide leading right into the water," Aaron said, a smile tugging on his mouth. "People might actually start coming out here for fun."

Alyen looked up at him, watching how the sunlight hit the gold flecks in his eyes. The corners of her mouth pulled upward in exhausted relief. "The best part is that now you know the truth, and we can be together again."

There was a pause. Something in Aaron's face shifted, and Alyen suddenly felt cold.

Aaron gave her a strange smile, rubbing her arm, but said

nothing. He glanced away for a moment in the direction of their rowboat, then turned back to her.

"Do you think you're ready to go back yet?"

Alyen cleared her throat, all relief vanishing. "Sure. I think so."

Aaron helped her to her feet, steadying her as she swayed. They made their way slowly to the rowboat and Aaron helped to settle her on the seat. He was caring and attentive, the way he always had been. But something had changed, and Alyen felt dread spreading through her gut.

As Aaron pushed the boat into the waves and leapt in to take up the oars, Alyen prayed that her worries were unfounded. That they were both just tired. That when they landed, they could have their talk on the sunny beach and everything would be mended between them, just as she'd planned.

Because as it was, she very much feared that Aaron's plan was different.

As the shore approached, Alyen clutched her cloak more tightly around her. Sunlight was glinting off the swells of the sea, but she shivered with exhaustion and uncertainty as she studied the expression on Aaron's face.

He hadn't said a word since they'd left the island. He hadn't even really looked at her since they launched the boat. Instead, his face had become increasingly closed off and pensive, turbulence rolling off him in waves.

The boat hit sand, and Aaron leaped out and dragged it onto the shore. Alyen tottered as she stood and Aaron held out his hand to steady her as she stepped onto solid ground. For a moment, their eyes met, Alyen's searching, Aaron's holding an expression she hadn't seen before. She tried for a thin, hopeful smile, but Aaron's brow drew together and he released her hand. Saying nothing, he turned toward the horses.

"Aaron, wait," Alyen called after him. "We need to talk."

Aaron stopped his back to her. Slowly he turned. "About what?"

"About … about us. And all the … Aaron, I know I hurt you. I didn't want to, and it was awful for me, too. I just want to make it right. Go back to what we had."

Aaron narrowed his eyes and looked away, his lower lip clamped between his teeth. "Alyen …" he began, then broke off with a huff of air and a shake of his head.

"Aaron, please! Tell me what I can do. Tell me how to make things better."

Aaron finally looked at her, anger and hurt and heartbreak in his eyes. "You can't, Alyen. That's the problem. I don't know if this is something we *can* fix."

Alyen felt her face blanch. "Of course we can fix it. We can *always* fix it. It's *us*."

Aaron flung his arms wide. "Alyen, you *broke* me! And you did it on purpose."

"Well, I didn't *want* to—"

"But you did. You had a choice, and your choice was to hurt me."

Fear at the meaning behind Aaron's words made anger rise in Alyen's chest. "What was I supposed to do, Aaron? I *tried* to involve you, and you walked out, leaving me to decide everything on my own. What would you have done if *you* were the one who had to make that choice? Let the world rip itself apart just to spare my feelings?"

"You made me believe you'd left me! I had to watch you go off with the faerie king every single night!"

"That was Faer Dinnán's doing, not mine! Don't blame me for things I had nothing to do with!"

With a growl of frustration, Aaron turned and strode a few paces away, hands running through his hair. When he turned back, his face was almost bitter.

"Look, Alyen. I want to really *be* with someone. To build a life with them. I want a home, a family … I want to be with someone I know and love inside and out, knowing that they feel the same way about me and that we have each other's backs. I want honesty and intimacy, knowing that there aren't any secrets or games or hidden agendas. I want a *partner*. And I thought that's what we had. I thought that person was you."

"It *was*, Aaron!" Alyen shouted. "And it can be again. Have you stopped to think about what the last few weeks have been like for me? Wanting to be with you, to tell you, to make everything all right for us again, and instead having to watch you be hurt and furious with me every single day? For something I hadn't even done? For the last time, I had no other choice, and this *wasn't my fault!*"

Alyen stopped, breathing hard. Aaron was silent for a space, and when he spoke his voice was softer, his face sad.

"I know. I can't even really be angry with you. Which is why … maybe if I want all those things … maybe you're not the one I should be with."

He turned and headed up the beach toward Soran.

Panic rose in Alyen's throat. She stood frozen on the shore, then scrambled after Aaron, boots scraping against the pebbled beach.

"Aaron, wait! We're not done!"

Aaron didn't look up as he adjusted Soran's bridle. "You'll always do what's best for Dúramair, Alyen. It's your job. I'll always come second to that."

"So what, you're just going to *leave*?"

Aaron glanced up, saying nothing, then moved to tighten the strap of his stirrup. "I need to think things over. I need to be alone."

Alyen's stomach clenched. "Where are you going?"

"Norhelm. I have to talk to the dragons. I haven't told them about Scala yet."

"When will you be back?"

Aaron swung up onto Soran's back. "I don't know."

"Aaron, *please*," Alyen almost begged. "Don't shut me out. I'll give you space, but don't shut me out."

Aaron snorted.

"We're still the Trianid! How are we supposed to work together like this?"

Aaron gathered his reins and looked at Alyen squarely. "The Trianid's not broken, Alyen. Just us."

He clicked his tongue and rode up the bluff where he kicked Soran into a canter, heading east.

He didn't look back.

Alyen sat on the rocky shore, her unfocussed gaze aimed across the lapping waves toward Illya. Eventually she realized she was no longer sitting alone: Faer Dinnán sat beside her, arms clasped around bent knees. He looked at Alyen, studying her features, his expression tentative.

"That did not go the way I had hoped," he said.

Alyen said nothing.

Faer Dinnán continued to study her, then asked, "Why Aaron? Why is he the one you choose above all others?"

Alyen didn't answer right away. She watched the sunlight dance on the waves, watched tiny clouds form and disperse. Her fingers traced the pebbles on the sand. Finally, she spoke. "Because he lights my fire and calms my storm."

The faerie king said nothing for a time. Together they watched the undines cavorting in the spray from the sea as sylphs swirled in the ocean breeze.

Suddenly, Alyen spoke, her voice far calmer than the tempest in her chest. "Why did you make me choose? You could have solved everything yourself by enchanting both of us without ever telling us about it. Why didn't you?"

Faer Dinnán's eyes moved over Alyen's face. "I didn't want you to be compromised," he said softly.

Alyen's eyebrow rose. "You lied to me."

"Lied?"

"You told me it was the only way. You pressured me into making that choice. You made me push Aaron as far away as I could when all along we needed to be together to succeed."

"Alyen, I didn't know about your melding magic at the Keeper's cottage. Everything I said was true for what we knew at the time. And you, yourself, wanted to protect Aaron—"

Alyen turned her head sharply toward Faer Dinnán, and he broke off at the expression on her face. "Don't pretend you had Aaron's well-being at heart. You took every chance you could to push him further away from me, and you didn't miss a single opportunity to needle him at the Lake of Leora. You never cared about him, and if you didn't care about him, you didn't truly care about me either."

By the end of this speech, Alyen's limbs were trembling with anger and she turned her gaze back to the sea.

Faer Dinnán sat in silence a moment, watching her with an unreadable expression. Finally, he said, "I'm sorry, Alyen." His voice was the sigh of the wind in dry grass.

Alyen didn't respond.

Eventually the faerie king tried again. "The darkling power, I believe it affected me more than I realized. I think if I'd been in a better—"

"Leave me," Alyen cut him off.

Bewilderment crossed the faerie king's features. "Leave?"

"I don't want to be around you right now." Alyen's gaze never moved from the horizon. "Leave."

Faer Dinnán was still a moment, then shifted as if to rise from the sand. Before he stood, he paused. "May I give you a piece of advice?"

Alyen looked at him. His face was earnest, his form strong and solid once more.

"Don't give up," he said.

Alyen began to shake her head, but Faer Dinnán cut off her reply.

"You've said it yourself. You have both fire and storm within you. Use them. And win him back."

Tears pricked the corners of Alyen's eyes and she closed them for a moment. When she opened them, Faer Dinnán was gone.

It was nearing midday. Alyen rose from the shore and made her way back to Lusa. She mounted and rode to the top of the bluff where she gazed eastward as the wind from the sea whipped her hair around her face. Far in the distance she could still make out a small dark figure moving across the grassy swells: Aaron on Soran, making his way to Norhelm.

She watched him for the space of a minute but did not turn Lusa's head in his direction. She wouldn't follow. Not now, not like this. Pleading with Aaron wouldn't fix what had been broken, and she didn't want him to take her back out of pity.

Instead, she turned Lusa to face south. Nah'dar and Brother Hugh would be waiting at the inn. And she would need to give her report at Castle Dúr.

With a final glance east, Alyen nudged Lusa into a canter, away from Illya and away from Aaron. If they were to come together again, it would have to be at the right time and in the right way. Once she had figured out what that meant.

Once she had mastered both fire and storm.

EPILOGUE

Lirianna stood looking out the window of her weaving room, a piece of paper clasped in the fingers of one hand.

She'd fallen in love with this room the minute she'd seen the curving tower wall and the tall windows looking out over Sheanen Crann. She'd known at once it was a place whose beauty would bring her peace and joy.

But today she felt neither peace nor joy despite the beauty of the setting sun streaming through the windows, turning the forest canopy into a lush carpet of emerald and gold.

She'd read the letter so many times, its words burned in her memory like fire. Her fingers tightened on the wrinkled paper as once more, her mother's voice rang in her mind.

"We woke yesterday to find the southern pen completely demol-ished, the fence razed to the ground. We can't imagine how it happened; we didn't hear a thing and there wasn't a storm either. I

suppose it's not the worst that could happen, but we'll have to use our money from last year's wool to rebuild it rather than buying the bull your father had hoped for …"

Lirianna sighed heavily and returned to her loom, stuffing the letter into the pocket of her robes.

She sat, but made no move toward the shuttles lying ready on the table beside her. She had no will to weave even if she did have the courage. She was a Seer who was changing the future with her own will, whose weavings brought mishap and destruction. And from what she'd heard from Alyen, she feared that things between the Keeper and the Slayer would never be truly mended. The Trianid was strained—she couldn't bring herself to use the word 'broken'—and the weight of it hung like a stone around her heart.

"Seer of Strands."

The voice startled Lirianna out of her thoughts and she whipped her head around to find who had entered her private workroom unnoticed.

It was Faer Dinnán. He stood before one of the windows, his ageless features set afire by the rays of the setting sun.

"Your Majesty." Lirianna stood quickly. "This is unexpected."

Faer Dinnán's expression was unreadable. "Your friends have split apart. Truly this time."

I guess he gets right to the point, Lirianna thought.

"It doesn't sit well with me," Faer Dinnán said, and Lirianna noticed that his eyes looked troubled. "It has thrown off the Balance within the Trianid."

Lirianna nodded. "I feel it as well. But Aaron and Alyen

will do whatever they must to keep the Trianid and the kingdom strong. They always do."

Faer Dinnán looked away out the window, his eyes narrowed. "I know. And that is what troubles me. They have both proven themselves far beyond what most in their positions are ever asked. And it's because of this loyalty that they have come to pain."

The faerie king turned once more to Lirianna, his eyes piercing into hers. "It's because of me that their bond has broken."

He feels guilty, Lirianna realized with some surprise. "No," she said gently. "It's because of Ylvain that their bond has broken."

A fleeting look of gratitude crossed Faer Dinnán's face. He drew a deep breath and exhaled, a sound like wind in the leaves. He crossed the room until he stood before Lirianna, his eyes searching hers. "I wish to help them. And not only for the Trianid or the Balance. I wish them to be happy together."

"Our wish is the same, then," said Lirianna. "But I don't know what we can do."

"I have a plan. But if it is to work, I will need your help."

"You need *my* help?"

"You have certain … *talents* that will prove essential."

Lirianna felt her body still. "What do you mean?" she breathed.

Faer Dinnán looked almost confused. "Aaron is the prophesied Second Slayer, and Alyen possesses elemental magic never before seen. What kind of balance could there be in the Trianid if Destiny had not found an equally exceptional Seer?"

His words struck her core, and Lirianna could only blink, speechless.

"Will you do it?" Faer Dinnán asked, leaning close, his gaze intent. "Will you help me bring them back together?"

Lirianna felt her breath quicken, whether from excitement, fear, or both she wasn't sure. "Yes," she whispered. "I'll do whatever I can."

The shadow of a smile danced across the faerie king's face. "Good. In that case, I shall return soon."

And suddenly, Lirianna was standing alone once more in a scarlet pool of sunset splendor, wondering what it was, exactly, she had just agreed to do.

Acknowledgments

When it comes to creativity, I have always gravitated toward solitude. In school, I preferred to work alone rather than in groups, and I concluded early on that this was how I produced my best work.

In part, it's true. I still find that the words flow more readily when outer silence allows me to hear the voices inside. But writing has also taught me that I can only go so far on my own; that some stretches of the journey are made smoother with hands to hold. And that my *truly* best work comes when my own magic melds with that of others. So, once again, there are many people whose love and labor went into making this book and to whom I must give thanks.

To my husband, my love: Even though this one doesn't end in happily-ever-after, I can dedicate it to no one but you. Thank you for being my rock, my support, my cheerleader, the one who is always there with tea and chocolate and a hug. I'm usually pretty good at the whole expressing-with-words thing, but they haven't made words good enough for you. So, for now, thank you will have to suffice.

To my children: Thank you for filling my life with love, purpose, and fun. Thank you for giving mommy time to write when I know you'd rather I was with you. You will always and forever come first.

To my family and friends: Thank you for your endless encouragement, for listening to me babble on about writing and publishing, and for supporting my dream and my choice to be an artist.

To my exceptional editor, Rebecca Heyman: Thank you for loving my stories. Thank you for never letting me get away with anything less than my best, and for ensuring I continue to raise the bar. Once again, your expert guidance and spot-on perceptions have made this book so much better than it would have been without you.

To my fabulous proofreader, Lucia Ferrara: Thank you for keeping my writing correct and consistent. Your ability to catch the smallest of details borders on superhuman, and my books are better for it.

To the fantastic designers at Damonza.com: This cover is everything I wanted and more. Thank you for giving my books absolutely magical imagery and making my fantasy worlds look real.

To the story itself: Thank you for sticking with me, even when I showed up to the page clueless, doubtful, or despairing. I have loved writing you and your characters more than I can say.

And to my readers: Thank you from the bottom of my being for reading my stories and loving them. They may seem like small things, but every kind comment, email, or review I receive means the world to me.

Stories are important. They do good things for the soul. I'm honored that you've made space in your life for mine.

ABOUT THE AUTHOR

Anne Mollova is an author and musician living with her family in Pittsburgh, PA. Aside from writing, she loves being in nature, making music, eating chocolate, drinking tea, and creating things out of yarn and needles.

"Thank you for reading! Please consider leaving a brief review of *Slayer of Monsters* on the site of your choice. Even a very brief one helps to ensure I can keep writing books for you. Please accept my gratitude in advance!"
—Anne Mollova

Connect with Anne
For books and updates visit: www.annemollova.com

Subscribe to Anne's newsletter at
www.annemollova.com/newsletter
and receive a free bonus scene.

g goodreads.com/Anne_Mollova
BB bookbub.com/authors/anne-mollova

www.ingramcontent.com/pod-product-compliance
Lightning Source LLC
Chambersburg PA
CBHW010727310726
48971CB00009B/2754